# the secret to letting go

## KATHERINE FLEET

Entangled Publishing, LLC
2614 South Timberline Road
Suite 109
Fort Collins, CO 80525
Visit our website at www.entangledpublishing.com.

Ember is an imprint of Entangled Publishing, LLC.

Edited by Karen Grove
Cover design by Lousia Maggio
Cover art from iStock

Manufactured in the United States of America

First Edition February 2016

*To Wade—thank you for always believing I could do this.*

To Debbie,
The lady with
the huge heart ♡
Hope you like it!

Katherine
02.18.2016

*Daniel*

# Chapter One

She walked into my family's sporting goods store on Main Street fifteen minutes before closing. Her old-fashioned flowered dress belonged in my grandmother's closet, and her faded jean jacket was worn through in spots.

"Can I help you?" Jocelyn, our front clerk, asked.

She shook her head, sending white-blond strands of hair flying around her face.

"Just let us know if you need anything." Jocelyn went back to flipping through a magazine.

The girl headed down the center aisle, her red canvas sneakers squeaking on the linoleum. She stopped to study a bin of sleeping bags, recently marked down, and stared up at the Fourth of July display I'd made from a pyramid of stacked camp chairs and an American flag.

Eventually, she wandered toward my corner, where I managed the golf inventory. In the fall, I was headed to Georgia Tech on a full golf scholarship. My dad dreamed of seeing me in the PGA, but for me, college was my ticket out of Canna Point.

I adjusted the collar of my Hudson's Sporting Goods polo shirt and watched the girl check out a rack of discounted sweatshirts. Threads jutted from her jacket where a button used to live. She reached the putting practice area.

Pulling a putter from the closest display, she glanced at me, like she worried about getting in trouble. When I didn't say anything, she held it backward with her left hand and tapped a ball toward a hole. It went wide. She frowned and lined up a second ball. It stopped short.

I stepped from behind my display case. "Are you left-handed?"

Her head jerked up, and I paused. Her eyes were the same crystal blue as the waters off the Keys on a clear day. I knew every person my age living in Canna Point, but this girl was a stranger. Odds were against her being a tourist. Our town sat too far north of Clearwater and St. Pete to attract the crowds that flocked to other areas of Florida. Maybe she was visiting a relative.

"If you're left-handed, you'll need a different putter."

She frowned, and her fingers tightened on the grip. I found the correct club and stepped up on the platform, feeling gigantic next to her. I offered her the putter, and she reluctantly exchanged with me.

"You grip it with two hands...like this."

I demonstrated the correct position with the putter she'd surrendered, the grip still warm in my hand. She copied my stance, the hem of her dress brushing the floor.

"Now, swing it like this." I putted the closest ball into the farthest hole and pumped my fist a little when the ball dropped in with a satisfying plunk. I looked over at the girl, but she just stared until heat flooded my cheeks. I cleared my throat. "Your turn."

Ducking her head, she adjusted her grip, sucked in a deep breath, and hit a two-foot putt toward the nearest hole. The ball teetered on the edge. *Fall in. Come on, fall in.*

Strange that I cared so much, but then the ball obeyed, and she beamed up at me. Her grin changed her quiet presence into something altogether different, something that made it hard to look away. There were lots of pretty girls in my hometown, including my on-again, off-again girlfriend, but no one who looked like this odd girl with her sprinkle of freckles and ragged haircut. Had someone attacked her head with a pair of scissors?

Realizing I'd stared way too long, I set the putter back in the rack and hid behind my best sales pitch. "Would you like to see some prices? We have some great specials on right now."

Her smile evaporated, and her brows knitted together. "Prices on what?"

"On golf clubs."

Her head tilted to one side. "Golf clubs?"

I looked away so she wouldn't see me roll my eyes. Who didn't know about golf? "That's a putter you're holding, and we have some great prices on ladies' sets. They include everything you need to get started."

She brushed a strand of hair from her cheek and shifted her weight from one foot to the other. "Sorry. I don't know much about sports."

I huffed, wanting to point out that she'd walked into a sporting goods store, but her shoulders hunched inside her jacket. The top of her head only came to my shoulder.

She handed me back the putter. "I wasn't planning on playing any golf, but you seem good at it."

I shrugged. Life without sports was as foreign to me as life without the sun, sand, and ocean. When my dad was younger, he played minor league baseball, with dreams of the majors. After a knee injury crushed his plans, he'd come to Canna Point, married my mother, opened his first store, and poured his dreams into me. I played Little League in grade school, spent four afternoons a week in middle school practicing basketball, and then in my freshman year, I'd swung my first golf club and been hooked ever since.

The girl looked away, playing with a braided bracelet tied around her wrist. I glanced at my watch. The store closed in five minutes. Around us, coworkers busied themselves with the mundane tasks of closing up—sweeping floors and counting cash.

"So, if golf is not your thing, is there something else I can help you with?"

She peeked up at me and nodded. "A camp stove."

"Ah…" So, a legit reason existed for her intrusion into my world. I slipped back into the familiar role of salesman. "They're over here." She followed me to the opposite side of the store. "We have single and double burners. Do you know what you're looking for?"

She shook her head. "They look expensive."

I glanced at the tags on the shelves, picking up the closest stove and inspecting it. "Looks like they start at thirty-five dollars."

She pulled some wrinkled bills from her pocket and flipped through them. "I only have nineteen." She stared over at the shiny green stove. "Maybe I could trade some homemade preserves to cover the rest?"

I returned the stove to the shelf and rubbed the back of my neck, hoping she'd miss the embarrassment heating my face. "We only accept cash or credit card."

She gave the stove another long look. "Oh…well, thanks for your help with everything. Playing golf was fun." Her sneakers squeaked when she turned toward the front of the store.

Watching her retreat, an unexpected guilt squeezed my lungs.

"Wait…" The second the word escaped, I regretted it. I should have just let her go, but then she stopped and looked back at me. Her hopeful expression hijacked my intentions. "We have two stoves at home, and we don't use the older one anymore. Maybe you could have that."

"Really? I can pay you." She pulled the small wad of money from her pocket and held it out to me.

For some reason, taking money from this girl felt like stealing from the offering plate at church. I sighed and shook my head. "What type of preserves do you have?"

Her eyebrows rose in surprise, but then she grinned. "Raspberry and strawberry. I picked the berries myself."

"Sounds good." I loved anything strawberry, so how bad could it be?

"Are you sure?"

"Absolutely. Who doesn't need more preserves?" I wasn't even sure what preserves were. Was she talking about some type of jam? "Just give me your name and number, and we can arrange a time to meet."

I pulled out my phone, ready to add her as a contact, but she frowned, chewing on her lip. "I don't have a phone. Can we just arrange it now?"

"Um…sure." How did a person survive without a phone? "I'm not working tomorrow. We could meet around noon. I'm Daniel, by the way, Daniel Hudson."

I offered my hand, but she just stared at it. Her fingers clenched into fists at her sides. For a second, I thought she'd refuse to shake, leaving me there with my hand stuck out in the air like an idiot, but she uncurled her fingers, wiped her hand along the side of her dress, and reached out. My fingers surrounded hers, and our hands pumped up and down. She smelled like lemons. Her hand slipped back to her side, and I rubbed mine against the sudden tight spot in my chest. Maybe the second chili dog at lunch hadn't been such a great idea.

"Hudson... Isn't that the name of the store?"

"Yeah, it belongs to my dad."

She looked around, her eyes wide. "He must have worked really hard."

"So he tells me at every opportunity. We actually own seven more throughout the state."

Her blue eyes widened further. "People must have a lot of money to spend on sports."

"I guess, but less now than they used to."

Dad wanted me to show more interest in the business, but I didn't plan on managing a store for a living. My father worried about the future of the sporting store empire he'd built, especially with the recession and expansion of the bigger chain stores, but I'd already been accepted into first-year engineering, and my twin sister, Amelia, planned to study art and design.

"You never told me your name," I pointed out.

"It's Clover. Clover Scott."

"Huh...unique name." But it suited her. Then again, unique was a polite term for her peculiarity. The lights at the back of the store dimmed, and we both glanced up. The other customers had already left, and the manager stood by the front door, waiting to let Clover out. "So, I'll see you tomorrow at noon?"

She nodded so hard, her teeth probably rattled. "I'd like that."

It wasn't like we were arranging a date, so why did her enthusiasm make me straighten up and puff out my chest? "We can meet at the beach next to the pier. My friends and I'll be surfing. You bring the preserves, and I'll bring the stove."

Uncertainty flickered across her face, and her mouth opened and closed, like a fish out of water.

I should have used her reluctance to back out, but instead I reassured her. "We won't be hard to find. We're just north of the pier, and this way we can meet on neutral territory."

Her expression turned blank.

"You know…in case I'm secretly a serial killer. There's always safety in numbers."

Her lips twitched upward, and she laughed. The sound tinkled through the air like wind chimes on a breezy day. "I already know you're not a bad person."

"Oh yeah?"

She nodded. Her unwavering stare made me want to squirm in my shoes. "True evil can never be hidden. It's always there, if you know where to look. When I look at you, I see only good things."

I snatched my gaze away from hers and tugged at the collar of my shirt. I wanted to know how she could talk with such authority on the subject. I wanted to know what evil she'd seen, but I wanted even more to escape the narrow store aisle. Warning bells pealed in my brain. *She's crazy. Don't get involved.*

Only politeness kept me from running. Leastwise, that's what I told myself. Instead, I cleared my throat. "So, noon tomorrow?"

She blinked at my abrupt change in topic, and her cheeks turned bright pink. "Sure. Tomorrow…I'll be the one with the jars."

"Got it."

I gave a small wave and forced my attention to tidying merchandise while she headed toward the entrance. The manager wished her a good evening, the door chimed, and then she was gone. Ignoring my better judgment, I followed her path to the storefront and stared out the window.

Clover stopped just outside, stooping to pet a dog lying in the shade. She straightened, and the mutt followed at her heels. So the scraggly dog must be hers. It needed grooming and was missing part of its ear, but its tail wagged when she scratched the top of his head.

She crossed Main Street and headed for the spot where Jaywalking Pete sat leaning against a brick building. He was Canna Point's only homeless person and most people avoided him. He'd served in the first Gulf War and had never been right since. He mumbled to himself, scaring little kids. His smell offended most. In an attempt to get him off Main Street, the police once arrested him for jaywalking, which is where he got his nickname, but he was back on his favorite street corner the next day.

I had a soft spot for old Jaywalking Pete ever since Amelia and I were ten. My sister had left the store on a Saturday to walk the short distance to the town library, when a group of older kids decided to pick on her. Jaywalking Pete appeared and scared them off. So sometimes, when Mom made two sandwiches for my lunch, I'd walk over and give him the extra.

Through the window pane, I watched Clover smile at him. She stooped to say something, then reached in her pocket and dropped some bills in his cup. She glanced back at the store, and I ducked, feeling stupid for spying. Who was this girl who couldn't afford a stove but gave her money away to a stranger?

Still, when I got home, I immediately dug through the shelves in the garage to find the promised stove. With a curious jolt of anticipation, I stowed it in my Jeep, knowing I'd see Clover Scott again tomorrow.

It was only when I was slouched on the sofa, watching television, I realized... For the first time in two years, I'd taken the most direct route home. For the first time in all those months, I'd driven home without passing by Grace's house... without remembering.

# Chapter Two

"Hurry up if you're coming." I drummed my thumbs against the steering wheel and revved the engine.

"Yeah, yeah. Cool your jets. I just needed my easel."

I glared at my twin sister, but Amelia ignored me, dropping a box of painting supplies in the back. I threw the Jeep into gear the minute her butt hit the passenger seat.

"Whoa, what's the rush? Thought we were just hanging out for the day."

"No rush." I reached out to turn up some tunes. "Just getting old sitting here waiting for you."

Halfway out the circular driveway, Mom stood up from her flower bed and flagged us down. She could afford to hire help for the weeding, but according to her, she loved the feeling of accomplishment when she did it herself. Leaning against the Jeep, she pushed back her tattered straw hat and squeezed my shoulder with one gloved hand. Her green eyes squinted against the morning sun. "Be careful today, hon." She nodded toward the surfboard I'd strapped to the roll bars. "Looks like Tropical Storm Delores may be upgraded to a hurricane. Watch those currents."

Amelia leaned closer. "I'll keep an eye on him, although I can't guarantee he won't do anything stupid."

"Like bringing you with me."

My mother tapped me. "Hey, be nice to your sister. She's the only one you'll ever have."

Amelia poked my other shoulder. "It's okay, Mom. I know he loves me. He's just anxious because Morgan's back in town."

Mom frowned, and I shot my meddling sister a warning look, relieved she knew nothing about the stove shoved in the back corner of the Jeep. Amelia merely smiled and played with her ponytail.

My twin sister was tall and lean, like me. We shared the same hair color, darker brown in the winter and lighter each summer, but our similarities stopped there. Amelia avoided anything athletic, focusing her energies on art and photography. She was also a poster child for that phrase about acting first and thinking later, while I tended to overthink everything. Being in the same class for thirteen years, I'd long ago given up on keeping secrets from my well-intentioned but incessantly nosy sister.

Mom wiped at her forehead with the back of one glove, leaving behind a streak of dirt. "I thought you and Morgan broke up before she left for boarding school."

"We did, but we keep in touch."

Skepticism showed on her face, but she still smiled. "Okay, I'm sure you know what you're doing."

That was my mom—always trying to support our decisions, even when she didn't agree. She'd never voiced her opinions about Morgan, but I knew how she felt. She worried that I used Morgan as an excuse to avoid "real" emotions, but Morgan and I understood each other. We'd dated on and off for just under a year before she'd left for boarding school at Christmas. She could be self-absorbed and ambitious, but I liked hanging out with her. Most importantly, she was independent. She didn't rely on me too much, which meant I didn't have to worry about letting her down.

"I gotta run, Mom. The guys will be waiting."

She leaned close, kissing me on the forehead. "Don't forget supper at Gran's tonight. Six o'clock sharp...you know how she gets. Amelia, not too much sun."

"I'm wearing SPF 60." My sister grinned. "See you at six."

I honked and continued out the driveway, Amelia blowing air kisses the whole way.

She stuck her bare feet on the dash, and in minutes, we reached the sun-bleached highway, whipping down the coast with the top down and music blaring. Canna Point sprawled along the Gulf coast, branching out from the older tree-lined streets and homes in the town center to the newer subdivisions where we lived. Everything was connected by the coastal highway, with the real heart of Canna Point being the beach and fishing pier. The pier wasn't as long or fancy as the one in Clearwater, but it still jutted out into the Gulf waters on wooden stilts that kept it fifteen to twenty feet above the surf.

Wind tugged at my hair and made my eyes water, the smell of the surf and Amelia's coconut sunscreen reminding me of the good parts of Canna Point. Days like these were almost enough to make me want to stay...almost. Still, I planned to make the most of this one last summer with my friends—two more months before I headed to college and everything changed.

Ten minutes later, I slid into a choice parking spot only feet from the beach. I untied my board and jammed the stove in the bag with my towel. I checked my watch—two hours to surf before Clover showed up. Would she wear the same dress to the beach? I tried picturing her in a tiny bikini, like the ones Morgan preferred. Stupid idea. I shook my head like it was an Etch A Sketch. I didn't care how Clover Scott looked under all those baggy clothes—none of my business.

"I'll be on the pier." Amelia balanced her stool and paint box under one arm and her easel and canvas under the other. "Lunch at the Shack?"

For thirty years, the Shack had been serving fresh seafood and the best shakes in town. It wasn't much to look at, but the food made up for its lack of style.

"Sure." I just needed to meet Clover first.

She left, and I headed for my friends. They'd already staked out a piece of beach.

"Hey, Danny boy." Luke slapped me on the back. "Surf looks awesome."

"Yeah, thanks to a wonderful lady named Delores," Jacob chimed in. "I'd kiss her if I could."

"You'll be kissing my backside when I leave you in my wake, buddy," Sam countered.

Jacob and Sam bickered constantly, but it was all for show. Jacob, Sam, and I'd been friends since our first day of school together—Miss Perry's kindergarten class. There was nothing quite like bonding over chocolate milk and scraped knees.

Luke joined our pack when he and his mom moved to Canna Point at the beginning of middle school. Luke's dad served and died in Iraq, and his mom moved back to be closer to her parents. Luke planned to enlist at the end of the summer. I admired his decision, but still couldn't picture my buddy in a uniform facing life and death situations. Only a few weeks ago, we'd been worrying about prom dates and struggling through final exams.

He puffed out his chest. "Chick alert," he whispered.

I turned, and Morgan launched herself at me, all long limbs, red hair, and warm tanned skin. "Daniel! How are you? You look amazing."

I hugged her back, realizing how much I'd missed her. She

was fun and confident, and she knew how to drag me out of my own head. Plus she always smelled fantastic. "I'm good. Boarding school must agree with you."

She pulled back and planted a kiss on my cheek. "Yeah, if only I could have brought a few more things from home, it'd be perfect." She winked before swinging around, her arm still wrapped around me. "I want to introduce you all to my friend Mia from school. She's staying with me for a few weeks. Mia, this is Daniel, Luke, Jacob, and Sam."

Mia was a brunette with legs up to her armpits and curves that made Luke's eyes bug out of his head. He jumped forward to shake her hand. "May I be the first to officially welcome you to Canna Point."

"Um...thanks." Mia gave a small smile, motioning to Morgan for help when Luke kept a firm grasp on her hand.

Morgan squeezed my waist before letting me go and advancing on Luke. "Down boy. Go do your surf thing while we work on our tans. We'll meet you later at the Shack. Daniel," she called out, walking backward and dragging Mia with her, "I want an update on everything over lunch."

I nodded, and Luke smirked. "Easy to tell what she's been missing at boarding school, Danny boy," he said as soon as the girls were out of earshot. "And now she comes home with a smokin' hot friend. God bless Morgan."

"Enough with the girls. Let's surf," Jacob grumbled.

"Easy for you to say," Sam said, pulling on his rash guard. Right now, Jacob was the only one in a steady relationship.

Jacob stopped waxing his board and looked up. "Hey, what can I say? When you got the whole package going on, it's not hard to find one willing to stick around."

"Yeah, how much do you have to pay her?" Sam asked.

"Nothing, bro. You just got to know how to treat a woman...or at least get up the nerve to ask her out."

I whistled at Jacob's low blow.

"Shut up," Sam snapped back.

Talking to girls was a sore point for Sam. To make the situation worse, he'd had the hots for my sister for as long as I could remember, which drove the "awkward meter" through the roof. Whenever Amelia appeared, Sam clammed up tighter than my waterproof phone case. He had two months before Amelia left Canna Point for college, so the situation pretty much sucked for him.

Luke and I shot Jacob the evil eye, and he ducked his head.

"Sorry, man."

"Forget it." Sam shrugged. "Are we going to surf or sit around yammering all day?"

"Surf," we all yelled.

And that was the trouble with the opposite sex. They had the power to twist you into knots, turn your life upside down, and suck everything from you. Was it really so surprising that I preferred Morgan's no-strings attitude? But for some reason, when I tried to picture her brown eyes and familiar features, I kept seeing blue eyes, freckles, hacked-off blond hair, and stupid jars of preserves.

I surfed, keeping one eye on my watch and the other on the sky. Our sunny day turned to high overcast with the approach of Delores, the surf building and pounding the shore. At eleven thirty, I glanced up at the pier. Amelia sat painting, gulls circling overhead, only she wasn't alone. A tiny figure with a shock of white-blond hair stood next to her. What the hell?

A wave crashed over me, and I sucked in a mouthful of ocean. The salt burned my throat and stung my eyes. I surfaced, spluttering and cursing, and motioned to the guys that I needed a break. The next wave carried me into shore. Propping up my board, I toweled off, pushed on my sandals, and headed up to the pier. Stubborn sand clung to my feet and worked its way between my toes. Halfway there, I slowed my pace. Why was I practically running? But I knew the answer. I wanted to know why Clover was with my sister. Were they talking about me?

For a weekend, the pier was pretty deserted, and when I finally made it to the end, they didn't notice me right away. They faced the ocean; Clover's dog sprawled at her feet. Clover pointed to something on Amelia's canvas, and they laughed. The melodic sounds grated on my nerves. Clover still wore her bright sneakers, but she'd lost the jean jacket. Her white, orange, and blue striped dress should have looked gaudy and outdated, but somehow it suited her.

I cleared my throat. Clover turned, her expression hidden by dark Wayfarers. The corners of her mouth tipped up in greeting. "Daniel."

My sister jerked at the sound of my name, and the dog at their feet stirred. He came over to sniff me. His misshapen ear twitched against my leg.

"Caesar, be nice."

I snorted. "You named this dog after Rome's greatest military leader?"

Clover's chin jutted out. "He needed a mighty name. I don't think his last owners believed in his potential. Right, boy?" The dog wandered back to her, eager to receive the belly rub she gave him.

Amelia stared at us. "You know each other?"

Clover smiled. "Yes, this is Daniel. Daniel, this is Amelia, a very talented artist."

My sister chuckled. "Thanks for the compliment, but the intro isn't needed. Daniel's my brother."

I blew out a breath, relieved that Amelia and Clover's

meeting was coincidence, relieved that she hadn't been stalking my sister.

Clover's eyebrows lifted behind her sunglasses. "Really? Now that you mention it, you do look alike, only Amelia's eyes are the color of spring grass." Her head tilted up toward me. "Yours are the whole forest—every shade of green and brown mixed together."

Sweat popped up on my forehead. When did it get so hot?

Amelia snorted. "Don't flatter him too much. His head is big enough. He's my twin, although I'm the oldest, and I therefore inherited the God-given right to boss him around."

"Yeah, I curse those eight minutes on a regular basis," I muttered, glancing back at Clover.

"So, how did you two meet?" my sister asked, not bothering to hide her curiosity.

"Clover came into the store yesterday." I paused, not sure how much to say. Would she be embarrassed by her lack of money and our planned trade?

"Your brother is a good person." Clover pushed her sunglasses on top of her head and squinted up at me. I swallowed. Her eyes were even bluer than I remembered. "I wanted to buy a camp stove but didn't have enough money. Daniel offered his old one in exchange for my preserves."

Amelia tapped the end of her paintbrush against her chin. "He did, did he? He must have forgotten to mention it."

I was about to tell Amelia that I didn't think it was important, when Clover's face fell. *Damn.* I'd obviously insulted her with my lack of enthusiasm. "I was keeping the preserves as a surprise…for my grandmother." I stumbled through my hasty excuse. "We're having supper there tonight."

Amelia almost fell off her stool at my blatant lie, but Clover accepted my improvisation with a genuine smile. "Well, good thing I brought some of my peaches as well." She reached into a battered canvas bag and pulled out a glass jar.

"Here are the raspberries."

"Hmmm…I love raspberries," Amelia crooned. She was clearly enjoying every minute of my awkward exchange with Clover.

I grabbed for the jar, my mind already working on the story I'd give Amelia later, but a gull swooped low at the same moment, squawking. Caesar jumped to his feet and knocked into Clover. The jar fell and rolled toward the edge of the pier. Clover cried out. Like a slow-motion movie scene, I shouted a warning, but she lunged for the stupid thing anyway.

If we'd been in Clearwater with proper railings around the pier, the story would have ended there, but the wooden railings surrounding the Canna Point pier were thin, weakened by sun and wind and salt. The crack of splitting wood filled the air.

Crap. Just like the preserves, Clover vanished over the edge.

# Chapter Three

Amelia screamed and scrambled to her feet, but I focused only on Clover's cry. The surf and wind swallowed the distant sound of her body hitting the water. Amelia jerked toward the hole in the railing, but I yanked her back. Kicking off my sandals, I dove through the opening, past a frantically barking Caesar, and over the edge.

I fell toward the ocean, smacking the surface and plunging under the water. My ears rang, and I thrashed, fighting for a few precious seconds to orient myself. Pressure built in my chest. I searched the murky depths for Clover's slight form. *Nada.* Out of breath, I kicked my way to the surface and sucked in air. I spun around, looking for a blond head, but I was alone.

Far above me, Amelia leaned over the pier's edge, screaming for help. My friends paddled in our direction, but they wouldn't arrive in time. Clover had been under too long.

Drawing in another breath, I dove deeper, under the pier. My lungs burned with the effort, but I pushed farther, swimming down toward the pylons. Where was she? Stars exploded in my vision. I floated toward the surface, survival instinct battling with my need to find her. If I surfaced one more time without her, she'd die.

And then I saw it. A flash of red. Clover's sneaker. Reversing direction, I reached down and found her wrist. Fire licked across my lungs. I needed oxygen. I kicked again. Clover's dead weight slowed my progress. Daylight illuminated the water above me, but I was out of air. Only a few feet separated me from air and survival, but the currents tugged and pulled at us, making the simple task hopeless.

Still, I couldn't let her go. I refused to release her weight and save myself. Time slowed. Water entered my nose and mouth, burning on its unnatural course inside my chest. Drowning was supposed to be peaceful, but I fought it with every fiber. I wasn't ready to join Grace. There was a time when I thought I was, but it wasn't true anymore.

*Please…not now. Not today.*

Fingers closed around my arms and bit into my skin. Relentless, they propelled us upward. My head broke the surface, and I gasped. Luke held the collar of my rash guard, supporting me.

"Daniel…I got her. Let go!" Sam shouted over the pounding surf, his blond hair plastered to his head. He'd positioned Clover on her back as best he could. I looked at her pale face and blue lips. He tugged again. Another wave crashed over us, and I released my death grip on her.

Jacob maneuvered his surfboard to help Sam with Clover. I hauled myself onto Luke's board and collapsed, letting Luke take over the work of kicking us to shore.

A crowd gathered on the beach. Other swimmers met us, helping. I staggered to my feet and barely made it to shore before collapsing and heaving up a gallon of seawater.

Luke slapped me on the back until I stopped coughing up the ocean. "Take it easy, man."

I accepted a water bottle from a stranger and guzzled it, trying to rinse away the taste of sea and sand. I spit and wiped the back of my hand across my lips. "Is she okay?" My voice was raspy, hardly recognizable.

"Sam's working on her. Someone called 911."

Ten feet away, Sam performed CPR on a limp Clover. He moved with speed and concentration. Thank God he'd worked as a lifeguard at the community pool for the last two summers.

"Daniel!" Amelia broke through the crowd and threw herself at me, panting. She squeezed me so tight, I started coughing again.

"Easy! Are you trying to kill me?"

"Not funny. You really scared me." Tears ran down her cheeks. "Where's Clover?"

I shook my head, stumbling over the words. "I think I was too late."

She followed my gaze to where Sam continued to work on Clover with a methodical rhythm. Caesar paced the length of her still body.

"No," Amelia whispered. She gripped my hand. "I don't understand. I was just talking to her and now…this."

I couldn't respond, couldn't find the words to comfort or reassure her. I felt hollow inside, numb, just like I had two years ago. Everyone watched as Sam compressed her chest and forced his own breath into her lungs. Her pale fingers sprawled on either side of her body. Caesar licked at them, but they didn't move. Only minutes had passed since she fell, but it felt like hours. It'd been more than enough time to replay our two brief encounters, and I wanted more…

It wasn't right. I didn't even know her, but no one was meant to die over a stupid jar of jam. Anger flooded me, filling the hollowness. I clenched my eyes shut. *Wake up, Clover.* Time stopped, and the beach fell silent. Even the wind seemed to die. *Fight…*

Someone gasped and convulsed.

*Clover.* My eyes flew open. She coughed. Water spewed from her mouth, and her eyelids flickered.

The beach erupted in applause and shouts of relief. Amelia sagged against me, and I squeezed her fingers. Sam helped Clover onto her side. She coughed up more water, her face too pale, like she still hovered between life and death… undecided. Stumbling upright on legs that felt like rubber, I covered the distance between us and fell to my knees at her side. I wiped her hair away from her face with shaking fingers.

"Clover, can you hear me? It's Daniel."

Coughing wracked her body, and I rubbed her back until the spasm ended. I met Sam's concerned look. "Thanks." The single word seemed inadequate, but Sam nodded, and I knew he understood.

Amelia crouched next to him. "Sam, you're shaking." She grabbed a towel off the sand and wrapped it around his shoulders.

"I'm fine," he mumbled. His cheeks turned red when she rubbed her hands over his, blowing on them, heating them with her breath.

"No, you're exhausted. Let me help."

When she gripped both hands in hers and held them to her chest, he turned so red, I worried he might actually choke, but somehow he managed to suck in a breath. His "deer in the headlights" expression turned into a smile.

Clover stirred. Her blue eyes searched for mine. "What happened?" she croaked.

I exhaled and bent a little closer. "You chased your preserves over the edge of the pier."

Her eyes widened. "You saved me."

I frowned. "Not just me. It was Sam and the other guys, too."

She blinked up at my friends and the other people gathered around. Her breathing sped up, and she struggled into a sitting position.

"Whoa," Sam said. He gently pushed her back on the sand. "You're not going anywhere until the ambulance gets here."

The sirens grew louder, and Clover thrashed against Sam. "No! I don't need an ambulance." She jerked upright before we could stop her.

Amelia caught her fluttering hands. "It's okay, Clover. They'll just check you out. You swallowed a lot of water."

She shook her head. "I'm not going with them. Please, Daniel." Clover grabbed at my arm. "I'm fine. Don't make me see them."

Maybe she was in shock. Someone handed me extra towels, and I wrapped them around her shivering body. Up on the road, a few swimmers flagged down the ambulance.

"Daniel…" Sam shot me a warning look, and I nodded in understanding.

"They're already here, so just let them check you over. You don't have to go to the hospital if you don't want to."

Sam nodded at me in approval, but Clover looked unconvinced. Seconds later, the paramedics arrived, and I stepped to the side. Clover answered their questions with one-word answers and shrank from their attempts to help.

One of the paramedics approached me. "Your friend's refusing to come to the hospital, but she needs to be monitored overnight. Can you make sure she's not left alone?"

"Yeah, sure. Of course."

The paramedic caught my gaze. "How are you? I understand you pulled her out."

"I'm fine. It was nothing."

"It's not nothing. You should be proud of yourself. You and your friends saved her life." He slapped me on the back.

"You barely left any work for us."

Once the paramedics left, the crowd slowly dissipated until only the six of us remained.

"I should call Mom," Amelia said.

"No. There's no need to worry her. I'll tell her at supper."

"She'll freak either way. You're just avoiding the inevitable."

I shrugged. "Probably. Come on, Clover, I'll take you home." I reached down, and she put her hand in mine, like it somehow belonged there. I pulled her up. She swayed on her feet, and I tightened my grip. "Amelia, can you bum a ride with one of the guys?"

"I can take her," Sam offered.

If Luke or Jacob had any thoughts on Sam's bold move, we were all too exhausted to comment. My body ached like I'd just run a marathon. Clover looked worse—wet, red-eyed, and pale. Her freckles stood out against her colorless skin. "Let's go, before you collapse."

I said good-bye to the group, and we trudged in silence to the Jeep, my surfboard dragging behind us.

"You don't need to drive me. I can walk."

I shook my head at her stubbornness. "I drive you home, or I drive you to the hospital. Take your pick."

She remained silent, so I prompted her. "Which is it?"

"Amelia was wrong, you know. You're the bossy one."

My shoulders sagged. I was too tired for a debate. "Just get in…please."

The girl was a mixed bag of contradictions. She fell off a pier trying to save a jar of jam. She didn't freak out at almost drowning but panicked at the thought of a hospital. She didn't have enough money to buy a stove, but she gave what little she did have to a homeless guy she'd never met before. Who could possibly understand the way her mind worked? I yanked on the rope securing my board, while she climbed in the front seat. Caesar jumped in the back.

I started the engine. "Which way am I headed?" Clover recited a street on the opposite end of town from my house. "That's up near the county park, isn't it?"

She nodded but didn't elaborate. Caesar poked his nose between the seats, resting his head on Clover's arm.

"You live there?"

"Temporarily."

"Visiting relatives?"

"Yes."

After that, we drove in silence. If she didn't want to answer my questions, I'd stop asking. I'd drive her home and be done.

"Thank you," she said finally, "for saving my life."

I kept my eyes on the road. "No problem."

"I don't remember hitting the water. Just the falling part."

"Maybe the fall knocked you out. You never came up at all."

She flinched and tightened her grip on Caesar. "I don't know how to swim."

"Maybe you should learn."

I felt her stare on me. "Maybe. The ocean is just so wide and open, but hidden at the same time. When I stand next to it, I don't know what I'm supposed to see."

I sped up to pass a car and tried to make sense of what she'd just said. The ocean was just the ocean. It wasn't complicated.

"Were you scared?" she asked.

The wind whipped through the Jeep, and I almost missed her soft question.

"I was scared I wouldn't find you." I didn't add that at the end, I was scared of letting her go and saving myself. I was scared of living with that guilt for the rest of my life. I already carried enough.

"If you hadn't, it would have been fine."

My head jerked in her direction, and my Jeep swerved on the road. Where did that come from? Had her fall off the pier been a suicide mission in disguise?

"I don't think I said that right." Her words rushed out. "I mean that I wouldn't have blamed you if you couldn't save me. It wouldn't have been your fault. I know you tried your hardest."

"Oh." My eyes returned to the road, and my heart returned to its normal rhythm.

We'd reached her street, and I slowed while she stared at the houses. At the end of the street, she pointed to a white bungalow with pink shutters and bright-colored window boxes. The driveway stood empty, the curtains pulled closed. "This is it. It's the prettiest one on the street, don't you think?"

"I guess." I pulled over next to the curb, blocking the driveway. It looked quaint and well-loved, like a happy, well-adjusted family lived there. So why didn't Clover have enough money to buy a camp stove? I deliberately derailed my train of thought—her money problems were her own business.

She unstrapped and slid off the seat. "Thanks again for everything." She stopped by the Jeep and looked up at me with red-rimmed eyes. Her hair stuck out at odd angles. It looked like the blond hair on the baby doll Amelia used to carry around with her—the one with the missing clothes and crayon markings over her body.

"I forgot to give you the stove," I said. "I don't even know where it is now."

"It's okay. You saved my life. I can manage without a stove."

I gripped the steering wheel with both hands. "Make sure you let the people you're staying with know what happened. They need to check on you tonight. I can come in and explain."

"No. You don't need to. Come on, Caesar."

The dog whined, and I gave him a pat before he hopped

down.

"He likes you, you know."

I chuckled. From what I could see, her dog was a cheap date. He liked anyone willing to scratch behind his ears. "So, I guess I'll see you around."

She nodded. "Yes…I mean, maybe." She shifted her weight, and her gaze darted around the quiet street. "Bye, Daniel."

"Good-bye, Clover." I put the Jeep in gear, but my foot remained on the brake, reluctant to make friends with the gas. "If you need me, you can find me at the store." Why did I say that? What made me think this strange girl might need me?

She gave a little wave, and I drove away, ignoring my uneasiness. I glanced back to see her walking up the front walkway and lost sight of her behind the bungalow's thick hedge.

The uneasy feeling grew. Why did she tell me that she didn't have a phone, when there was a phone line going from the street to her house? Why was the mailbox overflowing with mail and the lawn not mowed when the owners kept the rest of their house in good shape? Because whoever lived in the house was on vacation. Very convenient for Clover.

I slowed to a crawl and pulled over next to a magnolia tree. My suspicions multiplied. After a few minutes, a small figure appeared in my rearview mirror, walking in the opposite direction, a dog trotting next to her.

So, she'd lied about where she was living.

I wanted to drive away. None of this was my business, but I'd plucked her from the ocean, and now I felt somehow responsible. So, I'd follow her, make sure she was safe, and then be on my way. At least, that was my plan.

# Chapter Four

I trudged along the overgrown path, my shirt soaking up the humid air like a sponge. Branches scratched my legs, and mosquitoes buzzed in my ears. I slapped at one already sucking blood and cursed, wiping the bloody remains on my shorts.

I'd followed Clover into the county park, careful to keep my distance. At first, she'd kept to the main road, but then she'd veered onto an unmarked trail leading to a small lake. Passable to start, it narrowed to two thin muddy tracks slowly being reclaimed by nature. Somewhere along the path, I lost sight of her. Now where the hell did she disappear?

Ahead, something blue and metallic stood out against the trees. I circled the deserted sedan half hidden by knee-high grass and considered my options.

"Clover!" The woods remained quiet.

I kicked at the balding tires and peered in at a dog-eared copy of *The Grapes of Wrath*. It sat next to a stack of other weathered novels. Clothes and blankets and bags covered the backseat. An old-fashioned typewriter occupied the front passenger seat.

A tin bowl perched on the roof, and I looked inside—a half-used bar of soap, worn toothbrush, near-empty tube of toothpaste. A few feet away, a ring of stones contained the charred remains of a fire.

I'd stumbled on someone's home and, with a sinking feeling, I guessed the owner...Clover Scott.

I cupped my hands and yelled her name again, but only a bullfrog croaked in response. Fine. I kicked at the dirt and swung around.

An old camp chair sat next to the fire pit. I pulled it toward the sedan, squeezed my body into the seat, and crossed my feet on the bumper. I'd just wait until she got back. Then she could start explaining.

Something vibrated in my pocket, and I jolted awake, almost tipping out of the chair.

"Daniel, where are you?" Amelia shouted from my phone.

I winced and jerked it a few inches away. "Not so loud." I felt like crap. My head throbbed, my eyes burned, and the dried salt and sand on my skin itched in horrible places.

I pushed to my feet, pivoted, and my gaze landed on Clover's piercing blue stare. She sat on a blanket covering the ground, heating a pot over an open fire. She'd changed into plaid pants and a shirt covered with little flowers. Her hair floated in a soft halo around her face, unlike mine, which clung to my scalp along with what felt like half the ocean's grime. Only the dark shadows under Clover's eyes and the paleness of her face served as reminders of what we'd just been through.

"I've been home for hours." Amelia's voice snagged my attention. "Mom and Dad are going to freak if you don't get your butt home right now."

I glanced at my watch. I'd slept for three hours. Impossible. "You told them?"

"Yeah, but it's not like I needed to. People have been calling the house nonstop, asking about you and Clover. I even heard it on the radio."

I rubbed at my eyes, but it didn't erase the fuzziness in my head. "Wow. I'm a celebrity."

Amelia snorted. "Yeah, Hollywood will be calling for the movie rights any day now."

"And you're a regular comedian," I snapped. The other end fell silent, and I sighed. "Just tell Mom and Dad I'm fine. I'll be home soon."

"Gran's expecting us at six. You better go straight there."

"Right." I looked down at my shorts and swim shirt. "Do me a favor and bring me a change of clothes."

"Sure, but where are you anyway?"

I glanced over at Clover. "I'll tell you later." Once I figured out what to say. "How's Sam?"

Amelia didn't answer.

"Hellooo…you still there?"

"Yeah." She sighed. "Sam's fine."

"Really?"

"Uh-huh. Look, I've got to go. Just don't be late for Gran's."

I stared down at the phone. Nice. She'd hung up on me.

I shoved the phone back in my pocket, and Caesar trotted over to sniff my feet. Whose shoes was I wearing anyway? Luke's? I hadn't seen mine since I kicked them off back at the pier.

"Do you want some soup?" Clover asked.

I wandered over and stared into her boiling concoction of plants and berries and twigs. "No thanks."

She bowed her head, like I'd hurt her feelings. Great.

So far this day pretty much sucked. "I looked for you when I got here. Why didn't you answer?"

She ignored my question. "You looked peaceful when you were sleeping."

I jammed one hand through my hair and grimaced at the mess. "Yeah, well, you should have woken me."

She looked up and shrugged. "Turns out I like you being here."

Like some kind of magic, her honest words and soft tone made my anger evaporate into thin air. What was I supposed to do with this girl? It was like kicking little orphan Annie and her mutt. I didn't want to be the villain in Clover's sad little tale. I wanted no role in it at all, yet I still walked over and crouched next to her.

"You're staying here…by yourself?"

She looked away, but not before I saw secrets and shadows hiding in her eyes. She busied herself, scooping leaves and sticks into a bowl.

Huffing, I picked up a piece of firewood and poked at the ground. "Okay…you're obviously living out of your car. Don't you have any friends or family you can stay with?"

Her spoon dipped in and out of the bowl, but never rose to her lips. Eventually, she shook her head.

"Well, you can't just stay here, like this."

Her head lifted, and her expression surprised me. I'd expected tears, not fierce determination. "I can take care of myself."

Ouch…obviously a sore point. Not that I understood. I wasn't ashamed to admit that I couldn't even do my own laundry, and thank God for college dining plans. The most I could manage was spaghetti and sauce from a bottle and frozen burgers on the barbecue.

"I'm not saying that you can't take care of yourself." Of course, that's exactly what I thought. Who chased a jar of jam off a pier? "But it's dangerous for a girl to be out here by herself. What if an axe murderer comes along?"

"I'll hide in the woods."

"You could be sleeping."

"Caesar would warn me."

I scowled at her stubborn answers. "What about gators?"

"You mean alligators?"

"Well, I wasn't talking about the basketball team."

Ahhh…this got a response. A flicker of fear crossed her face, and her gaze darted around. "I haven't seen any."

"Don't be fooled. That little old lake over there is probably full of them."

She gritted her teeth and straightened her shoulders. "I can manage. I'm very industrious."

Who did she think she was…MacGyver's baby sister? "I can't just leave you here." There it was—the crux of the problem. Her situation offended my sense of right and wrong. At least that's what I told myself to explain the worry I felt, worry at the thought of Clover here, by herself, at night.

She smiled, and her eyes crinkled in the corners. "I was right about the good in you, but you don't need to worry. If evil comes, I can make myself invisible."

I snorted, the *crazy* detector beeping in my head again. What the hell did she mean by that? Was she serious? I tossed the stick into her dying fire.

"Besides, I'm just passing through. I'm leaving tomorrow."

I glanced over at her car's rust and balding tires, knowing they told a different story. "Where are you headed?"

"I don't know."

"Really. You came all the way from Virginia to Florida with no destination in mind?"

Her head jerked up. "Who said I came from Virginia?"

"No one." I pointed at her license plates. "I can read."

She blushed. "Oh."

"So what's with all the secrecy? Are you hiding?"

"No." She laid her bowl on the ground. "I'm looking… for a person."

"Who?"

She stood and planted her hands on her hips. "I like you, Daniel. You make me feel…safe, but it doesn't mean I have to tell you everything."

I rubbed my palms against my shorts and cringed at her "safe" comment. Did she see me as some kind of protector? I'd no interest in being anyone's knight in shining armor. I'd failed in that role once before. "Yeah, well, did anyone tell you that open fires are only allowed at official campsites?"

"I know. That's why I needed the stove." She glanced at her fire and bit her lip. "And I'm very careful. I make sure it's out before I go to sleep."

And we were back to me worrying about her alone in this isolated spot. "You can't stay here. The paramedics said you needed to be watched."

She gave me a steady look. "Go home, Daniel. I've been taking care of myself for a long time. I don't need you."

My moral compass warred with my growing desire to throw up my arms and walk away, but in the end, it won out. I crossed my arms and planted my butt on the ground, prepared to wait until she listened to reason.

"Daniel…" She sighed and stepped closer, laying her hand on my shoulder. "Please, just go. I'm fine."

I'd been ready to argue, but her soft touch—it scratched at my nerves and clawed at my lungs. It stirred a frozen place inside me that I wasn't ready to feel yet, a place that Morgan's touch never threatened. I bolted to my feet. Moral compass be damned.

"Fine. Have it your way."

I left without saying good-bye, but partway down the small lane, I looked back. She faced the fire, her back to me, her arm wrapped around Caesar. I captured the image in my head, wondering if this would be the last time I laid eyes on Clover Scott. My stomach twisted at the thought, but was it from relief or something altogether different?

"My grandson—the hero."

"It was nothing, Gran." I stooped and presented my cheek for her kiss. I was ten minutes late and, based on the cars out front, I was the last to arrive.

"I'll decide that after you tell me the full story." Gran's eyes narrowed on my muddy clothes. "By the way, you're a mess."

I ducked my head. "Sorry. Can I use your bathroom to clean up?"

"Yes, and I'll forgive your tardiness, as long as it doesn't become a habit."

My grandmother, Virginia King, or Ginny, as most people called her, valued a few things above all else: honesty, punctuality, cleanliness, and the Canna Point Historical Society, of which she was the founder and longest-standing member. She loved to tell me how her house was a founding structure of the town, constructed by my great-great-grandfather in the 1920s. It also served as the Society's headquarters.

"Thanks, Gran, and I'll be here early tomorrow to mow the lawn."

The house required constant upkeep, and since my grandfather passed away four years earlier, I'd taken over most of the physical labor. Mom once suggested that Gran sell the house and move into a condo. Bad idea. Gran wouldn't even speak to Mom for a week. For such a tiny package, with her slim size, soft gray hair, and hazel eyes, Ginny King intimidated the heck out most people. I'd learned a long time ago not to argue with Gran once she'd made up her mind about something.

She patted my shoulder. "I appreciate the offer, but if this hurricane continues tracking in our direction, I'll need help with the shutters instead. Forecasts are saying it could hit as early as tomorrow evening. The mayor's asking people to prepare."

My thoughts charged back to Clover. She said she was leaving, but what if she didn't? Her car wouldn't stand up to a hurricane. Still, I'd done what I could. She'd been clear about not wanting my help, and she wasn't my responsibility. But all my reasons for not worrying felt more like excuses.

"Daniel?" Mom appeared in the hallway, frowning. "I've been calling you for hours. Why didn't you answer?" She pulled me into a hug and, even after I straightened, her fingers gripped my arms, like she was afraid to let go.

"Sorry, Mom. I had to drive Clover home, and then I was so beat, I pulled over and slept. My phone was on vibrate, and I was completely out of it." The story wasn't far off the truth. Still, I couldn't look her in the eye.

"Why didn't you call? We would have picked you up."

I shrugged. "I didn't want to be a bother."

Her frown deepened. "You are never a bother. This Clover…is she the girl who fell in the water?"

I nodded.

"Amelia says that you pulled her out, and Sam revived her."

"Yeah. It all happened so fast. It's a bit of a blur."

She closed her eyes and finally let go of my arms. "Thank God it turned out well. I'm so proud of you boys."

"Meredith," Gran interjected, "let the poor boy clean up, so we can eat dinner."

Mom shook her head and sucked in a deep breath. "Of course." She produced a bag from the corner of the foyer.

"Some clean clothes for you, and we'll hold supper."

Fifteen minutes later, I found everyone gathered in the dining room, the smell of roast beef reminding me that I hadn't eaten since breakfast. My dad stood up to shake my hand, before hugging me and slapping my back. Ernie Hudson wasn't big on expressing his feelings, so this was a huge deal.

"I'm real proud of you, son. I'm proud of all you boys."

"How's Clover?" Amelia asked. I used the interruption to escape Dad's hold and slip into my chair.

"She's fine."

Amelia handed me the mashed potatoes, and I scooped a pile onto my plate.

"Is she living here or just visiting? I really liked her."

I forked out some roast beef and avoided the curious looks around the table. "She's just in town for a few days. She's leaving tomorrow."

"I found the rest of her preserves on the pier, along with your sandals. I think you left wearing Luke's."

I wiggled my toes. "I was wondering who owned them."

"Should we eat the preserves?" Amelia continued. "You never gave her the stove. I also found that on the beach."

"What stove?" Dad asked.

I shrugged, but Amelia chimed in before I could answer. "Our old camp stove. Clover came into the store looking to buy one but couldn't afford it. Daniel offered to exchange our old one for some homemade jam. That's why Clover was at the pier today."

I ventured a glance in the direction of my parents. Dad looked surprised, while Mom looked thoughtful. Not good. If she sensed I was keeping something from her, she'd be like a dog with a bone until she uncovered the truth.

"Too bad she's leaving," Gran said. "I'd have liked to meet this Clover girl."

"You'd like her, Gran," Amelia piped up again. "She's

different. Unique."

"Where's she staying?" Mom asked.

"With relatives, I think. I dropped her off at a house up near the county park." Perfect. It wasn't exactly a lie, but definitely not the whole truth. I wasn't sure why I hid the part about her car and makeshift campsite. Maybe I didn't want them to think less of her or, more likely, I didn't want them to think less of me for leaving her there.

"Oh, I wonder if it's someone I know," Mom said.

"Not sure. Can someone pass the gravy?"

I couldn't tell them the truth—that while I'd just saved her from drowning, everything about her made me feel like I was fighting for breath. I couldn't let Clover Scott's tiny presence, peculiar personality, and sad circumstances suck me in any further. Even her dog looked pathetic with his tattered ear and matted fur.

We all dug into Gran's cooking, and the conversation died off. My first five bites tasted fantastic, until I thought about Clover and her little pot of stick soup. In the middle of the table, heaps of food remained in the serving dishes, even after filling our plates. Did she eat things from the woods because she liked it or because she couldn't afford anything else? Guilt tainted the roast beef in my mouth, and I dropped my fork in frustration. She wouldn't even let me enjoy my supper.

In between mouthfuls, Amelia broke the silence.

"Morgan came by the house looking for you."

I retrieved my fork and pushed some peas around, trying to find my lost appetite. "She did?" Wow…I'd forgotten all about my promise to meet her for lunch.

"Yeah. They were already at the Shack when it happened, but she heard it from some friends. She wanted to see if you were okay."

I straightened in my chair. "What did you tell her?" Morgan knew about Clover. The idea made my fingers tighten around my fork and knife, but who was I trying to protect—Clover, Morgan, or myself?

"I told her you were fine…a hero. She liked that."

"Did you tell her where I was?"

"No…since I didn't know."

"Oh." I relaxed in my seat. "Right."

"Sam wants you to call whenever you get a chance."

"He's all right, isn't he? I mean, I didn't stick around very long after, but I assumed he was fine."

"No, it's nothing like that," Amelia rushed to explain. "Sam's…great." She picked up her napkin and held it to her mouth. Was she trying to hide her bright red cheeks? "I mean that he's fine…physically."

"He is?" I raised an eyebrow.

She huffed. "Argh…you know what I'm trying to say. He just wants you to call."

I winked at her. "Got it…"

Amelia threw her napkin on the table. "Let's talk about something else. Gran, how's your book coming?"

"Coward," I whispered, laughing. Asking Gran about her book on the history of Canna Point was a surefire way to change the topic. Gran loved talking about it more than anything else. It was like winding up the battery bunny and watching him pound on those silly drums for hours.

"Thanks for asking, sweetheart, but I'm afraid the news isn't great. Florence's grandson, Eric, was supposed to help with the writing, but turns out he's nothing but a condescending know-it-all."

"Doesn't he have a Masters in History?" Mom asked.

"I don't care if he has a Masters in going to the moon. He's consistently late, and it looks like he never brushes his hair."

Ahhh…there was Gran's thing about punctuality and cleanliness.

"He doesn't think we have enough documentation to support our book," she continued, "but we don't need every detail documented. Most of us lived it. He's trying to turn it into a textbook of dates and facts, when we want it to be the story of our town—the good and the bad."

"I'm sure it will work out," Mom said in a diplomatic tone. "Maybe you just need to explain your vision."

Gran shook her head before standing to clear the dinner plates. Amelia jumped up to help. "I've already tried, but he won't listen. Young people today…they have no respect for their elders."

Amelia hugged her with her free arm. "We respect you."

Gran smiled, planting a kiss on Amelia's forehead before shooting me a stern look. "I know you do. That's why Daniel will be on time for supper next time."

"Yes, ma'am." I accepted her scolding, but also caught the wink she threw in my direction before heading to the kitchen to retrieve dessert.

# Chapter Five

The next day, Gran stood with both hands on her hips and a worried expression on her face. "I appreciate the help, Daniel, but you need to get home. I don't want you on the road when the wind picks up."

At some point in the night, Tropical Storm Delores gained strength and set its sights on our stretch of the Gulf Coast. I'd woken to a town in full-scale preparation mode.

I took a final glance around the yard, looking for anything that wasn't tied down. Gran's patio furniture was already tucked into her shed, and I'd secured her windows and patio shutters. Her supply of batteries, candles, and bottled water sat ready just in case.

"Maybe you should come to our house to ride out the storm. Mom would be happier."

Gran steered me firmly in the direction of the driveway. "I won't be alone. Florence and Ruth are staying with me," she said, referring to her friends from the historical society. "Don't worry. This house and I have survived more than one hurricane. We know what to do."

I wrapped an arm around her shoulders and squeezed. "Keep your phone close and call if you need anything."

She returned my hug and tapped her hand against my cheek. "Go and be careful. If I hear that you or your friends are silly enough to watch it from the beach, I'll put you all over my knee and tan your hides."

I swallowed back my chuckle at the image and jumped in my Jeep, starting the engine. "Don't worry. I intend to watch Delores on television, at least until we lose power."

She blew me a final kiss, and I backed out of the driveway, one eye on the ominous clouds to the west. It was still mid-afternoon, but the dark sky made it feel like early evening. Everything and everyone was waiting for the mass of swirling weather to make its presence truly felt.

I drove along desolate streets. On the radio, the local forecaster repeated the same information I'd heard all day. A Category 2 hurricane was predicted to make landfall somewhere north of our town. He recited warnings for storm surges, hurricane-force winds, heavy rain, flooding, and even tornadoes.

I arrived home to an empty house and checked in with my dad. They were still working on boarding up the storefront, preparing for possible flooding. I'd no idea where Amelia was...maybe with a friend.

I poured a glass of milk and waited for my frozen pizza to finish heating in the microwave. When it beeped, I pulled out my plate and headed for the family room, settling into the wide leather couch. Flicking on the TV, I channel surfed, but all the local stations covered the incoming hurricane, alternating between weather radar images, warnings, and pictures of the damage left by past hurricanes.

*"If you are located in a low-lying coastal area, you are advised to move inland. This hurricane has picked up speed and will pack a punch. We are forecasted to be hit with the so-*

*called windy side of this storm, but don't be fooled. There will be rain, storm surges, and flooding."*

I gulped back my pizza, burning the roof of my mouth. Crap. The ominous predictions kept bringing my thoughts back to Clover. All day I'd debated driving out to check on her, to make sure she'd actually moved on, but all day I'd found excuses. I needed to help Gran. I needed to get my own family ready. What excuse did I have now?

I sat, snug and secure in my house, while Clover could be stupid and stubborn enough to ride this thing out in her beat-up car. The county park was all low-lying and could easily flood. I didn't even know if Clover's car radio worked. She could be oblivious to the danger.

I stood and paced, debating my options. Yanking out my phone, I called Sam.

"Hey. Thought I'd hear from you yesterday," he said.

"Yeah, sorry about that. I've been busy with the whole hurricane thing."

Sam snorted. "Tell me about it. I've been lugging supplies and crap all day. So, how's your friend Clover?"

I paused in front of the kitchen window. The wind kicked up and stirred the palm trees overhead. Hopefully my parents were on their way.

"For starters, she's not really my friend."

"Okay."

I recognized Sam's measured response, meaning he was waiting for whatever came next.

"And second, I don't know how she is. I haven't told anyone this, but the girl's living out of her car...alone...in a back part of the county park. She told me she was just passing through and she'd be leaving today, but I'm not sure I believe her."

"So call and check on her."

I winced at Sam's disapproval, but it did sound pretty bad

when I said it out loud. "She doesn't have a phone."

"Seriously…and you just left her there?"

"Yeah." I dropped into a chair. I'd rationalized my decision a thousand different ways, but the results were always the same—I was a jerk. "So what do I do now?"

"Go check on her, and if she's still there, bring her somewhere safe."

"She's stubborn. She may not want to leave."

"You're twice her size, man. Just pick her up, put her in your Jeep, and leave."

Sam made it sound easy, but we both knew it wasn't that simple. Still, I had to try.

"But you have to go now. Dad says that stretch of highway down to the park will be closed soon—flood risk." Sam's dad was a deputy sheriff in town, so I trusted what he said. "If she's still there, she'll be stuck."

I was already making my way to the garage, grabbing a few flashlights and a raincoat on the way. Thankfully, I'd put the top on the Jeep that morning.

The garage door clanged opened, and leaves sailed across the driveway. "Maybe we can keep this to ourselves for now. Your dad doesn't need to be involved."

Sam was used to walking this fine line between his father and his friends. He didn't rat us out for having a few beers or speeding occasionally, but this was different.

"Only if you keep me in the loop. If I don't hear from you, I'm calling him."

"Sounds fair."

I didn't bother with a note for my family, because my plan included being home long before they returned. If I ended up with Clover in tow, I'd figure out a way to explain her presence. Right now, I focused on reaching her.

The first spattering of rain started when I reached the town center. Amelia called, and I hit the speakerphone.

"Daniel, where are you? I just got home to an empty house."

I shook my head—so much for my plan. "It's a long story, but there's something I have to do before the storm hits."

I cursed. Ahead, officials erected barriers across the main road, turning back traffic. Breaking hard, I turned right, taking an alternate route that would get me back on the coastal highway...but further north. I just had to beat whoever was setting up barriers on the side streets.

"What's going on? What's wrong?" Her disembodied voice filled the Jeep.

"Nothing. It's fine."

"Really? So, why won't you tell me where you're going?"

I swung the Jeep around another corner. The speedometer crept up past the speed limit. "I said it's nothing. I'll be home soon."

She huffed in frustration. "Does Sam know what you're doing? He was acting weird on the phone."

"Why were you talking to Sam?"

"We were...I mean...he was just calling to check on me. He wanted to know if I was okay after yesterday."

Rain obscured the windshield, and I hit the wipers. "Amelia..."

"What?"

"Sam's a good guy. You need to go easy on him."

"Jeesh...you make it sound like I'm some kind of heartbreaker."

"When it comes to Sam, it wouldn't take much."

For a moment, she said nothing. "Fine. I promise to go easy on him. Now are you going to tell me where you are?"

I shook my head. Persistence was my sister's middle name. "No."

"No problem. I'll just get Sam to tell me."

"Amelia—" I warned, but she'd already hung up.

Ahead of me, the coastal highway appeared, with no barriers to block my progress. Making a rolling stop, I glanced at the pounding surf. Wind buffeted the Jeep, the exposed stretch of highway offering no protection. I drove with both hands on the wheel, my knee bouncing to the rhythmic slap of the wipers.

At the park entrance, I turned off the highway and headed down the side road. About a hundred feet off the highway, a barrier gate forced me to stop. The attendant booth sat empty, the sign in the window said, CLOSED BECAUSE OF DELORES. Great. I pulled up my raincoat hood and climbed out to check the gate. I yanked at the padlock securing the single metal bar, but it didn't budge. Now what? Clover's hidden campsite was a twenty-minute walk, less if I jogged, and we'd still have to make our way back. A gust of wind slammed into my body, and I braced myself.

Just off the road, a dried creek bed ran about two feet below road level. Maybe I could follow it past the fence and pop back up on the other side. In a shower of droplets, I climbed back in the Jeep, threw the gear in reverse, and maneuvered off the road. The plan was solid, but it didn't account for the rain turning the earth to mud. I made it past the gate, but before I could get back on the road, my tires spun out. Damn. I changed gear and gunned it, but the Jeep slipped sideways, deeper into the growing mud pit.

Five minutes later, I admitted defeat. I called Sam, and he answered after the first ring.

"I'm stuck in the mud just past the gate to the park."

"What's the plan?"

I hated leaving my Jeep in a potential flood zone, but what choice did I have? "I'll walk in to where I last saw her. If I find her, I'll head for the old camp building. It's two-story, so it should keep us above any flooding."

Back in the 1960s, the Boy Scouts built a large camp in

the park. When funds ran short, they'd sold the building to the county. For a while, the park ran a small canteen on the first floor. I still remembered buying ice cream there during the summer. Now it was used for offices and storage.

"Keep your phone with you," Sam said, "and let me know when you get there."

"Got it."

"I'm calling Amelia."

"Not sure if that's a good idea."

He sighed. "She already knows where you are. And if I don't hear from you, I'm calling my dad."

I'd have ribbed him for caving so easily to my sister, but a gust rattled the windows. "Whatever. I got to go." I had bigger problems than Sam and Amelia.

I hung up and shoved the phone and flashlights in my pocket. Above the teeming rain, thunder rumbled. The weatherman had predicted these—pockets of thunderstorms moving ahead of the hurricane. We'd yet to see Delores's fury.

I jogged down the muddy road, the last of the daylight losing its battle with the storm. Leaves and small branches swept around me, but they weren't my real concern. Before long, the wind would uproot whole trees. Even with my flashlight, I missed the turnoff leading to her car. I hit the northern campsites and knew I'd blown past it. Doubling back, I faced the growing wind head-on. My hood blew off, and rain trickled down my back. Water and mud soaked through my sneakers.

I slowed and peered through the darkness at the small road I'd missed the first time. No wonder. It now resembled a roaring stream. I sloshed down the trail, thankful for the dense trees that provided some protection from the wind. Lightning struck somewhere close, and the smell of sulphur tainted the air.

I was practically on top of the car before I saw it—so much

for her story about moving on. Now why wasn't I surprised? I rapped the flashlight on the back window, and a small yelp came from inside.

"Clover, it's Daniel. Open up!" I pulled at the handle, but the door didn't budge.

"Clover, unlock the door!"

I shone my light in, but the figure curled on the backseat cowered in the corner. Caesar's face filled the window. He barked and jumped from the front seat to the back.

"Clover...it's Daniel."

She didn't respond, so I shone the flashlight on my face. "See it's me," I yelled above the growing din of the weather. What was wrong with her? Why wasn't she moving?

I tried the driver's door. Locked. I stumbled through the grass to the other side. I pulled at her door and cursed when it wouldn't move, but my luck returned on the front passenger door. I yanked it open, and a frantic Caesar greeted me.

"Easy, boy."

I reached in to unlock the back door, and he sniffed at my hand.

Squeezing in next to Clover in the back, I slammed the door shut. Ahh...that was better. The noise level lessened to a dull and distant roar. Chilly air hit my wet clothes, and I shivered. I grabbed a blanket from the floor and dried off the worst of the mud and rain.

"Clover, we can't stay here."

A low moan came from the pile of limbs and blankets. I gripped the flashlight between my thighs and pointed it straight up. The car filled with light and shadows, and I pulled the blanket from her. Great. She slumped against the seat, absolute panic on her face.

Her wide eyes stared, unfocused. "Mama, I'm sorry..." she whispered.

What the hell? Was she hallucinating? "Clover!" I

grabbed her frozen hands and rubbed them between mine. "This whole area could flood."

She blinked. "Daniel?"

"Yes. We have to leave the car and walk."

"Thunder… I don't like it." Her icy fingers gripped mine. Not liking thunder appeared to be the understatement of the year.

"It's not the thunder you need to be afraid of…it's the storm surge and the hurricane winds. If one of these trees lands on the car, it'll crush us."

So maybe that wasn't the smartest thing I could have said. She cringed and shrank further into the seat.

Inspiration came to me. "What about Caesar? You don't want him in danger."

The dog responded to his name, dancing on the front seat. Clover looked over at her scraggly pet, and a wisp of sanity appeared in her near-hysterical gaze.

I jumped on the argument. "That's right. Let's go so Caesar will be safe. Do you have a raincoat?"

She stared blindly around her and then shook her head.

"Here. Take mine. I'm soaked anyway." I shrugged out of my coat and helped her shove her arms in. It swamped her. I pulled the zipper to the top and tucked her hair inside the hood like my mom used to do when I was little.

I reached for the door handle.

"Wait!" Her fingers dug into my bare arm. "I'm not ready."

"We have to go." I held her frantic stare. "Now!"

She frowned and motioned to her small stack of clothes. "You'll be cold. Take the sweater."

I huffed with impatience and dug through the pile until I found the wool sweater she pointed at. I pulled it over my head, thankful for its temporary warmth but knowing it would soon be soaked.

"Okay, we're going now, even if I have to drag you.

Understand?"

Her head twitched. It wasn't much of an acknowledgment, but I took it as a positive sign.

"Great. Let's go."

I cracked the door, and the wind caught it, flinging it wide. Wind tunneled through the car. It tore at our clothes and whipped her papers around. Rain soaked one side of my body. Instinct told me to stay in the car, but I knew better. We needed proper shelter. I climbed out and pulled her with me. Every moment, Delores got closer.

We made it two steps before lightning cracked overhead. Clover fought my grip. She sank to her knees in the grass and mud.

"Get up!" I shouted, but she didn't move.

Caesar licked her face, and she jerked a little. She kept mouthing something that looked like *I'm sorry.* She repeated it over and over, her eyes squeezed shut and her lips blue. Only I got the impression that it wasn't me she was apologizing to.

Great. What the hell should I do now? All I knew was that I wasn't leaving her behind. Not this time.

# Chapter Six

Adrenaline surged through me, and Sam's earlier words replayed in my head. I pulled Clover up by the armpits, almost lifting her clean off the ground. I'd throw her over my shoulder and carry her if that's what it took.

I met her wide gaze. "We can't stay here!"

She didn't respond, but when I wrapped an arm around her, she put one foot in front of the other. Together, we struggled toward the park's main road. At one point, she stumbled, and we both landed in the mud. I helped her sit up and wipe the dirt from her face.

"You okay?"

She gritted her teeth and nodded, scrambling to her feet.

My arms and legs shook from the effort, but we couldn't stop. We hit the main road and the mud lessened, but the wind gained in speed. It mocked our progress, toying with us. With the force of a freight train, it bowed trees at unnatural angles. A crack whipped through the air, and I pulled Clover close. The branch just missed us, crashing to the ground a few feet away.

"Caesar!" The dog bounded back to us. "Stay close." Did he understand? I maneuvered us around the falling debris, and he followed in our footsteps.

It should have been a fifteen-minute trek to the old camp, but it felt like an hour. Near the end, I half dragged and half carried a soaking-wet Clover. The building loomed ahead of us, and the promise of dry shelter gave me energy.

Propping Clover against the wall, I checked the door. Locked. I found a rock and swung it at the window in the upper half of the door. The glass smashed, the sound devoured by the wind. I reached in to find the lock, and the door swung wide, ripped out of my hand by Delores.

Clover and Caesar scurried inside, and it took my full weight to force the door shut. Wind still ripped through the broken window, clawing its way inside, but it was nothing compared to being outside.

Clover sagged against an old picnic table, and Caesar paced the floor at her feet.

"Don't collapse on me. Not yet." I prodded her tiny form. "We need to get upstairs."

My flashlight lit the path to the second floor, and we trudged together, leaving a trail of mud and dirt. I flicked the light switch at the top of the stairs, but nothing happened. The power was already out.

Most of the old dorm rooms had been converted into storage or offices. I checked each door until I found an unlocked room with no windows. Metal shelves lined the ten-by-ten-foot storage room. Great. No food, but we had enough toilet paper and cleaning materials to last us a decade.

Clover stumbled inside, Caesar at her heels. With the door shut, the flashlight cast a single beam of light in the darkness. "We have to get you out of your wet clothes before you freeze."

She tugged at the zipper, but her hands shook so badly,

it wouldn't budge. I brushed her hands aside and tackled the raincoat, tossing it in the corner along with her soggy jean jacket and my wet sweater. She collapsed to the floor, and I followed, rubbing my hands on the cold flesh of her arms. God, I needed to warm us up.

"Stay here. I'll go look for dry clothes."

"No." She grabbed at my T-shirt. "Don't leave."

She looked small and fragile, her skin as pale as one of Gran's porcelain figurines. I hated seeing her like this. I preferred the defiant girl who'd challenged me by the fire.

My hands itched to comfort her, to hold her until that girl came back, but I forced the feelings aside. I wasn't going down that road again—Clover already made me feel more than I liked.

"I'll just be gone for a few minutes, and Caesar's right here." I called to her dog and transferred her freezing hands from my shirt to his neck. He seemed happy to curl up against her, but I still felt a stab of guilt.

"I'll leave you this flashlight."

I dug out the second one and my phone. Great. I'd missed fifteen calls from Sam and Amelia. I tried both their numbers but only got the "no signal" message. Shit. We were on our own.

I looked back at Clover. Her eyes darted around the room, and her lips trembled. Was she going into shock?

"I'll be right back, okay?"

She nodded, or maybe it was just a shiver.

"Take care of her, boy."

Caesar looked at me and barked. As far as encouragement was concerned, I figured it was the best I'd get.

Ten minutes later, I returned with my arms piled high. Clover hadn't moved—she was still clinging to Caesar. The room smelled like wet dog.

"We're in luck." I dropped down on the floor, cross-legged, and laid our supplies in a line between us. "I've covered all the basics: shelter, food, and dry clothes. I checked the phone lines, but they're out."

I'd found a couple of T-shirts with the park logo on them in another storage room and a small pile of clothes that looked like they'd come from a lost and found. I tossed the smallest T-shirt in Clover's lap, along with some men's shorts that would likely float on her. "We need to get out of these wet things. There's a sleeping bag to keep us warm."

She clutched the T-shirt against her chest. "Thanks."

"No problem. I'll change in the next office, and you can stay here."

I'd raided someone's office mini-fridge and found an apple, banana, yogurt, jar of peanut butter, some crackers, and two granola bars. There was even a container of milk, still fresh. The banana was overly ripe and half the peanut butter was missing, but it beat starving to death. "Not sure how long we'll have to stay here, so we should probably ration the food. The yogurt and milk will go bad anyway, so help yourself."

She nodded but didn't reach for anything, so I opened the top of the yogurt container and squeezed half in my mouth. "Sorry…couldn't find any spoons." I wiped my mouth with the back of one hand and offered her the rest. "It's good. You should eat something."

She accepted the container with an uncertain look. "How long will we have to stay here?"

I shrugged. "Sam knows where I am, and as soon as the hurricane passes, they'll be looking for us." I didn't add that any number of things could kill us before then—flooding, falling trees, a tornado. The camp provided some protection, but we still sat in the middle of an evacuation zone.

"The wind—it's so loud. Like it's coming for us."

"Haven't you ever been in a hurricane before?"

She shook her head.

"This is what it sounds like. Of course, most sane people don't go for walks in it."

She grimaced, looking guilty, which wasn't my intention. I didn't blame her for getting us stuck in this situation. I blamed myself. If I'd checked on her earlier in the day, like I should have, we'd be sitting in my family room right now, eating a bag of chips by candlelight, safe, warm, and dry.

"I also found a radio. It should give us some news." The small battery-operated transistor belonged in another decade, but when I turned it on, the room filled with static and music. I spun the tuner, trying to pick up something other than golden oldies, but it only received in AM. Obviously, the station selection in the AM bandwidth was archaic.

"Sorry." I tuned it back to the original station. "Doesn't look like it'll be much good to us."

"I like it. Can we leave it on?"

"Sure." I set the radio on a shelf next to my phone. Clover released her grip on the T-shirt and gulped down some yogurt.

"I'll be right back. The building must be on a pump, so there's no water. I put some buckets outside to fill up." I'd wedged them between the building and the air-conditioning unit. Hopefully, they were still there. "You can change while I'm gone."

This time, she didn't try to stop me. "Take Caesar for company."

"You sure?"

She barely hesitated. "Caesar, go."

I scooped up my own change of clothes and left the room, Caesar at my side.

I retrieved my rain-filled buckets and secured the door. I'd stood outside for less than a minute, but I was completely soaked.

Outside the storage room door, I stripped off my wet clothes and rubbed at my dripping hair with a small hand towel I'd found in the bathroom. Gradually, life came back to my icy limbs.

I pulled on a pair of sweat pants, three inches too short for me, and tugged a park T-shirt over my head.

"Clover, it's me." I knocked at the door. "I'm coming in."

Other than the faint sound of music, silence greeted me. I opened the door a crack. Clover lay sleeping, curled on her side, her body covered by the sleeping bag and her head resting on some rolls of paper towels.

Caesar nudged my leg, and I shot him a warning look. "Shh." He seemed to understand. I opened the door wide enough for him to slip through, and he curled up in the corner, ready to follow his owner's example.

Closing the door, I grabbed some paper towel rolls and sprawled on the floor next to her. My half of the unzipped sleeping bag was too short, leaving my bare toes sticking out. Sighing, I sat up and dug in the pile of clothes from the lost and found until I located two mismatched socks. I tugged them on, not caring where they'd been or who'd worn them last.

I lay back down and stared at the ceiling. For a few minutes, I watched the shadows cast by the flashlight, then I clicked it off, reducing the room to darkness. Clover shifted next to me, her warmth pressed against my rib cage.

I barely knew anything about her, but lying next to her in the dark felt comfortable and familiar. The thought twisted my stomach. I didn't want to feel anything for Clover Scott. She may have been a stranger, but I already understood that getting sucked into her life would lead to nothing but complications. So how come I was alone with her, sleeping inches apart?

I was just doing the honorable thing; that was all. Clover had been in danger, and I was making sure she was safe. I'd do the same for anyone else.

Satisfied, I rolled away from her and adjusted my makeshift pillow. Lulled by the sounds of her soft breathing and despite the hardness of the floor and the viciousness of the storm kicking at our door, I closed my eyes and slept.

The building shook. Glass shattered, and Clover shouted.

I fumbled for the flashlight and shoved at Caesar, who'd curled up on my legs. "Get off!"

The dog jumped up, only to lick my face. "Seriously..." I grunted and wiped at the saliva he'd kindly left behind. Clover's dog needed to find someone else to like.

I clicked on the flashlight and swept the room for any damage, but the four walls of our shelter remained standing.

Clover touched my arm. "What was it?"

"Don't know." I pushed to my knees, getting tangled in the sleeping bag. "I'll check it out."

"I'll come with you."

"No." I stopped midcrawl and shone the flashlight back at her face. "Stay here."

She frowned and pulled the sleeping bag off her legs. "But..."

I scowled. "No buts. If you come, I'll have to worry about keeping you safe as well."

Her hands fisted on her lap like she planned to argue with me, but I couldn't back down. The girl had a proven record of getting herself in trouble.

"Caesar, stay here." I turned on the second flashlight and

tossed it to Clover. "If I'm not back in ten minutes, you can come looking."

Her eyes met mine. The shadows in the room hid her thoughts, but she nodded. "Be careful."

I turned the knob, and the door pulled from my hand, sucked immediately into the rush of wind. If the storm resembled a freight train earlier, it had grown into a space shuttle launch. I picked my way down the hall toward the office I'd invaded earlier. The top of a pine tree lay across the desk, sticking in through a smashed window and under a gaping hole in the roof. Wet pine cones and needles stuck to every surface. A rapidly growing puddle spread across the floor fed by the pounding rain.

I headed to the stairs to check out the first floor. Halfway down, the sound of lapping water stopped me. I swung my flashlight around. Two to three feet of seawater sloshed through the building, topped with floating debris. Fantastic. How fast was it rising?

I returned to our temporary shelter. Clover sat against the wall, gripping the flashlight. "How bad is it?"

I shoved the door of our cave shut. How much should I lie? If the waters continued to rise, we'd be trapped on the second floor, but Clover couldn't swim. Maybe we could climb out through the hole in the roof and get higher.

I worked to keep my tone even. "A tree fell. There's some water on the first floor, but not too deep. If it gets a lot higher, we may have to leave."

"Leave? Where would we go?"

I sank to the floor, my back propped against the wall. "I'll figure it out if we need to." I shivered, and she pushed the sleeping bag in my direction.

"Here. You're cold."

I pulled off my wet socks and tucked my legs underneath. "Thanks." I checked my watch—just past midnight, still hours before daylight returned.

A female voice crooned through the radio. It wasn't bad. "Who's this?"

Clover's lips twitched into a half smile, like she was remembering a happy time. "It's Patsy Cline. My mom loved her." She hummed a few notes under her breath.

"Where are your parents?"

She stiffened, and the humming stopped. "I don't like hurricanes," she said after a few seconds.

I snorted, letting her avoid my question. "You and the rest of the world. At least it won't be another Katrina."

Her forehead creased. "Who?"

"You know—Hurricane Katrina. The big hurricane that trashed New Orleans back in 2005," I continued when her expression turned blank. "Come on. You must have heard of it. It was all over the news."

"Oh." She shifted away from me, closer to Caesar. "I don't watch much television."

Man...what was up with this girl? Maybe her family was too poor to own a TV, but there were still newspapers and kids talked about stuff in school. Had she been living under a rock?

"Well, it was really bad. The levies broke and flooded parts of the city. A lot of people died."

She swallowed and plucked at her bracelet. "Yesterday, when I fell in the water, I'm glad I can't remember what happened. I don't want to know what it feels like to drown."

I remembered the burning pain of the water entering my throat and lungs. I remembered praying for peace. Only a second more, and I would have given up. We'd both have died. Clover waited for me to respond, but I couldn't think of anything to say.

"What do you think happens to people after they die?" she asked eventually.

Muscles twisted in my stomach. I'd thought too much about this question. I'd sat in the church and stared at Grace's coffin and wondered. Was she in heaven or was she just gone? Did Grace simply decay into nothing? I cleared my throat and dropped my head back against the wall. None of these thoughts were meant to be shared. Nothing against the girl sitting next to me, but I hadn't shared them with anyone.

"If you believe everything they tell you in church, the good ones go to heaven."

She leaned forward. Her pale skin glowed in the dim light. "What about the evil ones?"

"Why do you do that?" Frustration trumped my inbred politeness. "Why do you talk about evil and good…like we're living in a *Star Wars* movie? Like there's the Force and the Dark Side."

Her eyebrows squished together. "I don't know what you're talking about."

"Of course you don't. You've probably never heard of *Star Wars* or even been to a movie theater."

Caesar growled at my sharp tone, and I sighed, rubbing at the back of my neck.

"You're mad at me."

"No." At least I didn't think I was. "I just don't understand you. I don't understand why you say the things you do, or act the way you do."

"I shouldn't have come here." She pulled her knees to her chest and pushed her hair back from her forehead. After our trek through the hurricane and our short-lived sleep, her ragged hair stood up in clumps. Mine probably wasn't much better. I ran my hand through my hair, avoiding her hurt expression for as long as I could.

When tears welled in her eyes, I groaned. "Don't cry." I unrolled some of the paper towel and handed it to her.

She sniffed and rubbed at her nose. Thank God she

stopped. Crying females gave me hives. It's one of the things I liked about Morgan. She never cried, at least not in front of me.

"So, have you always been afraid of thunder and lightning?"

She traced a circular pattern on the sleeping bag with one finger. "How did you know?" Only a few inches separated our bodies beneath the sleeping bag. I could feel her warmth.

"Hmmm...I don't know. Maybe it was the shaking, or possibly the complete terror on your face. You kept saying you were sorry. What for?"

She cringed and squeezed Caesar until he whined. "Thanks for finding me. You saved me twice."

Once again, she redirected the conversation, side-stepping my questions. What was up with all the secrecy? "I should have checked on you earlier, and then we wouldn't be stuck here."

She made a sound in protest. "It wasn't your fault. It was mine."

I shifted on the tile floor and reached for the apple from our meager stack of food. Man, what I wouldn't give for a large pizza, extra pepperoni, extra cheese. "That's right. It is kind of your fault. So, why didn't you leave like you said you would?" I took a bite, too hungry to care about the bruised parts.

She shrugged. "The car broke down. I can't get it started anymore."

"You could have mentioned that before."

She stared down at Caesar, her lips clenched tightly together.

"You could trust me, you know." I offered her the opposite side of my apple. I figured she'd refuse it, but she reached for it, our fingers brushing. Her touch left a soft tingling on my skin. I swallowed and rubbed my hand against my thigh.

"Some people say I'm easy to talk to."

Of course, if I'd been even easier to talk to, maybe Grace would still be alive.

She took a bite from the apple and handed it back. "You are easy to talk to. I'm just not great at sharing."

"Well, I don't believe that. You shared your money with the homeless guy across from the store."

She frowned. "Do you mean Peter Walker?"

I nodded, wondering how she could possibly know his real name when I didn't.

She tilted her head and squinted up at me. "How do you know about the money?"

I choked on my apple. Damn. I couldn't admit to spying. "It's a small town." I cleared my throat. "So there are no secrets. Anyway, I'm just saying that you could talk to me if you wanted."

Why was I prodding her into confiding? It was none of my business, but I couldn't stop my fascination. She was a shiny Rubik's Cube, and if I could just spin the different color squares into the right position, I could figure her out.

She sighed and twisted her fingers together. "I'm not used to sharing. I'm not used to having a friend."

Friends? Is that what she thought we were? "So try something simple. Tell me just one personal thing, besides the fact that you're fanatic about your preserves."

Her features scrunched up in concentration, like she was in the middle of a math exam rather than a middle-of-the-night, middle-of-a-hurricane, passing-time conversation.

I rolled my eyes. "Just pick anything."

"But I want to pick the right one."

"There is no 'right' one." I huffed. "It's just a question."

She grinned up at me, cutting my impatience off at the knees. "I got it. I like to write."

Her unexpected response made me pause. "That's cool. I

saw the typewriter in your car. It looked pretty old."

"It belonged to Mama. Her father gave it to her." Her grin faded. "No—"

"What's wrong?"

"My typewriter," she whispered. "Do you think I'll get it back?"

"I don't know." My shoulders slumped. In my rush to save her, I'd never considered the fate of her belongings. "Were there other…important things in your car?"

"Not really." She shrugged, but her sad expression contradicted her words. "Just reminders of happier times."

"My grandmother says that things can always be replaced, but people can't." It was probably a lame sentiment when you'd just lost all your belongings, especially coming from someone whose house was dry and safe.

She nodded, a far-off look on her face.

"What will you do when the storm ends? Maybe your insurance can replace the car."

She shook her head, and my stomach churned.

"You could call some friends or family for help."

She hugged Caesar. "There's no one."

I crossed my legs and leaned back against the wall. This could not become my problem. What would I do with her? Take her home and say, "Hi, Mom and Dad, this is Clover. She's the complete stranger who I've had to save twice, and now I'd like for us to—" What? Provide her a home, give her a car, help her on her way?

"What about the person you were looking for? If you find them, they could help."

"Maybe."

A thump outside the building made us both jump. It was probably another tree, but it sounded like it missed the building.

"Daniel?" She looked up at me, her eyes the brightest

splash of color in our dimly lit world.

I used every ounce of my limited acting ability to hide my own fears. "It's okay. We're safe."

She chewed on her lower lip, and her eyes flashed with uncertainty. "I want to ask you something, but I don't know if I should."

My stare held hers. "Just ask. I don't bite, you know."

"Okay." Her chest expanded with air, and then she blew it out. "Could you hold my hand?"

I frowned, and her face fell.

"I shouldn't have asked," she whispered.

I shook my head. "No. I don't mind," I lied. The truth was, holding hands with Clover Scott scared the heck out of me. "It was just…unexpected."

Her hand rested on the floor only inches from mine. I sucked in a breath. What was the big deal? I'd held hands with Morgan a hundred times. I closed the distance and caught her slim fingers between my larger ones. Her warm skin heated mine and tugged at something in my chest. Her fingers tightened their hold, and I forced myself to not pull away, to slow my pounding heart.

The song on the radio switched to something I recognized—"Me and Bobby McGee." Janis Joplin's raspy voice filled the small room. Next to me, Clover yawned.

I cleared my throat. "We should save our batteries and maybe get some sleep."

She nodded, so I turned off the flashlight. We both shuffled into a flat position on the floor, our fingers still linked. I tried to sleep, but as tired as I was, that small connection to Clover kept my eyes wide open. My thumb brushed across the edge of her palm, finding the calluses I thought I'd felt earlier—calluses like the ones I'd gotten the summer I helped Dad build the pool in our backyard. But why did Clover have them?

I rolled on my side and faced her. "If you're in some kind of trouble, you could tell me." The words came from someplace deep inside, some need to protect this strange girl.

Her grip tightened on my hand, then slowly relaxed. "You're a good person, Daniel Hudson. For some reason, you don't seem to believe that, but I do."

How could she know how I felt? It was like she possessed some supernatural ability to see the things I hid inside. The thought made me stiffen.

Eventually, her breathing deepened, but even after she'd fallen asleep, I continued to listen to the rush of wind outside our isolated world. Only later I realized...she'd never denied being in trouble. I could only imagine what that might mean.

*Clover*

# Chapter Seven

"Clover! Wake up!"

My eyes snapped open. Fingers gripped my shoulder and shook me. Where was I? Why was my skin soaked with sweat?

I threw my arm over my face.

I'd been dreaming about Mama. For the first time in a while, she'd found me in my sleep.

Daniel leaned over me, propped on one elbow. "You were calling out in your sleep."

My hand fell away, back to my side. He was so close his breath touched my cheek. Staring into his eyes, I could almost forget about the nightmare. I could almost forget about Mama. Like the woods back in Virginia, his eyes changed color with his mood—greener when he laughed and darker, like now, when he was angry or worried. They were kind, serious, intelligent eyes that crinkled in the corners when he smiled.

It was hard, but I pulled my gaze from Daniel and looked around our tiny room. A thin crack of daylight snuck its way under the door. Where had the wind gone?

Daniel waved his hand in front of my face. "Earth to Clover…"

"I'm fine," I croaked, my tongue thick in my mouth, like I'd been chewing on cotton all night. "It's over?"

"Seems that way."

"I dreamed it was still here." Our walk through the mud and wind blurred in my memory. Death continued to taunt me like a bully, but now, somehow, it was Daniel who kept saving me. I didn't want to move. I liked having him close, but my body felt stiff and sore, and I needed to pee. I sat up, my muscles hurting even worse than the day after I fell off the pier. Caesar shifted by my side, and I stroked his matted fur. "How long do we stay here?"

Daniel frowned and sat up next to me. A clump of hair fell over his forehead, the brown strands tipped with gold. Bigger clumps stood out from the back of his head. "I'll check out the first floor, but we're probably stuck here until rescue arrives."

*Stuck here…with Daniel and his lopsided smiles.* I looked away. Staring at him made my chest feel funny, like there wasn't enough air to breathe. He looked like the boy in the picture frame Mama kept on the shelf in the kitchen. The boy in the photo stood with his arm around a girl. She laughed up at him, her smile so perfect you couldn't help staring. I'd asked Mama once who they were.

*"No one we know. They came with the frame."*

*"Oh…"*

*She crouched next to me and wiped away my disappointment with a stroke of her hand. "We could give them names and make up their story."*

*"Their story?"*

*She laughed, and the freckles on her cheeks danced. Her long, red hair trailed down her back. "Everyone has a story. It makes us all unique."*

*"What's our story?"*

*Shadows clouded her face, and she glanced around our cramped two-bedroom cabin. "My story is not what I thought it would be."*

"Because of Daddy," I whispered.

*Her lips flattened into a thin line, and she stood, turning her back on me. She stuck her hands in the dishwater and scrubbed at the frying pan. "You need to get back to your chores, Clover."*

*"But what about them?" I pointed to the frame she refused to look at.*

*"Not now."*

We never spoke about them again, but I still gave them stories. They lived in the sun and read books whenever they wanted and never had chores to do. Daniel was just like that boy—beautiful and good and smart, untainted by evil. Much later, after the nightmares came, I found the picture hiding behind the photo of the boy and girl—a picture of Mama, when she was younger, with a stern-looking man and a smiling woman that looked a lot like her.

"You must be hungry." Daniel rummaged through his small stash of food and handed me some crackers. "Want some peanut butter?"

He held out the open jar, and my stomach growled. I scooped a lump on the end of my cracker and took a bite. The peanut butter made my mouth stick together, but it tasted so good. When Daniel looked away, I stole a second scoop and stuffed it in my mouth.

Caesar stood and crossed the room. He sniffed and whined at the door. "Oh," I said, a few bits of crackers flying out of my mouth.

Daniel looked over, his mouth full of granola bar, and raised an eyebrow.

I sat up on my knees. "Caesar needs to pee. I do, too."

Daniel cleared his throat. "Right…of course."

He kicked his legs free of the sleeping bag and stood. I

tried to do the same, but my muscles argued back. My wobbly limbs tripped over the sleeping bag, and Daniel caught me. I grabbed a fistful of his T-shirt, and my cheek landed right against his chest. He felt warm and solid, and he smelled good. Would he notice if I leaned against him, just for a minute?

The need burned in my lungs and tingled in my palms, but he stiffened and took a step away. I let go, swallowing back disappointment.

Daniel pulled open the door, and the sudden daylight made me blink. I gasped at the weight of the air, heavy with the scent of pine trees and dirt and the ocean. An unnatural calm clung to the building, like time stopped. Only I knew it hadn't. I'd learned that much. No matter what else happened, time continued to pass, not waiting for fear or grief or memories.

"There's a bathroom down the hall. Second door to the right. We'll get one flush out of the tank, and then we can use water from the first floor. You go, and I'll take care of Caesar."

I wanted to protest. I could take care of my own dog, but I needed even more to find the toilet.

In the bathroom, I took care of business, and after, I stared at the mirror and frowned. No wonder Daniel thought I couldn't look after myself. I used the water left in the pipes to scrub at the dried mud on my cheeks and wet down the scraggly spikes of my hair. Someone had left a tube of toothpaste on the counter, so I squeezed some on my finger and rubbed it over my teeth.

I changed out of the shorts Daniel had found for me and back into my own clothes. They were still damp, but at least I didn't have to hold them up when I walked.

When I finished, I wandered down the hall and stared at the hole in the roof and the tree sprawled across the desk. I shivered, the floor tiles cold and wet under my bare feet. Through the hole, a single bird chirped. Was its nest in the tree? Had the bird lost everything, just like me? The thought of Mama's typewriter and my books, pictures, and writing buried in mud, cut through me like an ax. A part of me, that part anchored to Mama and the only good memories I had, had been hacked away. It hurt so much to think of it, even my teeth ached. I wrapped my arms around my belly and swallowed back the bitter taste. I knew I should be thankful. Caesar and I were safe, but hadn't I already lost more than my share?

Daniel met me outside the door of our room. "What do you want first—good news or bad?"

I forced the frown from my face. "Good news."

He smiled, like he knew what my answer was going to be. "Okay…the water level on the first floor hasn't risen, which means we are in no imminent danger of drowning."

I closed my eyes and said a little prayer. I hadn't even known that drowning had been an option. "That's good to know."

Daniel chuckled. "Yes, it is. Bad news is that we definitely aren't going anywhere on our own. We're here until someone comes for us."

"For how long?" I wasn't sure if being stuck with him fell under the good news category or the bad.

"Can't say for sure."

Caesar licked my hand, and I scratched behind his ears. We'd been together since South Carolina, where I'd found him wandering a campground, hungry and missing part of his ear. I'd always wanted a dog of my own. Daddy had kept dogs, but he'd raised them to be mean—to keep strangers away and to keep me and Mama in line. Caesar was different—friendly, brave, and loyal.

Daniel motioned to me. "You should come and see this."

He led the way to an office with a window. I shuddered at the sight—trees uprooted, lying crisscrossed like a child's toys, sticking out from under the water. Where was my car?

Daniel whistled under his breath, stealing my thoughts. "Dad's going to kill me when he finds out about the Jeep."

"I'm sorry," I whispered. "It was a really nice Jeep. When you drove me home that day, and the wind pulled at me, it was like I'd always imagined flying would be."

Daniel shot me a strange look. Had I said something wrong? "Don't worry." He shrugged. "Insurance will cover the damage, or if we can't find it, they'll replace it."

I stole another look out the window. He talked about rescue, but we were lost in a foreign, watery world. "No one will know where to find us."

"Not true. Remember Sam from the beach?"

I nodded. I remembered waking up with sand caking my skin and the taste of salt water burning my throat. I remembered the boy with blond hair and gentle eyes who'd held me down while I panicked at the thought of going to a hospital.

"I told Sam where we were headed. His dad is the deputy sheriff."

"A deputy?" The boy who'd helped save me was the son of a deputy sheriff? Cold crept along my skin, turning my limbs to lead.

"Yeah. I'm sure Sam's told his dad by now, and Mr. Garrett will send a rescue team."

The cold chewed at my body and numbed my thoughts. Daddy's voice roared to life. *"You can't trust them, Clover— the police and the government. They spy on us."*

"The police are coming for us?" I hid my shaking hands behind my back.

"Well, it will be the sheriff's office…but yes."

*"They watch for weaknesses, and when they find them, they'll show no mercy. Don't tell them anything, Clover."* Daddy's ramblings kept coming, like they always had, like angry bees swarming from a broken hive. *"Don't let them see*

*you. Stay invisible. You understand, girl? You understand?"*

I wanted to cover my ears and shut out his voice, but Daniel already stared at me like I was crazy. I closed my eyes, and my hands clenched tight.

"Clover?"

My eyes flew open.

"What's wrong?"

I shook my head and stared down at the crack in the tile next to my big toe.

"Clover, look at me."

I kept staring down, but when I finally lifted my head, I found something warm and concerned on Daniel's face. I'd expected disapproval or suspicion, but his expression made something blossom inside me and I couldn't look away.

"You're afraid of hospitals and thunderstorms." His minty breath fanned my face, making it hard to focus. "Now you're acting all weird because I mentioned Sam's dad."

God, his words made me sound like a coward.

"Were you in an accident? Is that what happened to your parents?"

My stomach knotted, breaking his spell over me. I spun away. *Was I in an accident? No.*

My forehead pressed against the cool glass of the window, and my fingers dug into the wooden sill. I'd prayed it was an accident—Daddy's shouting, the blood. I'd wanted to go to sleep and pretend it was a nightmare. Maybe I had, burying everything and everyone, ignoring it for two years. Then the local sheriff knocked at my door. His round stomach strained against the buttons of his shirt, and sweat stained his underarms. He'd pulled off his brimmed hat, but it left a mark across his forehead. I'd stood on the porch in the suffocating heat and stared at that line, refusing to meet his suspicious gaze, refusing to answer his questions.

"Talk to me, Clover."

Daniel's voice broke into my memories, and I spread my palm flat against the glass, grateful to his words for bringing me back. The past was a dark place I tried to avoid. "Do you ever wish you were someone else?"

"What do you mean? Like a rock star or a millionaire?"

I twisted to face him. "No." I sighed, wishing he understood. "Just someone different."

He found a chair and sat backward on it, facing me. "Not really. Sometimes I wish I'd made different decisions."

So did I, every day, but I also daydreamed about being someone entirely different. I'd driven though Savannah on my way to Florida, past tree-lined streets and fancy houses. The car had no air-conditioning, so I'd driven with the windows down. I'd looked at the kids riding their shiny bikes, and jealousy tightened my fingers on the wheel. Did their moms make peach cobbler from the fruit trees in their yards? Did their dads yell if the chores weren't done perfectly?

"Have you ever done something you're ashamed of?"

Daniel hesitated, but only a little. "Yeah."

I frowned and shook my head. "I don't believe you."

"We all have our secrets." His green eyes darkened. "Things we hold inside. Doubts that keep us awake at night."

"But you're a good person."

He shrugged, and his broad shoulders shifted inside his T-shirt. "So you keep telling me, but so are you."

I shook my head, but his gaze bore into me. "I saw the way you helped Jaywalking Pete, I mean Peter Walker, and even Caesar. You see the good in everyone else, so why don't you see it in yourself?"

I lowered my eyes, shamed by his praise. "Because we're the sum total of our parts. All our rights can't erase our wrongs."

Daniel folded his arms across the back of the chair and rested his chin on top of them. "Whatever it is, it can't be that bad."

I wanted to believe him. "You don't understand," I whispered. My head dropped. I stared down at my dirty, wrinkled clothes and knew I'd made an even worse mess of the life I'd been given. People made sacrifices for me, but I'd never been worth it.

"I would if you told me. What's the worst that could happen?"

For a minute, the worst came back to me. It replayed in my mind, and I couldn't turn it off. Clouds shifted outside. They blocked the sunlight, and I shivered.

"Clover…what happened to you?"

Tears pricked my eyes, and I lifted my head. "My story is not what I thought it would be," I said, borrowing Mama's words. Such a simple sentence to explain away so much.

Daniel blinked and looked down, leaving me to stare at his sun-kissed hair. Was it soft like mine or thick and coarse? His head rose, and I lost myself in his gaze, like walking through the woods, ferns brushing against my fingers, sun and wind and shadows dancing in the trees, rich soil squishing under my feet.

"You're stubborn. Did anyone ever tell you that?" He combed one hand through his hair, making it stick out even worse. "Your ability to evade questions is worthy of the CIA."

I knew what the CIA was. Daddy had taught me to fear them, too. "So maybe you should just stop asking."

His lips twitched, like he wasn't sure whether to frown or smile. My own tingled, and I pushed my thumb against them, confused by the sensation.

"Your eyes are so blue." He looked away again, like he was surprised he'd said the words out loud.

"Mama said they were the color of forget-me-nots."

Daniel cleared his throat, and his cheeks turned red. "Yeah, well, I don't think anyone could forget you."

"You're wrong." I scuffed my bare foot against the tile floor. "Like I already said, I can make myself invisible."

He shook his head. "You may think that, but trust me, Clover, everyone sees you."

But I'd already proven him wrong. I'd stayed invisible for two years. Daniel just didn't understand. Maybe someday even he wouldn't be able to see me. The thought made my chest ache right around the spot where my heart pounded.

Daniel stood up and stepped closer, a pained expression on his face. My fingers tightened on the wooden sill, and he reached over to catch my hair. He tugged a little, pulling my head to one side. "You don't believe me, but you should."

His thumb brushed my ear, and I held my breath. Outside, a soft rain fell on the roof and tapped against the window. Our hurricane had done more than change the world outside. It changed me. It tied me to Daniel in a way that was new and unsettling. Did he also feel it? I was scared that he did, and even more afraid that he didn't.

His mouth tightened, and he rubbed the top of my head, like he was petting Caesar. "Come on. You must be thirsty."

I nodded, but his sudden change of mood left me off-kilter.

He led me to the buckets filled with rainwater and handed me a plastic cup. I drank a full glass, and Daniel poured water into a makeshift bowl for Caesar before we headed back to our little cave.

After drinking his fill, Caesar sprawled on the sleeping bag like the king of the castle. "You're becoming spoiled," I scolded.

I pushed him to the side, and Daniel and I both sat. He stretched his legs out next to mine.

"So, I have to ask, are you going to freak out when help arrives?"

I hugged Caesar, ashamed of my behavior over the last

few days. Since meeting Daniel, I'd gotten myself in one fix after another, constantly needing him. I wanted to tell him that I wasn't normally like this. I'd managed on my own for a very long time, right up until the sheriff showed up. "You make me sound like a crazy person."

"Not crazy…but a little lost."

I sniffed. "I'm not lost." Maybe it seemed that way to Daniel, but I'd come to Florida because I was meant to. Mama's parents lived here. I'd never met them. They didn't even know I existed, but Mama had wanted us to find each other. But to meet them, I needed to do the impossible — confess the whole truth. I was still working up the nerve to find them when my car broke down, leaving me stuck. Now I'd lost the few things I'd owned, and I still wasn't ready to face them, but where else could I go?

Daniel looked skeptical. "Alone, then," he conceded.

"You're here, so I'm not alone anymore."

The warmth left Daniel's face, and he looked away. What had I said wrong this time?

"Daniel?"

He shrugged. "Yeah, I'm here until we're rescued."

I shivered at the coolness in his voice, taking it as a reminder that I shouldn't rely on him so much. If I did, what would I do when he left?

# Chapter Eight

The morning passed slowly while we waited for rescue. My belly quivered every time I thought about the deputy sheriff coming for us. Would he know that I'd run away from Virginia? The way Daddy talked, lawmen were always sniffing around, making trouble for honest folks. But then again, I wasn't exactly being honest.

The earlier awkward moment with Daniel passed to the point that I wondered if I'd imagined it. He found a deck of cards, and we played Go Fish.

He talked about his friends and Canna Point, and I listened, which was easy. He didn't waste words or use flowery phrases or talk down to me. When he spoke, he painted pictures, taking for granted things I barely understood—things like family, trust, friendship. I tried not to ask too many questions, in case they raised his suspicions. Not asking questions was tricky, though, because I'd always been curious about everything. When he talked about golf, my curiosity got the better of me, and I figured it was a safe topic.

"I still don't get it."

"I'll show you." He grinned and jumped to his feet.

I swallowed—an enthusiastic Daniel was a sight to behold.

"It'd be best to show you on a real golf course, but for now, we'll improvise." He found a broom and used it to "drive" a rolled-up sock toward an imaginary hole. He showed me something called a chip and a putt. They all looked the same to me, but Caesar loved it. He retrieved each sock Daniel hit.

"Nice!" Daniel pulled the drool-soaked sock from Caesar's mouth for the tenth time.

I laughed, and Daniel pinned me with his stare.

"Glad you think it's funny, because it's your turn."

I shook my head. "I don't know. I was awful in your store."

"You just need a good teacher, and I happen to be exceptional. Now, quit stalling and get your butt over here."

I stood, but nervous anticipation kept me rooted to the floor. Daniel caught my wrist and pulled me closer.

"It's a little tricky, because you're a southpaw."

He stood behind me, and I blew the hair from my eyes. "A what?"

"You're left-handed."

"Oh. Is that bad?"

His arms caged me in. He reached around and adjusted my grip on the broom handle. "No, it's just different than most of the rest of the world." He leaned so close, his cheek brushed my hair. "Bend your knees." He pressed his leg against the inside of mine, nudging my feet farther apart. "That's better. Now, relax your shoulders. This is supposed to be fun."

His words tickled my ear. I tried to breathe and let my muscles go loose, but his nearness made me feel prickly all over.

"Now, we swing. Like this." His arms guided mine, bringing the broom back and then all the way forward and into the air. Did I even hit the sock? "Follow through at the end." He gripped my hips and turned them.

Why did my heart keep faltering—beating in fits and spurts? And my stomach—it flipped and jumped like I'd swallowed a big old bullfrog.

The broom slipped from my fingers and clattered to the floor. Shoot.

I leaned over to pick it up, but so did Daniel. My head thunked into his.

He jumped back. "Are you okay?"

I rubbed at the tender spot, but he brushed my hands away. "Let me see."

"It's nothing. I'm fine."

"I think you'll live," he agreed. He stopped probing the spot and instead caught a strand of my hair between his thumb and finger. "Someday I'd like to meet the person who cuts your hair."

"I cut it myself."

He rolled his eyes. "Of course you do. It smells like lemons."

"It's the soap I made, but it's all gone now."

Gone…just like everything else I owned.

His expression turned somber. "Don't worry." His thumb moved to rub at the creases in my forehead. "We'll figure something out. I don't know how, but we will."

*But I'm not your problem to solve.* The words hovered on my lips but wouldn't take hold. Remembering his earlier coolness, I waited for him to turn away again, but he only clucked at me. Could he see my doubts and fears? "Trust me." His lips turned up at the corners, and my thoughts jumbled.

"Daniel…" I forgot what I wanted to say.

He took a step closer. His knuckles brushed the side of my face. Why was the room so hot? He lowered his head, his hazel eyes getting closer and closer. I blinked to keep from going cross-eyed.

I lifted my chin, afraid that if I looked away, I'd miss something important, and then it happened—

His lips found mine, as soft as a dragonfly landing, so soft that maybe I'd imagined it. Was he kissing me? My first kiss? My body froze. My hands curled into fists. He tasted like mint and warmth and goodness. I tried to focus on his features, but they were too close, so I closed my eyes and waited, waited for whatever was supposed to happen next.

Daniel's lips left mine. "Clover—"

I shook my head, keeping my eyes shut. I wanted more.

"Clover!"

My eyes flew open. Daniel had taken a step back, an odd expression on his face. He looked up. "It's a helicopter."

My fingers pressed against my lips. I thought the rhythmic *thwack, thwack, thwack* was coming from my chest, but it grew louder, vibrating the building.

"It's a helicopter. Come on. We have to signal them."

He caught my hand, pulling me along. We sprinted down the hall to one of the offices, where he threw open a window. He leaned out, shouting and waving.

"They see us, Clover," he called back to me, relief in his tone, but I didn't feel relieved.

I sagged against the desk, more confused than ever. What was I supposed to do when they rescued us? I was homeless. I had no money. All I had was my first kiss…from Daniel.

An hour later, I peeked past Daniel's shoulder and out the window at the approaching boat. Three men with orange life vests looked up at us. One of the men had short blond hair and wore a sheriff's uniform. He called out to Daniel, and Daniel shouted back.

"It's Sam's dad. Come on."

Daniel grabbed his things and headed for the stairs. I picked up my still damp jean jacket and muddy sneakers. They were all I owned now. Whatever I did from this point on, I was starting from scratch, at least when it came to my belongings. It took more than a hurricane to wipe out past actions.

Daniel charged ahead to the first floor. He waded into the murky water until it reached his thighs, but I stopped at the last dry step. Blocked by the smell of salt and decay and the darkness and floating debris, I couldn't go any farther. Caesar whined at my side.

"Daniel, you okay?" a voice called in from the boat blocking the doorway.

"Yeah, Mr. Garrett. We're fine." Daniel shot me an encouraging look. "Okay, Clover, time to get out of here."

I gritted my teeth, and tears stung my eyes. Why couldn't I be more like Daniel? I was used to taking care of myself. What was wrong with me? I held tight to the railing, but Daniel was right. I couldn't stay here. He stopped at the bottom of the stairs and reached for my hand.

"If you can jump off the pier and sleep alone in the park, you can handle this. Now, come on down here."

"Everything okay in there?" Sam's dad called out.

"Yeah. Just getting organized," Daniel covered for me. He climbed the stairs until only inches separated us. "Get on my back. I'll give you a ride."

I closed my eyes and wrapped my arms around his neck. My world shifted as he stood. Cold water sloshed around my feet, and I held on tighter. My cheek pressed against his neck, his skin cool and salty-smelling.

He coughed. "Clover, you're choking me."

"Sorry." I loosened my grip and peeked. Caesar swam ahead of us, and the men in the boat reached down to pull him in when he got close enough.

Too quickly, we also reached the door and then the bow of the boat. Daniel backed me up against the edge and strong hands reached for me, pulling me inside. *Just breathe. Don't panic.* The boat rocked, and I gasped as Daniel heaved himself inside and sat next to me on the middle seat.

"You gave your parents a scare," Sam's father said. I pictured the boy on the beach, and I could see the resemblance. They both had blond hair and blue eyes, only Sam's hair was longer and Sam's dad had a few more lines on his face. The deputy also had a gun strapped to his side. I tried not to look at it, but I couldn't help staring.

Daniel's shoulders fell. "Sorry, sir."

"What were you thinking, coming here on your own? You could have gotten yourselves killed. You should have called me."

I ducked my head, hiding from Mr. Garrett's disapproval, but Daniel didn't look away.

"I thought I could do it myself."

The deputy's tone didn't budge. "I'd expect a stunt like this from Luke, but not from you. I thought you had more sense."

I felt Daniel getting smaller beside me. "You're right, sir. I should have known better." He dropped his head in his hand, looking defeated, but it wasn't right. None of this was Daniel's fault.

I jumped to my feet and sent the boat rocking. Daniel grabbed the back of my shirt, catching me when I probably would have pitched over the side.

"Sit down!" The order came from four different directions all at once. Daniel tugged on my shirt, trying to pull me back to the seat, but I ignored it all.

"This wasn't Daniel's fault. It was my fault. So don't yell at him."

Mr. Garrett's eyes widened. "I wasn't yelling at him."

I leaned toward Daniel. "Well, it sounded like it. Daniel saved my life."

"It's okay, Clover," Daniel whispered. His cheeks had turned bright red. He let go of my shirt and gripped my hand, pulling until I sat back down. "He's just worried about us, and he's right. I shouldn't have tried this on my own."

Sam's father stared at our linked hands, an unspoken question in his eyes. It was easy to figure out Daniel's answer because he dropped my hand right away. It fell back in my lap, twitching like a dying bird.

"Sam tells me you're the same girl that fell off the pier two days ago."

I flinched, feeling very small. Did anyone else hear the suspicion in his voice? Wasn't it exactly what Daddy had warned about? I looked away and tried to stop the panic, pretending to be fascinated by the stands of half submerged trees we drifted past. The boat cut through the water, propelled by the long poles two of the men used to push us forward. A few feet away, a log floated past. It turned, and I shuddered, staring at the head and eyes of an alligator. Everything about Canna Point was foreign. I couldn't hide here the way I had in Virginia.

Daniel answered for me. "Yes, sir, she's the same girl. Mr. Garrett, this is Clover Scott. Clover, this is Andrew Garrett."

I turned back, and the deputy nodded his head, his brief smile more polite than sincere.

"So, what were you doing in the park? Park authorities tell me this whole area was gated and locked before Delores hit."

"Her car broke down in the park, and she didn't have a phone to call for help," Daniel said.

"Is that true? Is that what happened, Clover?" Mr. Garrett fixed me with another questioning look, and I nodded, lowering my head to stare at my dirty sneakers. Caesar rested his head on my lap and whined.

"Where were you headed before you broke down?"

I shrugged, my tongue too numb to form words. The insides of my belly churned like cake batter in a mixing bowl.

Daniel nudged my shoulder. "She came down to Florida to meet up with someone."

Mr. Garrett frowned. "Why don't you let Clover answer for herself?"

I lifted my head, but my shoulders still sagged. "It's just like Daniel said." Andrew Garrett's piercing blue eyes clouded with doubt.

"Look, Mr. Garrett," Daniel cut in, "it's been a really long night. We're both wiped."

Sam's father nodded at him. "For what it's worth, I'm glad you're both okay. This town doesn't need any more losses."

What did he mean by that? I wanted to ask Daniel, but a stretch of dry road appeared ahead. The men steered the boat toward several parked trucks, a boat trailer attached to one of them. We reached the road, and Mr. Garrett stepped into water up to his knees, pulling the boat in closer.

"Time to go, people," he ordered.

Daniel jumped over the side, followed by Caesar, who raced ahead, happy to be on dry land. Daniel reached back for me. He swung me up in front of him, and I clung to his neck.

"You okay?" he whispered in my ear, letting me slide to the ground.

"Yeah."

"Not going to panic on me?"

I shook my head.

"You defended me...you didn't need to."

I frowned. "He attacked you, but you didn't do anything wrong."

Daniel chuckled. "You looked fierce. He was probably

shaking in his boots."

"You're laughing at me." I took a step back. The thought made my insides twist. Since when did his opinion mean so much?

"No. You were kind of…cute. Like a mama bear defending her cub. I'm just not used to people considering me a cub."

"Everyone needs defending now and then. Mama used to say that if folks deserve defending, then we shouldn't be afraid to stand up." Of course, I'd been too afraid to do it when it counted most of all.

Shame flooded my body, and I turned away, afraid for Daniel to see it, but my gaze collided with the intense stare of the deputy sheriff. His eyes narrowed a little, and it felt like he could see right through me, all the way to the secrets I carried deep inside. I closed my eyes and rubbed my hand against my chest.

I needed to be wary of Andrew Garrett, because no matter what Daniel said, he'd hate me if he ever found out the truth.


"Any sign of my Jeep?" Daniel asked Mr. Garrett. They sat in the front of the deputy's truck, while Caesar and I sat in the back.

Mr. Garrett shook his head. "Sorry. The storm surge could have taken it anywhere. I'm sure we'll find it eventually. You have insurance, right?"

"Yeah, I do." Daniel looked back at me, and I knew he was thinking about my stuff. I couldn't let myself think about Mama's typewriter or the pictures or the writing I'd lost. If I did, the sadness would take over.

Sam's dad looked at me through the rearview mirror. "So, what's your plan now, Clover?"

"I don't know." I worked hard to keep my voice steady.

"Clover had most of her things in her car. We had to leave them behind."

"At least you're both safe. You need to be thankful for that."

Daniel nodded. "And the rest of the town?"

"There are trees and power lines down, but not a whole lot of damage. Streets closest to the beach flooded, but so far, everyone is accounted for."

I stared out the window at the branches and debris scattered across the nearly deserted road. To our right, angry waves still pounded the shore. We got closer to town and had to drive around downed trees. Yellow tape marked off live power lines.

"I'm dropping you off at your grandmother's. Your mom and dad are waiting for you there."

The truck pulled to a stop in front of a two-story house with bay windows and a wide front veranda. With deep yellow paint and black shutters, it looked like a giant sunflower.

Daniel jumped out, and I followed, but only because I had no choice. If I had to pick between staying with the deputy or facing Daniel's family, I'd take the choice that kept me closest to the one person I'd started to count on. Caesar raced ahead, not caring that he was now as homeless as I was.

Daniel led the way up the driveway, the deputy in the rear. The air, heavy and humid and thick with the smell of roses, clung to everything. The scent was almost enough to disguise the smell of mud and ocean coming from Daniel, Caesar, and me.

We clattered up the steps to the veranda, and the front door flew open.

"Daniel!" A slim woman, with green eyes the color of Amelia's, launched herself at Daniel. She closed her eyes and hugged him tight.

Envy streaked through me. It scorched my lungs. I tried to remember what Mama's hugs felt like, but it had been too long.

"Mom, I'm fine." Daniel hugged her back before stepping away.

"You scared me to death. Twice in one week." She pulled at a strand of hair. "Look. You've turned my hair gray."

"I'm pretty sure that was there before, but I'm sorry. I didn't plan on getting stuck."

"You could have called us." Her gaze flicked toward me. I wrapped my arms around my belly and backed up a few steps until I bumped into Mr. Garrett.

"Mom, this is Clover. Clover this is my mom, Meredith Hudson."

I wiped my hand on my pants before sticking it out. "Nice to meet you, ma'am."

"Nice to finally meet you, too." Her fingers closed around mine, and I caught a whiff of sweet-smelling perfume. "Your parents must have been concerned as well."

She released my hand, and I stuck it back in my pocket.

"Actually, I haven't seen my parents in a while."

Daniel's mom frowned. "Oh…that's a shame."

I shrugged and tried to think of a way to change the conversation, to fill the awkward silence.

"Daniel! Clover!" Amelia burst onto the veranda, followed by Sam. She hugged Daniel and then launched herself at me, her momentum almost knocking me clear off my feet. "I was so worried," she whispered in my ear. She hugged me tight and let me go before I had time to think or react.

Tears burned in my eyes, and I blinked them away. Is this how Daniel felt every day, being part of a family, having people that loved and looked out for him?

More people spilled onto the porch—a tall man who

Daniel introduced as his father, and a tiny older woman, his grandmother, who intimidated the heck out of me. Everyone talked at once. They hugged Daniel and shot questions at him. Soon people started looking at me, and I fidgeted under their curious stares.

"Clover lost all of her things in the hurricane," Daniel said. He didn't mention that they'd all been in my car.

Amelia grabbed my hand. "That's so sad. What can we do to help?"

"You don't have to," I mumbled.

"We don't have to, but we want to." Amelia looked around at the silent group. "Right, Gran?"

"Certainly." Daniel's grandmother watched me with a steady look.

"Where are you staying?" Daniel's mother asked.

"I don't know, ma'am."

"Maybe she can stay here with you, Gran, for a few days," Daniel suggested. "I know you have extra rooms."

Amelia's head bobbed up and down. "That's a great idea."

Mr. Hudson cleared his throat. "You're both putting your grandmother on the spot. That's not fair."

More silence descended on the group. Amelia squeezed my shoulder, but I just looked down at my feet.

Mr. Garrett turned to his son. "Sam, why don't we head home and leave the Hudsons to discuss this in private."

I released my breath, relieved he'd no longer be standing over my shoulder, quietly watching my exchange with the Hudson family.

"Yeah, sure." Sam stepped from the crowd and slapped Daniel on the back. "Glad you're okay, bro."

"Thanks for calling in the cavalry."

"No problem." He stopped in front of me. "Sorry about your stuff. Let me know if there's anything I can do."

I nodded, and he smiled back at me, but it was nothing

like the smile he gave Amelia before following his father down the stairs. He'd made it halfway down the driveway when Amelia stopped him.

"Sam, wait."

She flew down the steps, and they spoke for a moment, their heads bent close, before he headed to his dad's truck.

"What was that about?" Daniel asked when she practically skipped back to the house.

Amelia glared at him. "None of your business."

"Put it on hold, you two," Daniel's mom said. "We have more important things to discuss. Daniel, your dad is right. It's not fair to ask this of your grandmother. I understand that Clover needs help, but you can't assume that she can stay here."

Didn't they see me standing right in front of them? "I'm not looking for charity. I can take care of myself." I'd survived on my own before, and I'd do it again. I looked for Caesar, but he'd made himself at home, curled up on the veranda. Traitor. "Caesar…come."

My fickle friend stood and shook himself before moseying over. I snorted in disgust, not waiting for him before I started down the stairs.

"Wait…" Daniel bounded down the steps past me and blocked my path. "Where do you think you're going?"

I shrugged. I didn't know where I was headed, but I'd figure it out. I sidestepped, but he blocked me again.

"Don't be stupid. You have no money and no clothes. You have no one to help you."

My earlier tears welled and spilled over. "Thanks for reminding me." I wiped at them. My hands clenched into fists.

"Come on. I didn't mean it like that."

"Why not? It's the truth."

"It's not." He bent down to scratch Caesar between the ears. "You have me." Looking up at me, his goodness shone so bright, I had to turn away. I hadn't done anything to deserve his help.

"Why?" I whispered, unsure if he'd heard, but he answered.

"I wish I knew." His words barely reached me, he'd spoken them so softly.

It wasn't the answer I wanted, but what right did I have to ask for more? We hardly knew each other. Who was I kidding? He didn't know me at all.

"Daniel…" Ginny King approached, her stern expression making my knees knock together.

"Yes, Gran."

"I'd like to talk to Clover alone."

Daniel's uncertain gaze shifted back and forth from me to his grandmother.

"Are you sure, Mom?" Daniel's mother cut in.

"Very sure. I think it's time you head home, Daniel, and get cleaned up. I'll let you all know when I'm done talking to Clover."

By the way the Hudson clan hurried to their car, I understood that people didn't defy Daniel's grandmother. Before they left, Amelia gave me an encouraging smile and Daniel whispered "good luck" in my ear, and then I was alone with the woman, alone and shaking in my sneakers.

# Chapter Nine

A knock at the door sent me sliding lower into the claw-foot tub. A wave of bubbly water sloshed over the side. The door creaked open, and Ginny King appeared with fresh towels and clothes in her arms.

"It's been a while, so I thought I'd check on you," she said without apology. She dropped her load on the countertop. After the Hudsons left, Daniel's grandmother "suggested" I wash up and change before we talked.

"Sorry, ma'am. I lost track of time."

I didn't want to tell her how long it'd been since I'd bathed with hot water from a tap. The skin on my toes and fingers had all wrinkled up, but I couldn't stand to leave the sweet-smelling water.

"Well, I can't criticize anyone for wanting to be clean, and you can call me Ms. Ginny."

"Yes, ma'am."

She stared, one hand on her hip.

"Yes, Ms. Ginny," I corrected.

She held up a skirt and top. "This may not be the latest

fashion, but we look to be the same size." She leaned over to pluck my dirty clothes from the floor, and her nose wrinkled. "I'll throw these in the wash."

I gripped the sides of the tub, ready to get out but too embarrassed to stand up in front of Daniel's grandmother. "You don't have to do this. I know Daniel didn't give you much choice."

She shook her head and pulled a hairbrush out of a drawer, adding it to the growing pile of supplies. "Nonsense. As you will come to find out, I don't do anything that I don't want to do, and exactly how much I'm prepared to help has yet to be determined. We'll talk when you're dressed."

Ms. Ginny left, and I scrambled out of the tub, using a large, fluffy towel to dry off. I buried my face in it, inhaling the fresh scent of laundry soap. I pulled on the clothes she'd left. The top was a little loose, but the flowered skirt fit me fine. After, I lingered in front of the mirror. I tugged the brush through my tangled hair and sniffed at the perfume bottles and jars of cream lining the vanity. They brought back memories of Mama. When I was little, before Daddy got worse, she'd let me try on a little of her makeup. She'd even painted my toenails with bright pink nail polish.

I left the bathroom and wandered down the hall, stopping at each open door. Wrought-iron beds, homemade quilts, and flowered wallpaper turned the four bedrooms into a life-sized dollhouse. Sunlight spilled into the rooms through lace-covered windows. I knew Ms. Ginny waited for me downstairs, but I couldn't move past the room at the back of the house that overlooked the yard. The quilt, stitched with rings of green and pink, matched the braided rug stretched across the hardwood floor. The bed was so soft, I sank into the middle as soon as I lay down on it.

Curling into a ball, I lost myself in a memory of a life that was never mine. I lived in this house. My clothes hung in the closet in the corner, and Mama waited for me downstairs in the kitchen. It was my birthday, and she'd baked a chocolate cake. My friends came, and we ate cookies and drank iced tea in the shade of the trees in the yard. Daddy was there, too, but he was different. He told jokes and admired my birthday gifts. Later, Mama and I snuggled in my bed. She pulled out the special gift she'd kept until we were alone. It was wrapped in white paper with a big pink bow. I wanted to know what it was, but I fell asleep before I could open it.

I blinked and stretched. My hand stroked the soft, scented linens under my cheek. I pushed away the blanket and struggled to a sitting position. The only light came from a small lamp on a table in the corner. How long had I slept?

I found Ms. Ginny downstairs in the living room, curled up in an armchair with a book. Uncertain, I hovered in the doorway until she looked up.

"You're awake."

"I'm sorry. I didn't mean to…" My voice trailed off, and I shifted in my bare feet. I didn't mean to what—fall asleep in her spare bed, overstay my welcome, intrude in her life?

She waved away my apology. "You obviously needed the sleep. That room used to belong to Daniel's mother. It's always been my favorite."

My head bobbed. "It's perfect."

"You must be hungry."

I started to deny it, but my stomach protested loud enough for Ms. Ginny to hear.

"I'll heat you up some supper." She stood and laid her book on a side table. "We're lucky enough to have our power back already."

I followed her to the kitchen at the rear of the house.

"Can I help?"

She looked over, not even pausing in her trek from the fridge to the stove. "No, just have a seat."

Not used to being waited on, I perched on the edge of a chair. "Where's Caesar?"

"He's spending the night in the garage. Don't worry. He's got food, water, and a comfortable bed."

"Should I check on him?"

"If you'd like, but he's fine."

I wanted to go, just to see a familiar face, but I stayed put, worried that she'd think I didn't believe her.

Nearby, family pictures stood on an antique hutch. A younger version of Daniel posed on the beach, his arm thrown around a beaming Amelia. He looked different — more carefree and happy. What happened to change him? I wanted to know.

"He's called twice to check on you."

I swiveled my head to meet Ms. Ginny's stare, and my cheeks turned hot.

"I think he's worried that I'm going to put you out on the street."

"Daniel's been a good friend."

"Is that all?"

I tucked my fingers under my legs so she couldn't see them shaking. "What do you mean?"

"I'm old, Clover, which means I wasn't born yesterday. There's clearly more going on between you two."

The kettle whistled, and Ms. Ginny turned away to fill a pretty teapot with steaming water. I was glad for the distraction. It gave me time to gather my scattered thoughts.

Shrugging my shoulders, I tried to explain, not knowing if my words would make sense. "I met Daniel three days ago, but it feels like longer. He makes me feel like…like I could be a better person when he's around."

Ms. Ginny crossed the kitchen and laid a plate on the table. The smell of fried chicken and gravy made my mouth water.

"That sounds like a lot of feeling for someone you just met."

"Does it?" It was all so new to me. "Are there rules about how long it should take to have these feelings?"

She stood over me, hands on her hips. "No, but there are rules about respecting your elders and not biting the hand that feeds you."

I lowered my head and gnawed at my bottom lip. Once again I'd said something wrong, something to anger Ms. Ginny, but I wasn't sure what. Why did everything have to be so complicated?

Ms. Ginny walked back to the kitchen counter, and I started to breathe again. She poured herself a cup of tea, returned to the table, and slipped into the closest chair. "Look, Daniel's practically a grown man, and he's always made good decisions, but he's also my grandson. I want to make sure he's not getting involved with something or someone he shouldn't."

"Like me," I whispered.

"Maybe…"

My stomach clenched.

"But I'm not sure yet." She added a teaspoon of sugar to her cup and slowly stirred. "Lots of people go through tough times. It doesn't make them a bad person. It's how you choose to deal with the rough times that defines your character."

"Have you gone through…rough times?"

She sighed and looked over at me. Her expression softened a little. "You don't live to be my age without experiencing some rough patches."

"How did you get though them?"

"With the support of friends and family, and by having

faith."

I picked up my fork and looked at the mashed potatoes and fried chicken. Why wasn't I hungry anymore? "I don't really have any friends or family, well, except for Daniel, and I'm not sure that I have much left in the way of faith."

Ms. Ginny stared real hard, and I turned away, afraid of what she'd see.

"That's a shame. Everyone deserves to have people they can count on. What about your parents?"

I shook my head.

Her fingers brushed against mine, and I jumped. "You know, sometimes it helps to talk."

For a moment, I was tempted. I could open my mouth and let everything pour out, but then I remembered the sheriff back in Virginia and the gun Mr. Garrett wore strapped to his side. I swallowed hard against the lump in my throat and pulled my hand away. "And sometimes talking just leads to more trouble."

Ms. Ginny clucked. "That's a real big wall you've built around yourself." She casually sipped her tea. "Let me know when you're ready to start taking it down."

I pushed my chair back from the table. "I understand if you want me to leave."

"And if I did, where would you go?" She laid her cup back in its saucer. "If you left right now, where would you sleep tonight?"

I sprang to my feet and lifted my chin. "I'd figure something out." I squared my shoulders. With every breath, I fought the weight that seemed to press down on me. I couldn't let myself think about the pretty bed that waited upstairs.

"You could," Ms. Ginny said. She took another sip of tea, while I paced the floor. How could she sit, so calm, when I felt like I was back in the middle of the hurricane, scared and wet, but with no Daniel to cling to? "Or you could accept the help

I'm prepared to offer."

I stopped pacing and dug my fingers into the back of the chair. "But you want me to leave."

"I never said that, and it doesn't pay to jump to conclusions." She leaned back and looked up at me. "Daniel mentioned on the phone that you like to write. Are you any good at it?"

I shook my head, trying to understand what she was asking me.

She frowned. "So, you're not good at it?"

"No…I mean…I think I'm good at it, but I don't know. I've never let anyone read my stories." Not even Mama.

She crossed her legs and brushed a piece of lint from her slacks. "Hmmm…that could be an issue."

"An issue for what?"

"The job I'm planning to offer you."

I sank back into my chair. "A job?"

"Yes, a job. For several years, I've been working on documenting the history of Canna Point. It's a project that means a lot to me. So here's my offer—you stay here with me, and in exchange, you write our town's story."

"Really? You want to hire me to write a book?"

I let myself imagine it—staying in Canna Point, living with Ms. Ginny, seeing Daniel. Maybe, if I had enough time, I'd find the nerve to talk to my grandparents. It seemed too good to be true, like someone was playing a cruel joke.

"Maybe," she said.

My heart sank. Of course, she'd change her mind. Some people had rosy, shiny lives and others didn't. I knew my place in my world.

"There'd be ground rules—things you'd need to agree to."

"Ground rules?"

"Yes. Daniel can tell you that there are certain things I don't like, untidiness and tardiness being two of them. If you're going to stay here, I expect you to help with chores and be on time for meals."

I nodded my head. "I can do that."

"Of course, it would be on a trial basis. You'd actually be working for the Canna Point Historical Society, and the other members would have to agree that your writing is good enough."

"That sounds fair."

"And then there's the matter of my grandson."

I straightened in my chair. Would she ask me to stay away from him? Could I make that bargain if it meant a home for Caesar and me?

"Call me old-fashioned, but I don't agree with all this hanky-panky that goes on between young people these days. If you're living in my house, I want your promise that there'll be no inappropriate behavior under my roof."

Inappropriate behavior… I thought about Daniel's lips touching mine, the way I felt when he smiled at me, the way I felt small and protected when he carried me out of the boat earlier. Which part was inappropriate? I pushed my thumb to my lips. He'd kissed me, my first kiss, but I knew there had to be more. What else did boys and girls do? My cheeks heated again. Could Ms. Ginny see my curiosity about this hanky-panky business? Daddy always said I was too curious for my own good.

She glared at me. "Your behavior right now is not reassuring me."

My shoulders sagged. "I'm sorry."

"I can see that I'll have to have the same talk with Daniel. I know he'll listen."

"Yes, Ms. Ginny."

"Well, at least you didn't try to deny what you're thinking, which brings me to my last rule. This one is absolute. I don't tolerate lies. Is that understood?"

My heart sank all the way to the bottom of my belly. I'd learned over the years that lying was a complicated subject. Even good people sometimes lied to protect the people they loved. Mama had made lying to Daddy into an art form. Sometimes, lies were the only option...times like now. Sometimes lies served a greater purpose, at least that's what I told myself.

I crossed my fingers behind my back so Ms. Ginny couldn't see. "I promise. No lies."

I looked out the window, worried that a bolt of lightning would somehow appear and strike me where I sat, but the evening remained quiet. Ms. Ginny smiled, and I returned it. I'd passed her test, and the thrill of a fresh start charged through my body.

"So, it's settled then."

"Yes." My head bobbed in agreement.

"Tomorrow you can start going through the information we've already accumulated. I have to warn you there's a lot to look through. The other writer we hired, imbecile that he was, had already started condensing things into computer files."

"Computer files?"

"Yes, you can use the computer in the study." She saw the hesitation on my face. "You know how to use a computer, don't you?"

"Not really." I gripped the edge of the table, sure I was about to get fired, but Ms. Ginny only sighed.

"I'm not much for computers myself. Maybe Daniel can help you."

"Daniel?"

"Sure. He's good with computers, and I have the feeling he'll be here in the morning anyway."

Was she right? The thought made me smile.

"Now, get started on your supper. It's a shame to see good food go to waste."

I stared down at the fried chicken and found my appetite had come back, stronger than before.

That night I went to bed with a full belly and, even though I was sleeping in a strange bed, I felt somehow at home, like I was finally where I was supposed to be. I didn't dream about Mama. In fact, I didn't dream at all.

# Chapter Ten

The sun was just poking over the fence in the backyard when I woke up the next morning. I washed and dressed in the clothes Ms. Ginny had given me the night before.

I headed to the kitchen, my bare feet skidding across the hardwood floor. Ms. Ginny already stood at the stove, filling the air with the smell of eggs and bacon frying in the pan.

"Good morning, young lady." She'd tied an apron over her dress, her makeup and hair looking perfect for such an early hour. I brushed a hand over my own hair, making sure nothing was sticking up. "I'm glad to see you're an early riser. Breakfast is almost ready."

I glanced at the back door. "I'd like to check on Caesar first."

"Go right ahead. The garage key is hanging by the door. You can use the hose to fill his bowl. I borrowed a bag of dog food from my neighbor last evening. It's on the shelf against the back wall of the garage."

I slipped my feet into my sneakers. Ms. Ginny had washed the worst of the mud off, but the insides were still a little damp. I paused halfway out the door to take it all in—the scent of roses, the chirp of grasshoppers, the heat against my skin, the slight breeze tugging at my skirt. I tried to remember another morning that smelled so sweet, that smelled so much like hope.

Inside the garage, the shelves overflowed with decades of tools and toys and unfinished projects. Someone—I assumed Ms. Ginny—had cleared a spot for Caesar in the middle and laid out an old sleeping bag for him to lie on.

"Hey, boy." I gave him a long belly rub and breathed in the musty smell of old wood and forgotten things. "Sorry for deserting you last night, but it looks like you did pretty well for yourself."

He nudged my leg while I filled his bowl with food and used the hose to top off his water. While he ate, I nosed around the packed shelves. Eventually, he'd had enough and headed outside to explore, but I stayed.

Alone, I dug through the garden equipment and tools. Hidden behind some paint cans and a chair with a missing leg, I found a bicycle. A thick layer of dust covered the frame, so I wheeled it outside to take a better look. I wiped off the worst of the dust with my hand and hiked my leg over to test the seat—a little high, but I could touch the ground with the tips of my toes. Both tires needed air, but the chain looked good. I checked the brakes.

"That bike belonged to Meredith."

I turned to find Ms. Ginny watching me from the back door.

"It's real nice, but the tires are flat."

"There should be a pump in the garage. You're welcome to use it, if you wanted to clean it up."

"Are you sure?"

"I wouldn't have offered if I wasn't sure. It's better off being used than rusting away in the back of the garage. Do you know how to ride?"

I nodded, and a grin spread across my face. The bike I'd owned back in Virginia didn't fit in the car, so I'd left it behind. It wasn't as nice as this bike, either. It didn't have a deep basket and shiny red paint, but I still missed it.

I nudged the kickstand down with my foot and slid off, feeling mighty pleased with myself. I wanted to explore Canna Point, and I'd found the perfect way. Ms. Ginny disappeared back into the house, and I stretched my arms over my head and twirled in a circle.

Maybe I'd been wrong about some people not having shiny lives. Maybe Daniel and Ms. Ginny and even the bike were signs that it was my turn to be happy. I'd buried my past for two years, and until the sheriff's visit, I'd been doing a good job at it. There was no reason why I couldn't bury it again. This time I'd hide it so deep that no one would ever find it, not even Mr. Garrett and his prying looks.

I headed inside for breakfast, a grin on my face. As soon as I finished eating, I'd find the pump and tackle the tires.

It was a perfect day to start rewriting my life's story.

I rode toward the center of town, careful to avoid the streets still blocked with fallen trees and power lines, and ended up on the town's main street. A few storefronts were still boarded up from the hurricane, but most were open for business, including the sporting goods store. I thought about going in to see if Daniel was working but chickened out.

Reaching the town square, I stood my bike up close to a stone plaque. The years had worn at the words until they were barely legible. I could make out CANNA POINT and FOUNDED IN. The year was a mystery. I sat on a bench under the shade of a tree that was probably older than the plaque and chewed on the apple I'd taken from Ms. Ginny's kitchen. Sitting there, I noticed a group of old men gossiping around their checkerboards and walking canes.

I watched them for a while, and then one of them spoke to me. I'd been taught to be wary of strangers, but all I saw was a whole lot of loneliness and sadness hiding behind their grumpy expressions and sniping. So when they asked if I'd like to play, I couldn't say no.

Two hours later, I looked up from the checkerboard to see Daniel walking toward me. My eyes widened, and my mouth lifted into a smile. The morning sun bathed him in a golden glow, and I couldn't look away, not even when Mr. Wallace gloated over capturing another one of my checkers.

"Clover, I've been looking all over for you."

Mr. Wallace pointed a pudgy finger at Daniel. "Who's this? Your boyfriend?"

I pressed my palm against my chest and shook my head.

Daniel reached the table and crouched down beside me, frowning at the board. "What are you doing here?" He was dressed for work, wearing the same shirt and pants he'd worn the first time I met him. His hair was damp, and he smelled fresh and clean, like the air after a spring shower.

Hank Crawford answered from two tables over. "What does it look like she's doing? She's losing at checkers." Mr. Crawford claimed that his eyesight wasn't so good, but he'd already beaten me three straight games in a row. His wife died four years ago, and now he lived with his daughter, son-in-law, and granddaughter. He used to be an accountant, and before that he'd served in the army.

"You still haven't told us who he is, Clover." Mr. Wallace gave Daniel the evil eye, and I hid my smile behind my hand. Mr. Wallace had been told by his doctor to start getting exercise or he was going to die of a heart attack. So every day he told his wife he was walking, but instead he came here.

For the fifth time since I'd arrived, he pulled a chocolate bar out of his jacket, broke off a piece, and stuffed it in his mouth. Like the other times, he didn't offer to share.

I cleared my throat and pulled my lips into a straight line. "This is Daniel Hudson. He's a friend."

"Hudson," Mr. Crawford said. "As in Hudson's Sporting Goods? As in Ernie Hudson's son?"

Daniel didn't say anything, so I nodded for him. "I'm staying with Ms. Ginny right now."

Daniel straightened and took a quick look around the ragtag group. He stuffed his hands in his pockets and glanced back down at me. "I came because Gran said you needed help with her computer, but I've got to be at work soon." He gestured back to the road where a green pickup truck was parked against the curb, the store logo on the door.

"She can't be leaving in the middle of a game unless she plans to forfeit," Mr. Wallace said. He rubbed his hands together, ready to claim victory if I gave up.

"Hey...I know...aren't you the boy who was going out with that girl who died a couple years ago?" Mr. Mendoza, the man playing checkers with Mr. Crawford, asked. He scrunched up his face like he was trying to remember something important. "What was her name, Hank?"

"It was Bill Carter's daughter, Grace. I went to the funeral. Terrible time." Mr. Crawford's big voice boomed through the quiet morning.

Daniel stiffened. He pulled his hands out of his pockets and squeezed them into fists. "I've got to get to work, Clover. Have fun with your checkers."

"Wait!" I jumped to my feet, but Daniel kept walking. I ran to catch up, but he didn't stop until we were almost at the truck. When he turned, I saw sadness all wrapped up in anger, and I wished I knew how to wipe it away. I wanted to know who Grace was and how she'd died, but I'd already figured out the most important part. Whoever this Grace was, she was responsible for the change in him—the reason the carefree boy in the picture at Ms. Ginny's house had disappeared.

"What?" he asked, and I flinched at his tone.

"You're angry." I held my breath for a long time before letting it go. "At me?"

He didn't say anything, but then he sighed. "No. I'm not angry with you."

"Good." His eyes turned to green, and a weight lifted off me. "I wanted to thank you for yesterday—for rescuing me and finding me a place to live. Ms. Ginny offered me a real job."

"I know. I'm glad everything worked out." He looked at his watch and back at his truck. "I really have to go. Dad will kill me if I'm late for my shift."

I tried to keep the disappointment from my face. "Oh. I'm sorry that you spent so much time looking for me."

He rubbed one hand across the back of his neck. "I was worried. Gran wasn't sure where you were, and with all this debris around, biking is not the safest. You should at least wear a helmet."

A warm feeling spread through my body. He'd been worried about me. "I'm a really good biker. I can even ride with no hands."

Daniel groaned. "Don't tell me those things. Just promise me you'll try to stay away from life-threatening situations for a few days." His mouth lifted into a smile, like he was trying to keep things light, but then it fell back into a frown. "I need some time to recover from the last two."

I crossed my heart with my finger. "I promise."

He slapped his palm against his forehead. "Now why doesn't that make me feel any better?"

"I don't know."

"Of course, you don't." He motioned with his hand to my

bike. "I can give you a lift to Gran's if we leave now. I'll put the bike in the back of the truck."

I glanced over at the tables where my newfound friends stared at us, not even trying to be discrete. "I think I'll stay and finish this game."

He shook his head. "You're different from anyone I've ever met."

"Is that bad?"

"I'm not sure. I haven't figured it out yet."

He started toward his truck, and I followed.

"Why did you kiss me?"

His head jerked up. "What?"

I leaned against the hood, the metal warm and smooth under my hands. "Yesterday… I want to know why you kissed me. It was my first kiss, you know."

"I'm sorry." His cheeks turned red. "I shouldn't have done that."

"But I liked it."

"You did?"

"Yes." I tilted my face up toward the sun. "Maybe we could do it again sometime."

His eyes widened, and I knew I'd said something wrong again.

"I mean…only if you want to."

A slow smile curved his lips, and he shook his head. "If only your damn dog didn't look so much like Sandy," he said, before climbing into the truck and slamming the door.

I had no idea what that meant, but when he drove away, he honked his horn twice. My hand crept up to press against my fluttering heart. I smiled again, even bigger than I had that morning.

# Chapter Eleven

"What should I wear?" I chewed on my lip and looked at the few pieces of clothes hanging in my closet. Amelia flopped on the bed behind me.

"It's just a barbecue at my house. What you're wearing is fine."

Giving up on the closet, I picked up a brush from the dresser. My hand shook a little when I pulled it though my hair, smoothing it out. "Why do I feel so nervous, like there's a squirrel in my belly trying to get out?"

Amelia laughed and rolled onto her back. "I love talking to you. You crack me up every time."

I frowned. "Is that good?"

"It's great," she said. "You're unique, and we love you for it."

"Maybe." I dropped the brush back on the dresser and crossed to the window.

"What's wrong?" She sat up. "Come on. I can hear it in your voice."

I pulled the lace curtain aside so I could see the garden.

I couldn't tell her what was really wrong—that I didn't understand anything when it came to Daniel. He'd come to the house the day after he'd found me in the park, and I could tell right away he was different. He'd helped me with the computer. He'd shown me every step of opening, searching, and saving computer files. I still longed for my typewriter, but I now knew how to type, delete, and correct without using a single piece of paper.

But other than helping me with the computer, he'd stayed quiet. He'd left right after he finished helping, and I hadn't seen him since. I wanted to ask what I'd done wrong, but I was nervous of the answer. Maybe I hadn't done as good a job of hiding my secrets as I thought. Maybe he'd figured out that I didn't deserve someone like him in my life.

More than anything, I wished Mama were here so I could talk to her. I'd asked her once about Daddy and if she loved him. She'd told me that Daddy wasn't her first love. There'd been someone else, someone who broke her heart. She was nineteen, almost twenty, when I was born, so I figured she must have been around my age or younger when she'd fallen in love with this other boy.

I couldn't tell any of this to Amelia, so I lied and hoped that Ms. Ginny would never find out. "I don't think your parents like me." But this wasn't even a real lie.

Amelia sprang off the bed. "That's not true."

"Are you sure?"

She frowned and pulled me back over to the bed. "Look, you just have to understand my parents. My dad is all gruff and manly, definitely not in touch with his feminine side, and my mom is just…" She paused and blew out a breath. "She's just very protective over her family. She worries about Daniel, especially when it comes to girls."

What did that mean? Was it about Grace again?

"She just needs to get to know you, and then she'll love

you as much as I do."

My eyes swept her face. Amelia was beautiful, talented, and smart. I just couldn't figure out why she was being so nice to me. "I've never had a real friend before, besides Caesar. I just wanted you to know that I'm glad I found you and Daniel."

She met my gaze, her eyes sad. "I don't know why you grew up the way you did, but I'm sorry. You deserved better."

I looked away, not ready for the way her words made me feel. My eyes burned, and I couldn't quite catch my breath.

She sighed and rested her head on my shoulder. We sat like that without talking, listening to the crickets through the open window. I paid attention to every detail—the shadows on the floor, the smell of the late-afternoon breeze, the brush of the lace curtains against the windowsill. No matter what else happened, this was a moment no one could take away. Maybe someday, if I was lucky, I'd have enough of these good moments to outnumber the bad.

Daniel and Amelia's house was like no home I'd ever seen before, with marble floors, huge windows, and fancy columns. Ms. Ginny's house was beautiful, with her lace and antique furniture, but I could picture Mama in it. I could imagine her in the kitchen making pies and cookies. In Ms. Ginny's house, if I tried real hard, I could belong, but Daniel and Amelia's house was like a foreign planet. Even the kitchen was intimidating, with its shiny silver gadgets and appliances.

"What is that?" I whispered to Amelia, pointing to some fancy buttons on the fridge door.

Her eyebrows drew together. "It's the ice and water dispenser. Watch." She pulled a glass from a cupboard and pushed it against a lever. A light came on and ice clinked into the glass. She pressed another lever and a steady stream of water poured out. She handed it to me, and I eyed it with suspicion, watching tiny bubbles swirl their way to the top.

"It's okay. You can drink it."

I sipped, but it didn't taste anywhere near as good as the water we got from the creek back in Virginia.

"Everyone must be outside." Amelia led me from the kitchen and through a room with a giant couch covered in pillows and a huge television set mounted to the wall.

In the corner of the room, something that looked like a bicycle sat on a big black stand. I stopped in my tracks. "What's that?"

Amelia rolled her eyes. "An exercise bike?"

"But how does it move?"

"It doesn't. See." She climbed on and started pedaling. A panel above the weird-looking handlebars lit up. "This tells me how far I've ridden and how many calories I've burned."

"But why would you want to ride a bike if it can't take you anywhere?"

She climbed off. "To stay in shape."

"But when you ride outside, you feel the wind on your face and you see things."

"Tell that to my mother. She rides that thing for an hour every morning."

I shook my head. Was this the way people lived? I understood so little, but I wasn't sure how much I wanted to know. Had Daddy been right to keep us close to home? Was the world full of greed and corruption? But that couldn't be right, because Amelia and Daniel lived here, and they were good people.

Amelia touched my arm. "Come on. You're going to love the backyard."

"Ahhh…good. You're here." Daniel's mom smiled at me from across the patio, dressed in a pair of denim shorts and a plain white T-shirt. Maybe Amelia was right when she said I wasn't underdressed, but I still felt out of place.

A wooden table, long enough to seat a small army, took up most of the covered area. Mr. Hudson stood in front of a big, shiny barbecue. He waved at me and then turned back to his cooking. Further down the patio, rocking chairs sat in front of a stone fireplace. Plants spilled out of clay pots and lined the matching stone walkway, which led to a gigantic swimming pool that looked more like a pond. I gasped at the waterfall and the slide.

Someone jumped off the rock wall and landed with a splash in the middle of the pool.

"That would be Daniel." Amelia snorted and whispered under her breath, "I wonder who he's showing off for?"

I shrugged, but I watched the surface until I saw his head pop up, a grin on his face. Only his smile didn't last. It disappeared the exact moment he saw me. Frowning, he dove back under and resurfaced closer to the edge. He pulled himself out, the muscles in his upper arms bulging. I gulped, suddenly feeling too hot.

He grabbed a towel from a nearby chair and used it to dry his hair. After, he hooked it around his neck, but I could still see his bare chest and lean waist. My mouth felt dry, like it was on fire, so I gulped back some water.

"Amelia," Mrs. Hudson said, "could you please bring out the salad? We're almost ready to eat. Clover, I hope you like hamburgers and potato salad."

I nodded. "Yes, ma'am. Thank you for having me over. I don't want to be any trouble."

Her long look made me want to squirm, or maybe it was Daniel. He'd reached the table. Water dripped from his swim trunks and left a small puddle under his feet. I set my glass down on the table and avoided looking at his bare chest, but I felt his stare on me.

"It's not any trouble," Daniel's mom said. "Daniel, you're dripping. Are you planning to change before supper?"

I peeked over at him, needing to look up to see his face. How could I have forgotten how tall he was? Was he growing, or maybe I was shrinking?

"Nah. I'm probably getting back in later." He looked down at me. "You made it."

"Yes."

"Clover…" Mrs. Hudson looked at me again. "Did you bring your swimsuit? Maybe you'd all like to swim after supper."

I lowered my head. "I don't know how." I didn't add that I didn't even own a swimsuit.

"That's too bad. If you're going to live in Florida, it's a handy skill to have. You never know when you might fall in the water and need to save yourself."

"Mom!" Daniel glared at his mother, but she only shrugged.

"I'm just saying that it would be useful. Wouldn't you agree, Clover?"

"Yes, ma'am."

Daniel took a step closer to me. "I'm sure Clover will learn to swim when she's ready."

Mrs. Hudson looked like she wanted to say more, but Amelia appeared on the patio with a large bowl of potato salad, and Mr. Hudson dropped a platter of burgers on the table.

"Let's eat," he said. "I hope you're hungry."

I nodded. "Yes, sir."

Amelia pulled out a chair and sat down. "Here, sit next to me."

Daniel sat on the opposite side of the table, next to his mom. Everyone started serving themselves. Even after a couple of days in Ms. Ginny's house, I wasn't used to so much food, but the Hudsons seemed to take it for granted. I already understood that Daniel had never climbed into bed with hunger pains twisting his belly.

"So, Clover, how's the book going?" Mr. Hudson asked.

I cleared my throat. "I've really just started. Ms. Ginny has so much information to go through." That was the understatement of the year. She'd dedicated an entire room on the first floor of her house to the history of Canna Point— old newspapers, books, legal documents, letters.

"Well, good luck. Hopefully, you'll last longer than the last guy."

The conversation turned away from me and onto a discussion of the hurricane. Grateful, I busied myself with my food, and as if I wasn't there, the Hudsons fell into their natural rhythm—the rise and fall of questions and answers, joking and interjections. I didn't understand half of what they said, but I laughed when everyone else did and frowned when it seemed I was supposed to. Mostly, I watched.

Was this the way most families were? Sharing with no fear, saying whatever came to mind, being opinionated, loving, and respectful all at the same time? Had we ever been like that—me and Daddy and Mama? I remembered a time when I was little. We'd driven to the ocean in the same car I'd lost in the hurricane. Daddy was having a good spell, and we'd had a picnic on the beach. We'd driven home in the dark. I'd sat in the backseat and stared out at the stars, feeling really small. I felt even smaller when they started to fight. I'd closed my eyes and pretended to be asleep, but really, I'd just lain in the back and silently begged Mama to take me somewhere far away. She never did.

"Clover…"

I jerked upright in my seat and met four sets of curious eyes. "Yes, ma'am," I said to Mrs. Hudson.

"I was just asking how you like the burger. You haven't

eaten much."

I stared down at my half-finished meal. "I'm just a slow eater, but it's the best burger I ever remember tasting."

Mr. Hudson's chest puffed out, and he smiled at me from the head of the table. "Well, you can just come on back here the next time we have a barbecue."

"Thank you, sir."

Amelia elbowed me in the side. "Good one. You compliment my daddy's barbecuing, and you've made yourself a friend for life."

"Speaking of next time," Mrs. Hudson said, "you haven't told us how long you're planning on staying in Canna Point."

"I haven't decided." Because I had no idea how long I'd be welcome at Ms. Ginny's house.

"You seem awful young to be here on your own. How old are you?"

I swallowed. "I turned eighteen in March."

Mrs. Hudson leaned forward in her seat. "Did you celebrate with your family? I know you said you hadn't seen your parents in a while, but there must be someone."

"Mom!" Daniel shot his mother another warning look. Just like earlier, he came to my defense, but I didn't understand why. He'd barely spoken to me during supper.

Mrs. Hudson shook her head. "I think it's perfectly reasonable for us to know a little more about the young woman living with my mother."

"Not if she doesn't want to tell you. She has a right to her privacy." Daniel's jaw clenched. His angry tone made me feel awful. I'd heard enough fighting to last a lifetime. I didn't want to be responsible for more.

"It's okay, Daniel. Your mother's right for asking. She's only looking out for her family."

I bit my lip hard, the shot of pain somehow giving me the courage to answer Mrs. Hudson. "There's only me…and

Caesar. It's been that way for a while. I don't have any money, I don't have any clothes other than what I'm wearing and what Ms. Ginny gave me, and I don't have any place to sleep other than her house. I was living out of my car, and when the hurricane came, I lost everything. I'm not proud of it, but I'm trying hard to start over."

I finished talking and sucked in a breath.

The table fell silent, everyone frozen in position like they'd been hit by a witch's spell that could stop time.

Embarrassment sent heat licking across my cheeks. "If you'll all excuse me…"

I pushed back my chair and fled inside. I wanted to go home to Ms. Ginny's house, but I had no idea how to get there, so I settled on finding a bathroom to hide in.

In the front entryway, I opened a door, but it was a closet. Shoot.

"Clover, wait."

I turned to find Daniel's mom a few feet away, her eyes wide and her body stiff.

"I owe you an apology. I—" She took a deep breath and clasped her hands in front of her. "I was feeling protective over my family, but I was also judging you, which wasn't fair. If both Amelia and Daniel tell me you're a good person, it should be enough. Regardless, you're a guest in my house, and there's no excuse for my being rude."

I knew her words were meant to make me feel better, but they only made me feel worse. She was apologizing, but if she knew who I really was, she'd be right to kick me out, to ask me to stay away from her family.

"I'm really hoping you'll forgive me."

"Clover?" Daniel appeared in the doorway behind his mother. "You okay?"

I swallowed back tears, but they still pricked at my eyes and clogged my throat. "Yes, I was just looking for the bathroom."

Mrs. Hudson's hand brushed my arm. "And we're okay?"

I nodded. "Yes. Maybe you could just tell me where it is?"

"Of course. It's down the hall, first door on the left."

Mrs. Hudson retreated to the kitchen, but Daniel lingered.

I cleared my throat. "I'm fine…really."

"I know. I just wanted to say that I was proud of the way you stood up to my mom. You shouldn't be ashamed of who you are."

I wrapped my arms around my belly. "I'm not." I only felt tired, tired of lying, tired of being different, tired of never belonging.

"I was also hoping that you wouldn't hate my mom. She's really great, most of the time."

How could I hate a mother for looking out for her kids? It's what I always wanted from Mama. "She loves you."

"Yeah." He leaned back against the wall, his bare feet stuck out in front of him. His swim trunks made wet patches on the T-shirt he'd pulled on.

"She worries about you." I hadn't planned to, but I took a step closer. I stopped when my toes were only inches from his. I was tired, but being this close to Daniel made me feel tingly. It made my heart race.

"That, too."

"I've got to go."

Daniel's foot stretched out and nudged my toes. I looked up at him, not understanding what I saw in his stare. "Not yet. Stay a while."

I sucked in a breath. I was definitely having inappropriate thoughts about Daniel Hudson. "I mean that I have to go… to the bathroom."

"Oh." He chuckled and straightened, towering over me. "Then I'll see you later."

When I came out fifteen minutes later—the length of time it took to calm my pounding heart—Amelia waited for me just outside the bathroom door.

"Sorry about earlier with my mom."

"It's okay. She already apologized."

Amelia stepped closer. "I still feel bad, but I have an idea." She caught my hand in hers. "Let's go to my room."

I followed her up the curved staircase and down the hall. If my room back at Ms. Ginny's was a life-sized dollhouse, Amelia's room was like stepping inside a painting. The white walls were blank canvases on which she'd created the most vivid images I'd ever seen—splashes of fuchsia and purple and turquoise.

"It's beautiful. Did you do all this?"

She grinned. "Yup. It practically gave Mom a heart attack."

I leaned over her bright blue desk to stare at a wall of photos. Amelia snapped on a lamp so I could see better.

I recognized almost everyone in the pictures, except one person—a laughing girl with black hair and brown eyes, her arm wrapped around Amelia or Daniel or both of them. Amelia was busy opening and closing drawers, but I continued to stare at the faces I knew and the one face I didn't.

"Okay. I'm done," she said eventually. I turned to find her standing next to a small mountain of clothes.

"Done what?"

"These are all the clothes that don't fit me or I'm not going to wear anymore. I want you to have them."

I picked up the closest piece of clothing, a green silky top, and held it to my chest. I sank to the bed but couldn't speak.

Amelia looked at my expression and started pacing the floor. "Oh my god, please tell me you're not offended. It's just that you said you didn't have any clothes left, and I have so much I don't even use. Daniel always says I act without thinking." She stopped in front of me, her eyes wide. "Please say something. Tell me you're not pissed off or totally freaked out."

My chest hurt like I'd been running. "Your family keeps giving me so much. More than I deserve, and I don't know why," I whispered.

"So…you're not pissed off?" she asked with a hopeful look.

I shook my head.

"Excellent." She grinned and disappeared back in her closet, emerging a few seconds later with a duffel bag. "You can use this to take everything back to Gran's house."

"Are you sure your mother won't mind?"

Amelia stuffed the clothes inside without pausing. "Are you kidding? She'll be ecstatic. She's always at me to clean out my room and get rid of the stuff I don't need."

"You really don't wear any of these clothes?" I held up a yellow sundress. "They're so beautiful."

Amelia grimaced. "Most of these clothes I outgrew freshman year, when I became the second tallest girl in my class."

"I wish I was taller."

"Are you kidding me? Short is way better. You don't have to worry about finding a guy who's taller than you. Do you know how many times I've worn flat shoes so I wouldn't tower over my date? Shorter girls have this whole 'cute' thing going on. Makes the guys feel all manly and protective."

I looked up at her and shook my head. I couldn't believe that beautiful Amelia worried about being too tall. "Have you been on lots of dates?"

She winked at me. "Daniel would say it's been too many. He says I'm flighty."

"What's it like?"

She stopped packing and tucked her hair behind her ear. "Sometimes fun, sometimes boring, and always nerve-wracking. Here." She tossed two scraps of fabric at me.

I caught them and held them up. "What are they?"

"Bikini. Let's get changed, and we can swim…in the shallow end."

I choked so hard, she had to slap me on the back.

"What's wrong?"

"I can't wear this in front of everyone."

"Sure you can."

I shook my head. "It doesn't cover anything."

Amelia grinned. "That's the whole point—showing off your assets. And it does cover the important parts."

She ducked back into her closet, reappearing two minutes later in a black bikini as small as the one she'd tossed at me. "Your turn."

But ten years wouldn't have been enough time to build up the nerve to wear this tiny swimsuit in front of Daniel. "No way." I crossed my arms over my chest.

She stared down at me, both hands on her hips, but I didn't budge off the bed. "You're really not going to wear it?"

I shook my head, and she sighed, closing her eyes. "Fine. Just give me a minute to think." A few seconds later, her eyes snapped open. "Aha, I got it."

Ten minutes later, I followed Amelia to the backyard, my feet dragging the whole way. Amelia kept telling me I looked great, and it was going to be fun, but to me, it felt a whole lot like facing a department full of police officers in the middle of a thunderstorm.

# Chapter Twelve

Daniel lowered himself in the pool right next to me, and I tightened my death grip on the wall. Just looking at him, my belly churned with nervous excitement. "You came back."

When Amelia and I stepped out of the house earlier, only his mom and dad were still in the yard, watching the sunset. I'd hidden my disappointment from Amelia.

"Sorry." Daniel treaded water with hardly any effort. His legs and arms moved in circles and created little eddies of water that spun around my waist and legs. "I had to drop something off for Jacob."

A few droplets of water fell from his hair. He shook his head, like Caesar after a bath, and I ducked to avoid the spray. The pool lights lit everything from below, making his eyes glitter like the stars overhead.

"You look different tonight," he said.

"It's Amelia's swimsuit." The navy one-piece with stripes down both sides covered more of my body than the tiny bikini did, but I still felt pale and exposed.

"I know. I recognize it from the one semester she spent

on the swim team. She's never been one for team sports."

"She gave it to me."

"It looks good on you."

My cheeks felt hot, and I looked away.

He glanced toward the deep end. "My sister deserted you."

I shrugged. When we first got in, Amelia and I stayed in the shallow end, but then Sam showed up. Now she sat in a floating chair at the far end of the pool, which Sam clung to, talking and laughing with her. Tired of sitting alone, I'd waded out until the bottom of the pool started to slope away under my feet and I'd needed the wall to keep me from sinking. I was stuck, too afraid to go any further and too stubborn to return to the shallow end. "I guess they wanted to be alone."

Daniel grimaced. "Yeah, it's a real party, watching my best friend pant after my sister."

"You don't like them being together?"

"Sam's had a thing for her for a couple of years but never had the nerve to act on it." He shrugged. "I'm used to looking out for Amelia, but Sam's a good guy. So which side do I take when it ends badly?"

I thought about his words. "Maybe it won't end badly."

He frowned and shot another eddy of water swirling in my direction. "Happily-ever-afters only happen in books and movies."

I didn't want to believe him, but maybe he was right. Maybe love and good intentions were never enough. He gripped the wall a few inches away from me and dipped his head backward, wetting his hair. A pang of jealousy sputtered through me. Everyone else was so at ease in the pool, while I kept thinking about how far below the surface I'd sink before I reached the bottom.

"So how come you never learned to swim?"

"I don't know. Probably because I didn't have anyone to

teach me."

He stayed silent for a minute. "Do you want me to teach you?"

Did I? It would be nice to conquer one of my fears. It wasn't even a real fear, not like thunderstorms. I was just afraid of drowning because I didn't know how to stay afloat.

"Come on." He pointed to the center of the pool. "It's much more fun out there than it is here."

I gave him a half-hearted smile. "Fine."

The grin he returned was so big, his eyes crinkled in the corners. "Really?"

"Sure." I liked the feeling of pleasing Daniel, of making him happy, even if it meant my possible death. Then again, he'd already proven he could rescue me from the ocean. What did I have to lose?

"Do you trust me?" he asked.

"Yes." My answer came so quick, I think it surprised both of us.

"Good. Stay here."

He hauled himself out of the pool, his arm muscles bulging. A wave of water sloshed in my direction, and I gulped.

A minute later, he lowered himself back in and laid a yellow foam board on the water between us. "Hold on to this with both hands. It will keep you afloat."

My mind was willing, but my fingers wouldn't loosen their grip on the wall.

Daniel swam behind me. He wrapped one arm around my waist and nudged me backward until my back pressed against his bare chest. A shiver danced up my spine despite the warmth of the water. "I've got you. Go ahead and grab the board."

"Are you sure?" I whispered.

His fingers spread across my hip. They dug into my skin, but not in a way that hurt. His cheek rested against my ear, and my belly clenched. "Trust me."

His breath tickled my neck, and for some reason my palms ached, but maybe they were just cramping from clinging so hard to the wall. It was a small thing, but it felt huge when I pried my fingers off and grabbed for the board.

"Good girl."

My heart sang at his praise.

"I'm going to let go now."

"No!" I jerked, wanting to reach back for him but afraid to release my death grip on the yellow board.

"I thought you trusted me."

I grunted. "I do…in theory."

"Then relax."

*Easier said than done.*

"I'm going to move slowly." His fingers left my hip, brushed against my belly, and I forgot to breathe. His other hand gripped the opposite end of the board, and he let my waist go completely. A second later, he faced me across the board and our bodies glided out toward the center of the pool. I glanced back at the wall, already more than an arm's length away.

"You're doing great. Just let your legs float out behind you. I'll do the work."

At first, all I could do was grip the board and try not to panic, but Daniel continued to pull me in slow, lazy circles around the pool. Somewhere along the way, I stopped being scared. He talked the whole time, his voice low and steady, and I forgot about how deep the water was below me. Instead, I let the warmth of the water and the quietness of the night lull me. Low murmurs came from Sam and Amelia, and an occasional laugh from Daniel's parents still sitting at the table drinking wine.

Daniel's face hovered above the water, only inches from mine, close enough I could see the tiny droplets of water clinging to his eyelashes and the faint outline of a scar above his right eyebrow. I wondered how he got it. He was telling me about a fishing trip he went on with his dad, and right in the middle of his story, I blurted out the one question I kept wondering about.

"Do you regret meeting me?"

His green eyes widened. His gaze darted over to Sam and Amelia and then back to me. "Why would you ask that?"

He stopped pulling, and my legs started to sink. My fingers dug into the board. "Because sometimes I think you like me and other times I'm not so sure. Like earlier, during supper. You never talked to me at all, but then you defended me to your mother, and after, you asked me to stay."

"Clover…"

His mouth opened and closed, but nothing came out, so my words kept coming, filling up the silence. "I'm not very good at this whole boy and girl thing. So I don't know if I'm doing something wrong. Maybe I shouldn't have asked you about the kissing."

He spluttered. "God, Clover, you really know how to put someone on the spot."

I frowned. "I'm not trying to make you feel bad. I'm just trying to understand."

He sank into the water and blew out some bubbles. When he came up, he sighed. "I know you're not, but the truth is that it's…complicated for me."

"Because of her?"

Daniel tensed. "Who?"

I took a deep breath. "Grace."

His mouth snapped closed, his expression all set to shut me out. I recognized the look, the same one Mama used to get when I asked too many questions about her and Daddy. The look meant I should just stop asking if I knew what was best for me, but I'd proven long ago that I didn't always do what was best.

"The girl in the pictures on Amelia's wall—the one with the dark hair and eyes—it's her, isn't it?"

Daniel looked up at the stars, his lips set in a hard line. He nodded.

"She was beautiful."

"Yes."

"How did she die?"

He stared at me. "You avoid telling me anything personal about yourself. In fact, you told me to just stop asking, but I'm supposed to talk to you about Grace, just because you ask? It doesn't work that way."

"I'm sorry." I ducked my head, feeling ashamed, but he didn't understand. My past wasn't just painful. If he knew what I'd done to Mama and Daddy, he'd never look at me again.

Daniel said nothing. He just stared into the water like he thought it might hold some magical answer.

"Really, I'm sorry. Please don't be mad."

He groaned and rubbed his hand through his wet hair. Then he reached for the board and started pulling me toward the shallow end. "I'm not mad. I just don't want to talk about it."

My feet scraped the bottom of the pool, and I knew I could stand on my own. Still I clung to the board, my only connection to Daniel. He must have known I could touch, but he continued to tug me until the very end. When we reached the steps, he finally let go.

"That's enough swimming lessons for now." Without looking back, he climbed out and left me behind.

I stood in water up to my waist and shivered when the night air hit my wet skin.

"Daniel?"

He looked back, impatience all over his face. "What?"

I thought about chickening out, telling him to forget about it, but despite my mistake with Grace, I needed to know.

"You never answered my question. The one about whether you regretted meeting me."

Daniel reached for me. He held my hand while I climbed up the stairs. I squeezed his fingers, but he let go as soon as I reached solid ground. He threw me a towel, and I wrapped it around me as tight as it would go, covering my thin bathing suit.

"Go and get changed. I'll drive you back to Gran's."

My face fell. Why wouldn't he answer?

I dressed, said good-bye to everyone, and climbed into the truck next to Daniel. He sat perfectly still, not starting the engine, not talking.

"Daniel?"

"I never expected you, okay." He stared out the windshield toward the darkened street. His fingers clutched the steering wheel. "But I also don't regret meeting you. You make me feel confused, and I don't like it. I'm sorry if it's not what you want to hear, but I'm trying to be honest."

His last words came at me like little daggers. I didn't know much about boys and girls being together, but I was pretty sure that honesty was an important part. I could keep thinking inappropriate thoughts about Daniel, but I was also lying to him. My secrets were a snare. The more I struggled, the more I flailed, and the more I flailed, the more the wire tightened around my throat.

# Chapter Thirteen

"What do you think of this one?" Amelia held up a striped top and raised an eyebrow.

"I don't need any more clothes."

"Don't be silly." She led me to the mirror on the store wall and stuck the shirt in front of me. "Every girl can do with more clothes, and this one makes your eyes look even bluer."

"I don't have any money to buy it."

"I'll get it for you."

I shook my head and pushed the shirt away. "No way. You already gave me half the clothes in your closet."

She snorted and hung the top back on the rack. "Trust me…it wasn't half the clothes in my closet. It hardly made a dent."

She moved to the next rack, her sandals clicking on the shiny, wooden floor. I stayed in front of the mirror. I barely recognized the girl staring back. The pink flowered sundress donated by Amelia actually fit.

When she'd arrived at Ms. Ginny's earlier to pick me up, she'd frowned before leading me back upstairs to the bathroom. I sat on the toilet seat, and she'd dumped a small heap of jars and tubes from her purse onto the counter. She'd brushed and spread and stroked her magic products on my face, and when she'd finished, I looked like this—a glittery-eyed, rosy-cheeked, shiny-lipped stranger.

"Smile." She'd snapped a picture of me with her phone and held it out for me to see. "Now it's time to shop."

We'd driven south from Canna Point, down the coastline to the next town. Two weeks had passed since Hurricane Delores hit and life on the Gulf Coast had returned to its normal pace. The mid-July sun blazed down on the bleached highway. Amelia drove with the air-conditioning and radio blasting, and we'd parked on the town's main street. We'd spent the next hour combing through a stretch of small shops and boutiques.

Amelia held up a skirt. "This would look so cute on you."

I brushed one hand over a rack of silky dresses and sighed. "I'm not buying anything. It's bad enough that I'm here and not working on Ms. Ginny's book right now."

"You needed a break." She flipped her hair over her shoulder and hung the skirt back up. "You've had your nose stuck in those papers all week. Even Gran agreed this trip was a good idea, so don't spoil the fun."

But I'd agreed to the trip not knowing how I'd feel. I'd never minded not having money. Life might have been easier with it, but I'd managed just fine without it. Being around Ms. Ginny and the Hudsons made it harder—seeing all the pretty things I'd never have for myself. Not that I needed a lot, just a few things that were mine, that weren't charity offerings from my new friends. Had I grown greedy? Had Daddy been right?

"Aren't we shopping for a dress for you?"

"That's right." Amelia twirled around to look in the mirror. She held up a strapless gown in a swirl of blues and greens. "What do you think of this one?"

It floated around her like a mermaid's tail. "It's beautiful."

"I'm trying it on. It's perfect for the dance." She headed to the fitting rooms, while I waited on a bench outside.

Two minutes later, she emerged. "Well?"

"Wow," I whispered, intimidated by the perfection of my new friend. She looked like a princess with her frothy skirt.

She spun around. "I don't know why I'm so excited about this year's dance. The country club holds it every summer. I've been going for years, but this time feels different."

"You're going with Sam?" I tried to keep the envy from my voice.

"Yup… I actually invited him." She piled her hair on top of her head and stared in the mirror. "He was so surprised, I thought he might pass out on me."

"I'm glad. You look happy together."

Her eyes turned dreamy. "Things between Sam and I have been simmering for a while, and thanks to you and that day at the beach, they boiled over big time."

"Daniel worries that it might end badly between you."

She let her hair fall and lifted one bare shoulder. "You have to understand, Daniel worries too much." She sat next to me on the bench and smoothed the dress down her thighs. "And I compensate by not worrying enough."

"It's because of Grace, isn't it?"

Her eyes widened, and she frowned. "You know about her?"

"A little. I saw her picture on your wall. I know she died, but Daniel got upset when I mentioned her name."

Amelia blew out a long breath and shook her head. "Don't take it personally. He doesn't talk to anyone about Grace. It's hard, because she was my friend, too, long before she and Daniel became a thing."

My fingernails dug into the padded top of the bench. "What was she like?"

"Fearless and beautiful. She made me look like I was standing still. But her highs were really high, and her lows were really low."

My stomach clenched. She'd looked beautiful in the photos, beautiful and full of life. "How did she die?"

Amelia closed her eyes and leaned her head back. Tears glittered on her eyelashes when she opened them. "She killed herself. I'll never forget the day we found out. Daniel and I were getting ready to leave for school when we got the call. I kept hoping there'd been some mistake or it was all a bad dream. I cried for two weeks straight."

I released the breath I'd been holding. It sounded so sad, like a terrible waste, but I also understood about secrets, about hiding parts of ourselves that we don't want other people to see. Grace must have had secrets of her own. "And Daniel?"

"It hit him the hardest. He felt guilty. We all did. We wondered if there was something we could have done to change things, but Daniel more than the rest of us. For a few months after, he mostly avoided us, until Mom threatened to take him to a therapist."

I winced. The idea of Daniel going through all that made my chest ache. "I'm sorry for bringing it up, for making you sad."

"No, it's okay." She sniffed. "It's good to remember her." She pressed her hands to her cheeks and wiped at her eyes. "Grace deserves to be remembered. She would have loved you, by the way."

I thought about that. Were we alike—Grace and I? Did our similarities make Daniel sad?

"Okay…" Amelia jumped to her feet and spun around again. "So, what do you think? Should I buy it?"

"Yes. You look beautiful, and it will definitely make Sam have inappropriate thoughts."

Amelia spluttered, and then her splutter turned into

laughter. "I hope so. That is the whole idea."

"What's it like? The dancing…the music…"

Amelia looked at the price tag on the dress without flinching. "Like any other dance, only a bit fancier."

"But what does it feel like?" I'd read the story of Cinderella, the prince, and her glass slipper. When I was little, I wanted it to be my story. When I was older, I wondered if Mama still longed for it to be her story, too.

"You must have been to a dance before."

I lowered my head and scuffed at the floor with my new shoes, the ones Ms. Ginny had given me to go with the dress. "No."

Amelia didn't respond, and I kept my head bowed, afraid she finally understood how much I didn't belong in her world.

"Oh, honey, I'm sorry." She sank back down, and her arm hooked around my shoulder. "I didn't realize."

Guilt twisted in my belly, and I swallowed back a lump of regret. She was apologizing when I was the one lying to her. "It's not your fault. It's just that sometimes I wish I hadn't missed so much."

She winked at me in a typical Amelia way. "Well, I can't change everything, but I can definitely take care of your first dance."

"Really?" The possibility shimmered in front of me, blinding in its implication, like staring at the sun too long.

"Sure. You just need to be invited by a member of the club."

"Oh." The sun sank, leaving me back in the dark.

"And Daniel's a member."

I sighed. As much as I would have loved it, I doubted if that particular sun would ever rise.

"We just need to make sure he asks you."

I looked away, avoiding her misplaced enthusiasm. It only made me feel worse. "He won't."

"But I thought you two were really getting along. He's been to Gran's house every day this week."

"Yes, but he just comes for my pie and cookies."

Amelia jerked upright. "Clover Scott, what are you talking about?"

I wrapped my arms around my belly, feeling a whole lot of embarrassment. "It started with the rhubarb pie I baked on Sunday. Daniel came by to mow Ms. Ginny's lawn and smelled it baking. He liked it so much, he said he'd come back for more the next day. So I baked him tea biscuits."

He'd scarfed them down as fast as I could put them on the cooling rack, loaded with so much jam it dripped on the kitchen counter.

"The next day, I made oatmeal cookies."

"And…"

"Yesterday, I made a lemon loaf…" My voice trailed off.

Amelia shook her head. "I can't believe it. My brother is using you for your baking."

"I don't mind," I rushed to explain.

I liked baking for Daniel. I liked sitting in the kitchen with him. He talked about his work at the store, and I listened. Maybe he was there just for my baking, but he made me laugh. He also listened when I told him about the research I was doing, and he gave me good ideas. I liked the way he thought about things—logical and thorough. He planned to be an engineer, and when he explained to me what they did, I knew he'd be a good one, that one day he'd help build amazing things.

We both avoided talking about the things we didn't want to share. I didn't ask him any more about Grace, and he didn't ask me about Mama and Daddy. Of course, there'd been no more kissing, but I thought about it every time I was with him, and even sometimes when he wasn't around. I'd even dreamed about it, dreams that made me wake up feeling hot and all out of sorts.

Amelia frowned. "It still doesn't sound right."

"Daniel's done so much for me. He saved my life twice, and he helped me find a job and a place to live. Baking him a pie and some cookies is not much in return."

Amelia clucked at me. "None of us are helping because we expect anything in return. We're helping because we care about you."

Tears welled in my eyes, and I blinked them away, not wanting to embarrass us both by bawling like a baby in the middle of the store. "Thank you, but I still feel like us being friends is lopsided, like you're doing all the giving, and I'm doing all the taking. Doing this for Daniel makes it feel a little more even."

She sighed. "I guess, but I still think Daniel is being an ass. He never even offered to share your baking with me."

I closed my eyes, horrified that I'd not given him any to bring home to his family. "I'm so sorry. I'll bake you something tomorrow, just for you."

Amelia rolled her eyes and headed back to the changing room. "I'm kidding, Clover." She stuck her head out from behind the curtain. "But in case you're wondering, lemon loaf is my favorite."

# Chapter Fourteen

"Let's have lunch," Amelia suggested. "There's a café in town that makes chocolate cake to die for."

"Sure." I had a few dollars in my pocket. In addition to room and board, Ms. Ginny agreed to pay me a little for the time I spent working on the town's chronicle. It wasn't much, but enough to pay for my meal.

"Are you okay walking? It's not far, and I may not find another parking spot."

I nodded despite the ripples of heat rising from the asphalt. The humidity stuck my dress to my back, but Amelia didn't seem to mind. She perched her sunglasses on the bridge of her nose, and her shopping bag swung at her side.

"Did Daniel tell you that he's playing in a charity golf tournament tomorrow? You should come. Most of the town will be there."

I squinted against the sun. "Maybe. Daniel gave up trying to explain golf to me."

"It's pretty straightforward. There's a ball about this big." She held up her thumb and finger to make a circle. "You hit it with a club and try to get it in a small hole in as few strokes as possible. You do that eighteen times, and the person with the fewest strokes wins."

I laughed. "Where were you when Daniel spent an hour explaining this?"

"Ah, yes…well, my brother has a tendency to overthink and overcomplicate things."

We left the last of the low brick buildings that housed the shops and started past older, two-story houses set back from the street. The neighborhood reminded me of Ms. Ginny's, with lush lawns and flowerbeds bursting with color.

Amelia called out to an older man just stepping from a shiny black sedan in front of an intimidating two-story brick house. Lions' heads topped the pillars guarding either side of the driveway's entrance. It was beautiful, but cold and lifeless compared to the other houses on the street. A lone clump of pink bougainvillea grew next to the house.

Amelia slowed and waved. "Mr. Alexander…hi."

*Mr. Alexander?* My head jerked.

Amelia gave her shopping bag another swing and leaned toward me. "That's Mr. Alexander. He used to be my grandfather's law partner."

But I wasn't listening. My heart pounded. Alexander was a common name. It had to be someone else. It had to be a coincidence…but it wasn't.

He was the man from the picture I found—the one with Mama and the older woman. He was older now. He wore a light-color suit and straw hat with a narrow brim that covered most of his silver hair, but I still recognized his face. He'd been stern-looking in the photo, but now his shoulders hunched, like he carried the weight of the world, and his mouth drooped in the corners.

Mr. Alexander nodded at Amelia but didn't look pleased to see her.

Undaunted, she took a few steps into the driveway. "Do you remember me? I'm Amelia—Ginny King's granddaughter."

I lingered on the sidewalk, wiping my sweaty palms against my dress and trying my best to be invisible.

He made an unhappy noise, something halfway between a grunt and a sigh, and pulled a handkerchief from his pocket. He dabbed at the line of sweat on his forehead. "How is your grandmother? I haven't seen her since Bill's funeral."

"She's great. Still trying to write the history of Canna Point."

"Hmmph. She's been at that for years. It's high time she gave up on that impossible project." Mr. Alexander shifted and looked longingly in the direction of his house. He clearly wanted to escape, but Amelia didn't seem to notice.

"Oh, I don't know. I think we should never give up on our dreams, and now she has someone to help her."

"And who might this miracle worker be?"

She turned and waved me forward with one hand.

I willed my feet to move one step after another. My stomach heaved and churned. I wanted to throw up right on his pristine, white crushed stones.

"My friend Clover. Clover, this is Henry Alexander. Mr. Alexander, this is my friend Clover—"

"Nice to meet you," I interrupted before she could say my last name. I stuck my hand out, worried they'd notice the way it trembled. His hand closed around mine, his grip firm. Our eyes met and, for a moment, I saw what hid behind his gruff exterior. He was a broken man, and nothing I had to say could fix him. The knowledge squeezed my chest. I pulled my hand free, needing to escape.

"I've got to go," I mumbled, twisting away from his sad eyes and hightailing it out of the driveway.

After a few seconds, Amelia's sandals slapped the

sidewalk behind me. "Clover! Wait up."

I pressed my palms against my cheeks and slowed down a little.

"What happened? Are you okay?"

I nodded and tried not to sniff.

"Are you crying?"

A lizard peeked out from a nearby bush. "It's nothing," I whispered.

"It doesn't look like nothing. You can talk to me. You can trust me."

My heart raced, and my knees shook. The lizard darted out of sight. Why couldn't I disappear that easily? "It's just that he reminded me of someone. Someone I haven't seen in a long time."

"Oh." Her skeptical gaze met mine. "Are you sure that's it?"

I nodded. "Sorry for running away like that. He must think I'm rude."

"Who cares?" She cocked her head to one side. "It's not like he's Mr. Personality, so I wouldn't worry."

We continued toward the café, and when we reached it, Amelia claimed an outside table under an umbrella. We ordered drinks, and the waitress left us alone to study the menu, only I couldn't concentrate. The words kept blurring together.

"Why is he so sad?"

Amelia glanced up from her menu. "Who? Mr. Alexander?"

"Yes. He seems so lonely. What about his wife?"

She shrugged. "She passed away a few years ago, but he was grumpy even before that. I think there was some family tragedy, but I don't know the details. You could ask Gran if you really wanted to know. Mr. Alexander and my grandfather were law partners for years."

And that was the problem. Did I really want to know? But like a scab on a cut, I'd already picked at it a little, and I knew I couldn't leave it alone even if it ended up leaving a huge scar.

At home that evening, I found Ms. Ginny in the kitchen.

"Amelia and I saw someone today who knew you—Henry Alexander."

Ms. Ginny looked up from her potato peeling. "He and my husband were business partners, but I haven't seen him in a few years."

"He seemed sad."

She chuckled. "That's one word to describe him. You could also call him a crotchety old grouch."

"Why is he like that?" I leaned against the counter, trying to act casual, like the question and the answer weren't that important to me.

"I'm not sure, but he's probably always been that way."

"Mama used to say that all babies are born good and innocent. Evil enters into people along the way, and there has to be a reason for it."

She threw me an odd look that made me squirm. "Well, I don't know about evil, but I think Henry was never a particularly happy person. He set high standards for himself and expected the same of people around him. Things really went downhill after his daughter left."

My heart pounded at the mention of Mama, and I wondered if Ms. Ginny could hear it. I worked hard to keep my voice calm. "She left?"

"Yes. The year after Meredith got married, so that must be close to twenty years ago."

I picked up a potato and an extra knife and started

peeling. "Why did she leave?"

"I don't know all the details, but I think they had a falling out." Ms. Ginny moved on to slicing the carrots. "I know Henry regrets that she left."

"Why didn't he look for her?"

"He did. But why all the interest?" Her hands stilled, and her iron-hot gaze scorched my face. "It's ancient history."

I ducked my head, almost cutting myself with the knife. "I don't know. He just seemed so lonely, and maybe this can go in your town history."

Ms. Ginny shook her head. "He doesn't live in Canna Point, and I don't want our book to be based on gossip."

"Oh." I tried to keep the disappointment from my voice, but she must have heard it.

"Is there another reason you're interested in Henry Alexander?"

"No," I lied.

"Listen, Henry may not be my favorite person in the world, but he was heartbroken when his daughter left. He was also a close friend of my husband and, therefore, I will look out for his best interests. Do you understand what I'm saying?"

I gulped, and my head bobbed up and down. I needed to make sure Ms. Ginny never found out my real interest in Henry Alexander…my grandfather. I'd come to Florida because it was Mama's plan for me. The thing was, I no longer believed her plan was in anyone's best interest—not for me and definitely not for Henry Alexander.

I walked downstairs the next morning to find Daniel waiting for me at the bottom of the steps. He wore a navy blue golf shirt and fitted pants. A ball cap sat low on his forehead, with only a few tufts of his dark hair sticking out. He looked so vivid and alive, it made me blink, like looking directly at the sun.

"Daniel...hi."

He grinned. "Are you ready for the golf tournament?"

I frowned. "The tournament?"

His jaw clenched, and he muttered something under his breath about interfering sisters. "Amelia told me that you wanted to go. I was supposed to pick you up."

"Amelia mentioned it, but I told her I wasn't sure."

He lowered his head, making his expression difficult to read. "You don't have to go. You'd probably find it boring anyway."

Was that disappointment in his voice? Horrified, I jumped off the last step. "No...I want to go. I just didn't know if you'd want me there."

He straightened. "Why wouldn't I want you there?" His hazel eyes flashed. "I thought that after this week, we'd become friends."

I bounced on my toes. "I hope so."

"And I don't think you can get yourself in any life-threatening situations on the golf course."

"Ha, ha. That's funny."

He raised an eyebrow. "Not really. So, come and watch me play. Who knows...you may actually like it."

He smelled like sunscreen and aftershave, and I wanted to tell him that I'd like anything if it meant I could watch him. "Okay. I'll come."

He made it all the way out the front door before he realized I wasn't following. He looked back and held the screen door open with one hand. "Geesh, Clover, are you waiting for a written invitation?"

"But..." I stared down at my outfit. My blue and white plaid pants had survived the hurricane, although the mud left a few stains. The top came from Amelia, more tight-fitting and stretchy than the clothes I'd lost in the storm.

"But what?" He stepped back in the porch.

I shook my head. "I'm not sure what I'm supposed to wear."

"What you're wearing is fine." He plucked a straw sun hat from his grandmother's front closet and dropped it on my head. "And now, it's perfect."

I called out a quick good-bye to Ms. Ginny, and then we headed for a small car parked on the street. Sam sat in the driver's seat.

Daniel shot me an apologetic look. "Sorry, still waiting for the insurance check so I can replace the Jeep."

Guilt surfaced at the reminder, and I ducked into the backseat.

"Hey, Clover." Sam gave me a quick smile. "Just move all that junk out of the way."

I pushed aside a couple of comic books and some snorkeling gear and fastened my seat belt.

Sam slipped the car into gear and started driving. "So, how is life with Ms. Ginny?"

I pulled off her hat and leaned forward. "Well, she watches a show called *Jeopardy* and knows all the answers. She always looks perfect, even in the morning, she doesn't like anyone leaving a mess in her kitchen or when you're late for supper, and she gives really good advice."

Sam laughed, and I knew I'd said something wrong again. I looked at Daniel, wanting to understand why I kept messing up.

He twisted in his seat. "Most people would just say 'fine.'" Our eyes met and I saw something unexpected there... acceptance. "Don't worry. You'll never be most people."

A weight lifted off my shoulders, and my shyness disappeared. After that, Sam, Daniel, and I talked nonstop. I learned that the tournament raised money for the children's hospital, and Hudson's Sporting Goods was a major sponsor.

Eventually, we pulled up in front of the fanciest building I'd ever seen, with archways, marble columns, and floor-to-ceiling windows. Daniel told me it was the clubhouse. I stepped out of the car and stared in wonder at the rolling green grass that seemed to stretch on forever. Palm trees lined the property and swayed in the breeze. A young man even parked Sam's car for him.

Inside, I followed Daniel to a lounge area where his parents, Sam's parents, and Amelia sat drinking coffee. With a sinking feeling, I stared at the pretty dresses worn by the ladies, but what bothered me even worse was facing Mr. Garrett again.

Ernie Hudson and Andrew Garrett stood up. "Boys," Mr. Hudson said, "ready to play golf?" They all sported matching ball caps with the store logo.

"Yes, sir," Sam answered.

I stepped from behind Daniel, and Mr. Hudson's eyes widened in surprise. Amelia jumped up and squealed. She rushed over to hug me.

"Clover, you came."

"Yes, she did," Daniel answered. "Funny thing, though… she didn't know I was coming for her."

Amelia plastered a bright smile on her face. "Wow. There must have been some mix-up in communication, but at least she's here now."

"Hmmm…yes, she is."

Sam introduced me to his mother, Cheryl Garrett, who looked nothing like her son. Her shiny black hair brushed the tops of her shoulders, and her warm brown eyes tilted in the corners. Sam obviously took after his father.

"Clover, nice to meet you."

I shook her hand under the watchful eye of Sam's father.

He wasn't wearing a uniform, but I still felt the familiar wave of panic, the one that made me want to run. For Daniel's sake, I forced myself to stay put.

"Clover," Mr. Garrett said, his tone squeezing the air from my lungs. "I didn't realize you were still in town."

Amelia grinned. "She decided to stay with my grandmother."

"How long are you staying?" Mrs. Garrett asked, a polite expression on her face.

"I'm not sure."

"What about the person you came here to find?" Mr. Garrett asked.

I blinked. How did he know? But then I remembered Daniel telling him the day he came for us in the boat.

He gave me a hard stare. "If you tell me more, I might be able to help you find them."

"I haven't, I mean, I can't—" I tried to answer, but my voice trembled and faltered like a spin top winding down. Did anyone else notice the suspicion in his stare? He knew nothing about me, nothing about my past. He couldn't. So why couldn't I find the words? Why couldn't I slow my breathing?

Shoot. Tears filled my eyes as I struggled against the familiar rush of panic. Not now. Not in front of everyone.

# Chapter Fifteen

"Maybe we should go and register," Daniel cut in, squeezing my shoulder. His hand held me in place, like he knew I was about to take flight.

Mr. Garrett still stared at me, waiting for my answer, his steady gaze holding me captive.

When the silence stretched on, Mrs. Garrett cleared her throat. "That sounds like a great idea. We'll stay and finish our coffee. Andrew, did you remember sunscreen?"

Mr. Garrett turned to his wife and nodded, releasing me from his silent stare. I blew out the breath I'd been holding.

Daniel's hand moved to the small of my back, applying a not so subtle pressure. "I just need to speak to Clover first." Without waiting for my response, he marched to the corner, taking me with him.

"Are you okay?"

He stood in front of me, blocking my view of his family. I stared at the collar of his shirt and nodded.

"You're sure? Because you don't look okay."

My eyes darted around him, looking for the exit.

"This is supposed to be fun."

"I know," I whispered. Lots of things were supposed to happen in life, but there was never any guarantee.

"Hey." He tilted my chin up with one finger, and our gazes locked. "Just breathe. Nothing bad is going to happen. Sam's dad is a good guy."

"Really? He carries a gun and enforces the law. He doesn't make you nervous?"

Daniel tilted his head to one side, looking confused. "No, because I believe the sheriff's office is here to serve and protect, and Mr. Garrett has always been fair. So what's going on, Clover?"

He let go of my chin, and I looked away, avoiding the suspicion in his eyes. "He doesn't like me."

"That's not true. He just doesn't know you."

I dropped my head back against the wall. "None of you know me."

"I know enough, and I'd know even more if you decided to trust me."

Blood rushed to my head, pounding in my ears. "We agreed to not talk about our pasts." Daniel could never find out what I'd done.

"It wasn't an agreement." He shoved his hands in his pocket and rocked back on his heels. "I just said that it wasn't fair to ask me about Grace when you refuse to talk about the secrets you're obviously keeping."

His voice rose, and I glanced down at my feet. "Maybe I should go."

"No." He sighed and rubbed the back of his neck. "I want you to stay. I just wish this wasn't so complicated."

I looked at him—at the ghost of a smile tilting up the corners of his mouth and the determination in his eyes. His fingers brushed mine, sending shivers across my skin.

"When you look at me, it's like I can't catch my breath," I

whispered, "and I don't know why."

But maybe I did, and it scared the heck out of me. I'd started to count on Daniel, to rely on the way he made me feel. It had been a long time since I'd let myself count on anyone.

Daniel's nostrils flared, and my skin heated under his stare. "I've got to play golf for the next couple of hours, but promise me you'll stay. We need to talk. Okay?"

He captured my gaze, making my heart race. Finally, I swallowed and nodded.

"Good. Let's go back. I'm sure my family is staring and wondering."

*And probably disapproving.* "I need the bathroom first."

He frowned. "More hiding?"

"No."

He looked skeptical but gave me directions anyway. "If you hide in there too long, I'm sending Amelia to find you."

I didn't doubt him. Inside the bathroom, I stared at my reflection, at my bright eyes and flushed cheeks and clothes that didn't belong in this fancy clubhouse. I tucked a stray strand of hair behind my ear and turned slightly when the door opened. A redhead wearing a tight dress walked in. She balanced on high heels that made me dizzy just looking at her.

She smiled, but the expression didn't reach her eyes. "Clover, right?"

I turned fully. "Yes…"

Her smile widened into a grin, and she flicked her hair over her shoulder with a painted nail. "I'm Morgan Fletcher… Daniel's girlfriend."

*What?* A buzzing noise filled my ears.

"Are you okay?" Morgan's face turned into a sympathetic mask, only I knew it was just that…a mask. "You don't look well."

Sagging against the counter, I curled my fingers around the marble edge. Morgan dampened a paper towel and handed it to me. I accepted it without thinking, holding it to my chest, but it didn't numb the pain. I thought Daniel kept his distance because of Grace, because of a ghost. How could he have a real girlfriend and still kiss me? I thought there were rules about these things, but reality seemed messy and chaotic and hurtful.

"So I gather Daniel didn't mention me. He tends to be private with his personal life, especially after what happened with Grace."

"Grace?"

Her eyes narrowed. "Sorry. I shouldn't have mentioned her. Daniel wouldn't appreciate me sharing that part of his life with a practical stranger."

It took a moment to understand that I was the stranger she was talking about.

"Daniel told me how he saved you after you fell in the ocean and after you got yourself stuck in the hurricane. He's such a good Samaritan."

"Yes…he is." The blood drained from my head and pooled in my limbs. The thought of Daniel telling this perfect girl all about me hurt more than I thought possible. Had they pitied me? Laughed at me?

Morgan stepped closer to the mirror and pulled a tube from her purse. She ran the lipstick over her lips before tucking it away and leaning back against the counter. "And now you're staying with his grandmother. I'm sure you must be anxious to get out of Canna Point and get on with your life."

"Yes."

It wasn't a lie. I'd come here looking for Henry Alexander but had found Daniel instead. Morgan was right about me being a stranger. I barely knew Daniel and his family, and apparently I knew even less about his girlfriends. I'd made the stupid mistake of assuming that just because I thought about him all the time, maybe he also thought about me.

The door called to me, the truth now crystal clear. Mr. Garrett was obviously suspicious, and a relationship with either Daniel or Henry Alexander would just cause more hurt. It was time to move on.

Morgan straightened to her full height. "Well, it was nice meeting you. I've heard so much about you."

I lifted my chin. I couldn't let her see how much her words had shaken me.

She shot me another look, the expression in her brown eyes hard to read. "I know it's not my place, and I really hope you don't mind me saying this, but…" She took in a deep breath and slowly exhaled. "After what happened with Grace, Daniel has a hard time walking away from anyone in trouble. Maybe its guilt, but I'd hate to see anyone take advantage of his nature. It's not good for him."

*You're not good for him.* She didn't say it out loud, but she didn't need to. She smoothed her dress over her hips and looked at my outfit with pity. "I hope you find a place where you fit in, even if it's not Canna Point."

My mouth snapped shut. I watched her leave in her beautiful dress and spiky shoes and, at some point, my limbs unfroze enough so I could splash cold water on my face. I pulled my shoulders back so far my muscles shouted in protest, but it still hurt less than the ache in my heart.

Back at the entrance to the main room, I watched Morgan approach Daniel's family. She and Daniel hugged, and I let out the breath I'd been holding. They looked right together, both beautiful and complete and happy. Not damaged or hiding secrets.

Stuffing Ms. Ginny's sunhat back on, I headed to the doors, squinting against the bright sun. I marched down the driveway, past the rolling green course, and turned left on the main road, back toward Ms. Ginny's. It was easily an hour walk, but I didn't mind. I needed at least that long to figure out a new plan for my future—one that didn't involve Canna Point.

"Clover, where have you been?" Ms. Ginny met me at the front door, creases in her forehead. "Daniel's called three times."

Sweaty and tired, I fell into one of the porch rocking chairs. "I walked home." Caesar stood up from his new dog bed and shook himself before trotting over to lick my hand. He looked good, fatter and healthier than before. The engraved dog tag on his collar jingled when I scratched behind his ears—a gift from Amelia.

Ms. Ginny frowned. "I can see that. But why did you leave without telling anyone? You worried people."

"It was wasted worry." I kicked off my sneakers and stretched my bare toes. I had the makings of a good-size blister on one heel. "I'm fine."

Ms. Ginny huffed. "I've already told you that I have no time for dishonesty, and that's a crock if I ever heard one." She settled on the rocker next to me, lacing her fingers together. "What happened?"

I pulled my legs up to my chest and let Caesar lick my toes. "It wasn't what I thought it was going to be."

"Oh. So you've decided that you don't like golf?" Missing the sarcasm in her voice was next to impossible.

I rested my chin on my knees and stared out at the street. Cars passed—people with things to do and places to go. "I thought that maybe I belonged there, but it turns out I don't. I'm not sure where I belong."

Ms. Ginny sighed. "Those are some pretty heavy thoughts for a Sunday morning. Something must have happened to bring them on."

I grimaced and pictured Morgan Fletcher with her long hair, tight dress, and high heels. A fresh wave of hot anger rushed through me. At first I'd just been hurt, but at some point during my long walk under the midday sun, anger had joined the hurt. Why was Daniel kissing me if he had a girlfriend? If this was the way things worked between guys and girls, I didn't want any part of it. Before Morgan, everything about my time with Daniel felt good and right, and now somehow it was tainted and spoiled.

"I assume this has something to do with my grandson."

I tilted my head to find Ms. Ginny looking at me, one eyebrow arched. "I may be old, Clover, but I'm not stupid."

In front of the house, some kids rode by on their bikes. They looked happy, oblivious to how lucky they were. "My mama saw life in stories. She used to say that everyone had a story worth telling, but I'm not sure I believe that anymore."

"She sounds like a smart lady." Ms. Ginny pushed off with one foot, setting the chair into a rocking motion. "What did your father think?"

"Daddy?" My mouth tightened. "He didn't like stories at all."

"What did he like?"

"He liked order and being in control. He liked…fear."

Her chair stopped, just a little reaction, but enough to make me realize I'd said too much. I'd been distracted by Daniel and his girlfriend, and I'd messed up. I jumped to my feet and crossed to the rail. Caesar nudged my leg, like he knew I was in trouble.

A floorboard creaked, and Ms. Ginny's hand appeared on the railing, inches from mine. "Sometimes confiding in someone can help."

I shook my head with fury. She didn't understand. It wasn't that simple.

Her hand patted mine. "Maybe not now, but when you're ready. By the way, for what it's worth, my grandson sounded pretty upset on the phone. I don't know what happened, but he was really worried."

I swallowed back the familiar taste of bitterness. "Daniel's a good person. Concern comes easy for him." Now that Morgan had pointed out the truth, it all made sense. I'd been someone Daniel needed to save. That's all.

"Clover—" She cleared her throat and looked out over her green lawn. "I don't have a magic answer to whatever's eating at you, but maybe you just need to give this place and the folks living here another chance. Maybe they'll surprise you, if you let them."

Part of me wanted to. I didn't want to leave this house or Ms. Ginny or Amelia, but the risks of staying were just so big.

Finally, she nodded. "I'll call Daniel and tell him you're safe. The rest is up to you."

A few hours later, I sat cross-legged on the floor of the study, surrounded by stacks of old newspapers. I'd started working to keep my mind off Daniel, but somewhere along the way I lost myself in the town's stories. With my face buried in the yellowed, musty papers, I didn't even hear him come in.

"What the hell was that about?"

He planted his feet in front of me, and I had to lean way back to see his face. *Shoot.* Angry Daniel was a sight to behold. If I hadn't been sitting, my knees might have knocked together.

He yanked off his ball cap and slapped it against his thigh. "You left. You promised you'd stay and you just left."

I straightened. "Don't yell at me."

"Then don't do stupid things, like leaving without telling anyone."

Morgan's perfect face appeared in my head. I lifted my chin. "I don't have to tell you everything." My words were childish, but I didn't care.

He knelt in front of me. His cheeks glowed from hours in the sun. "That's bull. Anyone with a shred of common decency would have said something. We were all worried."

I tore my gaze from him and muttered, "Not everyone." I didn't understand a lot of things in Daniel's world, but he'd been wrong to kiss me and make me feel special while he had a girlfriend. I knew that much.

"What is that supposed to mean?"

The angry knot in my belly twisted tighter, and I looked away, moving papers from one pile to another. "Nothing."

"I want a real answer, and I can wait all afternoon if I need to."

I tried to shuffle some more articles, but he snatched them from my hand. "Stop stalling and just tell me. Did someone say something to you?"

Huffing, I met his fierce gaze. "Fine...Morgan."

The single word shut him up pretty good.

After a long, silent minute, he dropped down on the floor next to me. "Ahh...Morgan."

His soft tone cut through me like a butcher knife, like her upsetting me was inevitable. I looked down at a stack of articles. I didn't want to see his pity, but I still felt his stare. Then his hand snaked out to grip my elbow, and I jerked. He lifted me to my feet like I weighed no more than a sack of flour and started leading me to the door.

"Stop! What are you doing?"

"Something I should have done a while ago."

His look gave nothing away. I couldn't tell if he was angry or something altogether different. I dug my heels into the floor and folded my arms across my chest. "I'm not going anywhere with you."

Daniel smiled. "When you get to know me better, you'll understand that I don't back down from a challenge."

*Daniel*

# Chapter Sixteen

I took Clover to my favorite spot in the world—the beach. The clean-up effort continued, but even with debris scattered across the sand, the ocean stretched in front of me as far as the eye could see. Waves hit the beach in a constant rhythm, a rhythm you could count on. How many times had I looked out over the same surf wondering about life and fate and Grace?

Caesar bolted ahead of us, sniffing at a pile of wood and seaweed. Clover walked in silence, a condition she'd maintained on the drive from Gran's house. She stooped to pick up a piece of driftwood, tracing the knots and swirls with her thumb. She'd changed in the short time I'd known her. Clover looked at everything in her unique, unfiltered way—a mix of innocence, compassion, and frankness. Somewhere along the way, cynicism had crept in. She'd grown a little jaded. Had she learned that from me?

"Are you planning to tell me what Morgan said?"

She stopped and tossed the stick in the ocean. We both watched it bob and spin, pulled along by the current. "Oh… you mean your girlfriend?"

She'd also learned sarcasm. That came from hanging out with Amelia.

"Is that what she told you?"

She shrugged and started walking again. My strides easily matched hers.

"It's true that we used to date before she left for boarding school."

"So she's not your girlfriend?"

"Technically—no. Although we didn't officially end things. We left it open-ended, waiting to see what happened."

She shook her head, and her blue eyes flashed. "It's like you're playing a game with me, and I don't know any of the rules. But I don't want to play anymore, not if it makes me feel this way."

Blood rushed into my face, and I looked away. Like always, Clover brought me to my knees with her frankness. I wasn't proud of how I'd been dealing with Morgan. She'd called several times, clearly interested in starting things up again, but I'd put her off with excuses, avoiding anything concrete. In a way, it was Clover's fault. She had me on edge, not sure of what we were to each other or what I wanted us to be.

She'd turned to look at the ocean, and I stared at her stiff profile. She'd pursed her lips, and her chin jutted out, but I could see the hurt behind her anger.

"Clover, I'm sorry. I should have let Morgan know exactly where we stand."

"Fine. Now, can you please take me back to Ms. Ginny's?"

She called out to Caesar, heading for the parking lot, but I blocked her path. "You can't leave."

She glared at me, and I ducked my head. A lump lodged in my throat. "Please stay." Taking a chance, I looped my arms around her. "Please."

She didn't pull away—a positive sign. The wind picked

up. It tugged at our clothes and mussed her hair. She tensed against me, her hands hanging at her side.

"I'm not good at this." Her lips moved against my chest, and I strained to hear her words over the rush of the waves. "I don't understand what we're doing. This past week when you were at Ms. Ginny's, I felt so happy, I was afraid to close my eyes in case you disappeared. But today, when I saw you with Morgan, it hurt so much even my teeth ached. Feeling like that scares me."

My heart raced. Her confession scared the hell out of me, too. I didn't want anyone to rely on me that much, and definitely not Clover, someone who needed saving every time I turned around. Unfortunately, my body refused to listen. I squeezed her tighter, more afraid to let go.

Her hands crept up to my waist. "You never did tell me why you kissed me…after the hurricane?"

I tracked a seagull as it dove for its supper. "I don't know. It seemed like the right thing at the time. Does there have to be a reason?"

She pressed her cheek flat against my chest. "I don't know, but I think about it. A lot," she whispered.

I closed my eyes and groaned. "Me, too." She still smelled like lemons, and her tentative fingers resting at my waist made me think about a whole lot more than just kissing. I shifted away from her, hoping she didn't notice.

"I want to do it again," she said. "But I'm afraid."

"Of what?"

She looked up at me, her eyes clear and blue. "Of getting hurt. My life is getting all tangled up with yours, but what if you don't like being tied to me?" Her voice shook. "I'd have to figure out how to be alone again."

I tightened my grip, terrified of the raw feeling I saw on her face. "I can't promise anything." There were no guarantees. Life could spin on a dime, and I didn't want to be responsible if things didn't work out. She said nothing but held me so tight, my ribs started to hurt.

"I'm not asking for any promises, and if that day comes, I'll make do. I always have," she said finally, her voice muffled against my shirt.

We stood like that for a long quiet moment. My reservations about getting closer to her still existed, but somehow they were less important than the way I felt every day this past week when I'd sat across from her in Gran's kitchen. I liked talking to her, I liked being with her, and I loved holding her like this. Wasn't that enough?

Amelia always complained that I overthink things and that sometimes I just need to go with my gut. Now my gut told me that I needed Clover in my life as much as she needed me.

Her fingers moved restlessly across my back—bold and shy at the same time—and I let out the breath I'd been holding.

She tilted her head back, and I couldn't look away from the pattern of freckles on her cheeks. "By the way, Amelia says you're just using me for my baking."

God, her eyes were so blue. "Amelia needs to mind her own business." My hands dropped to her hips, and I pulled her closer.

"So it's not true?"

I laughed. "Hey, I'm not denying my love for your cookies, but it's not what kept me coming back to Gran's house." I frowned, feeling serious again. "I like talking to you. You make me see things differently."

She blinked, and her fingers stilled. "Really?"

"Yeah. You notice everything, even the small stuff that other people assume is unimportant, and you're so... committed to life. You make me think about the things I take for granted, like maybe I've been just getting by for the past two years and maybe it's not enough."

"You mean the two years since Grace died?"

"Yeah." I stepped back and yanked off my ball cap, jamming my fingers through my hair. There were questions on her face, but I needed a minute to think.

I headed toward the water and stopped just short of the incoming waves. My family understood. They didn't bring her up anymore, but Clover kept wading right in. It was different with Morgan. She'd gone to school with Grace and basically knew what happened. She never tried to cross that unwritten boundary with me, but was it out of respect or because she just didn't care enough about that time in my life?

I should have known Clover would follow.

"Did you love her?"

Love… I wasn't even sure anymore how I'd felt about Grace.

I wish she'd just dumped me. That would have been easy. My heart would have been broken a little. I'd have spent a few weeks hiding out in my bedroom and listening to her favorite music. She'd pass me in the hall at school, and I'd miss her dry sense of humor, the way she hogged the popcorn at the movies, the way she called golf a sport for old men. Maybe we'd have remained friends. We'd started out that way— hanging out at the beach, surfing together. She was athletic, smart, independent, overachieving.

"I thought I loved her."

"Amelia told me she killed herself." Clover's voice penetrated the wall I'd erected.

I pushed my hands in my pockets, hiding the fists that formed whenever I thought about the end. I knew what happened. It was the "why" part that haunted me and everyone else who'd loved her.

The sun vanished behind a cloud and sent shadows scattering across the waves. "She overdosed in her room on a Tuesday night in May. Her mom found her in the morning."

The steel band was back again. It wrapped around my chest and squeezed my lungs. In those first few months, it was a near constant presence, and I wondered if I'd die in my sleep from a heart attack. Now it came only occasionally. I rubbed at my chest, trying to relieve the pressure, but it remained.

"I was the last one who spoke to her. She called me, but I cut it short. I needed to finish an English essay I'd put off until the last minute. I don't even remember what I got on that paper, but somehow, at that moment, it was more important than talking to Grace."

"I'm sorry." I recognized Clover's strangled tone—the tone of someone who'd experienced similar loss—the anger, the pain, the helplessness. "It wasn't your fault, though. She chose her own path."

Her reassurance came quickly, and it was my turn to be silent. I'd heard this particular line from almost everyone— my parents, my friends, Amelia, the counselors at school. Of course, the people I hadn't heard it from were the only ones who really counted—Grace and her parents. Grace was an only child. She killed herself without any note or explanation, leaving her parents with nothing. So we avoided one another whenever possible. Maybe they blamed me, or maybe I just reminded them of what they'd never have again.

Clover's touch pulled me back to the present. She tugged my hand from my pocket, unfurling my fist and intertwining her fingers in mine. "You don't believe me, but you should."

"Why?"

"Because even if you bury yourself in guilt, you can't go back and change what happened. You can't go back and talk longer on the phone. Even if you could, even if you talked to her all night, she could have killed herself the next morning or the next night. You'll never know because you can't change any of it." Her voice rose, more adamant with each word, and I wondered who she was really trying to convince. "Your guilt can only make you suffer. It can never save Grace."

"I know that in my head, but not in here." I pointed to my heart. I'd been over it so many times. There must have been signs, something I missed. "I only know that I can never go through that again."

Her fingers tightened around my hand. "You mean worrying that you didn't do enough to save someone?"

"Maybe," I hedged, suddenly understanding where she was headed.

She pulled her hand free.

"Morgan said you spend time with me because you're a good Samaritan." Her lower lip jutted, defiant, but I saw the pain hiding underneath. "Do you think I need saving?"

The grain of truth in her accusation made me defensive. "I don't think so. I know so. Remember the dive off the pier? And the hurricane?"

"I didn't ask for your help."

"Did you expect me to stand by and watch? To do nothing?"

Her mouth clamped shut, her face frozen in a mutinous expression. Caesar chose that moment to return and lick at his owner's stiff hand. She didn't move, so I bent on one knee and scratched behind his ears. He whined and dropped to the sand, legs up, offering me his belly.

"Is that why you spend time with me? I make you feel less guilty? You think I need rescuing?"

The sun found a patch of cloudless sky. I looked up and squinted. "I never claimed to be perfect. After Grace, I never wanted anyone to rely on me again. I don't need that responsibility. I don't want it."

"And you feel responsible for me?"

A crab scurried across the beach a few feet away, and Caesar bounced to his feet to give chase. I stayed on my knees and picked up a stick, drawing aimless patterns in the sand.

Another girl might have let me off this particular hook, but I knew Clover would wait forever. So I stood and flung the stick away.

"It happened so fast, I never had time to decide. One day it was just me, and then you showed up in my store. You looked kind of lost, and then I offered you that damn camp stove and you accepted. Pulling you out of the ocean just solidified the deal. I want things to go back to the way they were, but I can't stop worrying about you. I want to know what you're thinking and what your damn secrets are. I want to make sure you're okay."

My speech came to an abrupt end, and I was afraid to look at her, afraid of a tiny girl who somehow had power over me. When I'd realized she was missing from the clubhouse earlier, I'd been crazy with worry. I'd seen the twin looks of concern on my parents' faces when I'd searched the building and the grounds. They were remembering the way I'd been after Grace died. Even after Gran called and Dad convinced me to finish the tournament, my game suffered. I prided myself on my ability to focus, to block out every distraction, but today, all I could think about was Clover.

She crossed her arms over her chest. "It sounds like you're here, but you don't really want to be. Maybe you'd be better off with Morgan."

I took a deep breath and faced her. Her forehead wrinkled, and her lips clenched in a tight line.

"This is not about Morgan. It's about me spending way too much of the last two years overthinking things." I blew out a breath, the truth of my statement resonating in my head. "I like hanging out with you. I like kissing you. I don't know what the future holds, but can't that be enough for now?"

I expected Clover to make this difficult, but she surprised me again. The worry lines eased from her face, replaced by a tentative smile.

"Okay."

"Okay? That's it?"

"Yes."

I grinned, afraid of exactly how happy she'd just made me. "That seemed too easy."

"Maybe I'm also tired of overthinking things." She bounced up and down, her grin as wide as mine. "So what do we do next?"

"Actually, I have a question. The golf club has an end-of-summer dance each year. It's kind of a formal event that we all dress up for." I didn't add that this year the dance was on the last weekend before I left for college. We'd just agreed to not worry about these things. "Anyway, I wanted to know if you'd like to come with me."

She nodded with such vigor, her teeth probably clattered together.

"Whoa…" My fingers reached out to grip her shoulders. "Calm down. You'll make yourself dizzy."

"Amelia told me about the dance and…" Her voice dropped to a whisper. "I really wanted you to ask me."

"So it's settled?"

She nodded, and then the moment turned awkward. For some reason, I felt nervous. Maybe it was because I really wanted to kiss her. I'd done it before, but that time I hadn't thought about it. I just did it. Now I was thinking too hard. Still, a guy had to try.

I stepped closer and reached for her hand. I tried to be smooth, but Clover threw herself at me so hard I stumbled backward. I caught her in my arms, and she pushed her lips against mine, knocking off my hat and smacking her nose against mine.

"Whoa…take it easy. It's kissing, not a wrestling match. It's supposed to be fun." I grinned and puffed my chest out a little, her enthusiasm a definite ego boost.

"Sorry. I've just been thinking about it for a long time and you look so nice…"

I cut off her explanation with a proper kiss, catching her little gasp of surprise. Her lips were soft—she tasted like lemonade—and the kissing was just as good as I remembered. She wrapped her arms around my neck, and I hooked my hands around her waist. The ocean breeze tugged at us, and a wave swirled around our feet. It soaked my shoes, but I didn't care. She fit perfectly against me, all tiny and soft and eager. If I didn't need to breathe, I could have just kept kissing Clover.

"Wow. I love kissing," she said, when I finally pulled back. She pushed her palms flat against my chest. "Why don't people spend all their time doing that?"

I cleared my throat and brushed her jaw with my thumb. "Because there's school, work, life."

She shivered, and her eyes swept closed for a few seconds. "None of that compares to kissing. It's even better than peach cobbler."

I laughed. Another wave surged over our feet, and she looked down at her soaked sneakers in surprise.

"Come on." My fingers found hers, and we headed back up the beach. My stomach rumbled, reminding me I hadn't eaten since breakfast. "Do you like pizza?"

She nodded.

"Good. Let's go find some. I'm starving."

She called to Caesar, and we walked back toward my borrowed car, our fingers linked the whole way. It felt right, just like talking to her about Grace. The steel band had lifted from my chest, and my steps felt lighter than they had in a very long time.

There was only one thing nagging at my otherwise perfect moment—Clover's secrets. She didn't seem capable of hurting a fly, but based on her reaction to Mr. Garrett, I couldn't help wondering if she was not only running from her past, but maybe also from the law.

I wanted to ask her, but she just looked so darn happy—and another part of me was scared of the answer.

She pulled her hand free and twirled around. Her blue eyes danced with happiness. "I'll race you back."

I snorted. "Seriously. You're a midget, and my long legs will crush you."

But she was already running, leaving me to chase the sound of her laughter across the sand.

Of course, I caught her. I lifted her high against me, and when she slid slowly back down to the ground, her heated stare on my lips, I forgot all about my questions. At least, for now.

That night I called Morgan. It was time to make a clean break.

"It's because I talked to Clover today, isn't it?"

"Partially." I sat in the backyard, alone under the stars.

"Are you angry with me?"

"No. It's my fault for not being more upfront with you."

She sighed. "Even now, you're being the good guy. You can't help it."

"I'm sorry if I hurt you."

"I'll survive, but it's you I'm worried about. Clover's a stranger. She's living with your grandmother, and you know nothing about her. She's using you."

My mouth snapped shut. I'd no intention of discussing Clover's refusal to share her past.

Morgan huffed in my ear. "You don't have to talk to me, but don't say I didn't warn you."

I unclenched my muscles and stretched out on the lawn chair, listening to the peepers. "I'll be fine."

"I hope you are. So I guess this is good-bye."

I gripped the phone. "It's for the best."

The line went silent for a moment. "I wish things had turned out differently, Daniel. I really missed you these last few months."

"Morgan—"

"It's fine. I don't need you to say anything. I just wanted you to know."

She disconnected, leaving me staring at my phone and feeling like a jerk. Today, with Clover, it felt like I'd made the right decision, but now I wondered if Morgan's warning might come back to haunt me.

# Chapter Seventeen

A couple weeks later, Clover bounced in the seat next to me, so excited she literally couldn't sit still. She looked up at me, her blue eyes hidden behind her 3D glasses. "It's so big."

I plucked them off her face, so I could see how wide her eyes had grown. "What—the movie screen or that bag of popcorn you're holding?"

"Both." She grinned and scooped another handful of popcorn into her mouth. "This is amazing—the smell, and the taste, and the glasses. We should do this every night."

I draped my arm across the back of her seat, and she leaned into my shoulder. "If you like it now, just wait until the movie starts."

She popped back upright, and I groaned. I'd been really comfortable with her tucked under my arm. "How much longer?"

I checked my watch. "Three more minutes."

Her head bobbed up and down. "And first they show us the other movies that will be coming soon, and then we see the one about the superheroes, right?"

I crossed my legs. "Yup. Previews first and then the main

attraction."

I didn't bother asking her how she'd never been to a movie theater before, because I knew she'd only dodge my question. She was an eighteen-year-old American who knew nothing about boy wizards with lightning marks on their foreheads or mind-reading vampires that glittered in the sun. But as much as I questioned her, she'd perfected the art of avoidance, redirection, and flat-out refusal.

It was a catch-22. I loved watching her discover all the things I took for granted, but I hated the constant reminder that she didn't trust me. Even after I'd told her everything about Grace.

My mind kept coming up with possible explanations for Clover's lack of experience with the modern world. Some were far-fetched like she was a time traveler or an alien, but deep inside, I knew the truth was something dark and ugly. I also knew her fear of storms and law enforcement came from that same shadowy place. More than anything, I wanted to help her, but it was impossible until she trusted me.

My fingers squeezed her knee. "Here, try this." I tore open my bag of M&Ms and sprinkled them on top of her popcorn.

She didn't need any extra encouragement. She tucked into a handful and then moaned. "It's so good." A piece of popcorn flew out. She slapped her hand over her mouth until she finished swallowing, and her cheeks turned pink.

I grabbed some, popping the pieces into my mouth one at a time. "You're welcome, by the way."

She leaned closer, and her lips settled against mine. Her kiss may have been salty from the popcorn, but it still tasted warm and sweet, like Clover. Her hand curled around my neck, and her popcorn bag crinkled between us. I buried my hand in her soft hair, anchoring her to me.

When she lifted her head, I couldn't stop grinning. "What was that for?"

"Because you're amazing, and I feel like doing that pretty much every time I'm around you."

She grabbed my arm and settled it around her, leaning back into my shoulder.

"You're the one who's amazing," I whispered, but I wasn't sure if she heard because just then the screen lit up, and she gasped.

Her gasp turned to a grin as the previews started.

I'd been excited about seeing the movie, but once she put on her 3D glasses and the action started, I only had eyes for Clover. She jumped and cringed and laughed and held tight to me. Being with her made me feel like a kid again. When had I stopped feeling this way?

When the movie was over, she hugged me for a full minute, while everyone else filed out of the theater. "That was incredible. Can we come again tomorrow?"

I chuckled. "Maybe next weekend."

Around us, staff swept the aisles, cleaning up before the next showing. Clover noticed and, before I could stop her, she was up helping—finding empty popcorn bags and drink cups and running them to the trash cans.

I wanted to call her back and tell her that people just didn't help out like that, but she was so enthusiastic. She talked to the movie attendants while she worked, and they actually seemed to appreciate her help.

I hovered near the exit, and when she was done, she ran up to me.

"You know that they're paid to clean up. It's their job."

I wondered if she'd feel embarrassed, but she looked at me like I was the one with the extra head.

"It doesn't matter, Daniel. People appreciate it whenever you lend a hand." She hooked her arm though mine, and I didn't know what to say.

The next day at work, whenever I was idle or waiting

around for a customer to come in, I made sure to ask if there was anything else I could help out with.

At the end of the day, Dad slapped me on the back. "I heard from everyone that you did a great job today. I'm proud of you, son."

Dad beamed at me, but I didn't deserve the credit. That belonged to a tiny blond girl with amazing blue eyes.

A week later, we stood together in the town library. Clover looked around at the stacks of books, her mouth open and awe on her face, like a little kid on Christmas morning. "There are so many. Are you sure that anyone can check them out?"

"As long as you have a library card." Nothing in Canna Point was particularly big or fancy, so what I really wanted to know was how a small-town library could possibly be that exciting.

"And how do you get a library card?"

I pointed to a librarian seated behind a desk. "You'd have to ask her, but I think you need ID and proof that you're living in town."

Clover's face fell.

"You must have something…driver's license, birth certificate, student ID?"

She looked over at the children's section where another librarian was putting on a puppet show for some kids. "Everything I owned was in the car."

I frowned. "I'm sure you can get replacements. I could help with the paperwork if you tell me where you used to live."

Her mouth snapped shut, and she dropped the book she'd just picked up.

"You seriously won't tell me?"

She stared at her feet for a long minute, and when she

lifted her head, her eyes pleaded with me. "I can't. Why can't you accept that?"

"Because I don't understand why you won't trust me."

She stood in stony silence, so I yanked my wallet out of my pocket. "Forget it. Just use mine."

She glared at the card I held out. "You're mad at me."

I shook my head. Maybe I was, but it didn't matter. On some level, I knew I couldn't force her to trust me. It was her decision. "I don't like that you won't trust me, but I don't want to fight."

Her shoulders slumped inside her jean jacket. She still wore it, even over the pretty flowered sundress that stopped at her thighs and left the rest of her legs bare. I stepped closer and dropped a kiss on her stiff lips.

"I'm sorry." I breathed against her mouth. "This was supposed to be fun."

Her forehead pressed against mine. "Please don't be mad. I feel like I'm ruining everything."

I pulled her into a quick hug. "Nothing's ruined. Just use my card and go get some books. I know you're dying to."

A smile tugged at the corners of her mouth. "How many can I get?"

"A lot."

She spun out of my arms. "And you'll wait for me?"

Grabbing a magazine, I dropped into the closest chair. "I'll be right here."

Music pumped through my earbuds while Clover darted back and forth from the stacks to my chair, showing me each book she added to her growing pile.

Eventually, my fingers caught the hem of her dress, holding her in place. "Enough. You already have too many."

She chewed at her bottom lip. "But it's so hard to choose."

"We can always come back. They'll still be here."

She frowned. "Maybe." She held up two novels. "But

which one should I read first?"

I let go of her dress and tugged on her wrist. She fell into my lap, giggling and dropping the books on the floor.

"What are you listening to?"

I handed her one of my earbuds, and she pushed it in her ear.

"I like it." She shifted on my lap until her head lay on my shoulder, one hand stretched wide on my chest. She hooked her legs over the arm of the chair. Her foot bounced to the music, but I was distracted by the smooth tanned skin of her bare legs.

We sat like that through the next three songs. Eventually, I reached for her bracelet—the braided strands she never took off.

"You never told me where you got this."

I expected her to avoid my question, but she actually responded. "Mama and I made them together."

"Them?"

She stiffened, but only for a second. "Yes, I made her one, too."

"It's pretty. Does she still wear hers?"

She stared at the strands for a moment before handing me back my earbud. "They're not hard to make. I can make one for you if you like."

I released the breath I'd been holding, and disappointment tightened my chest.

"We should get going." I pushed her legs off the armrest. "The library closes early on Saturday."

Clover's lower lip quivered. I'd told her I wasn't mad, but couldn't she see what her secrets were doing to us? She stood and reached for the book pile, but I got there first.

"I got them."

"I can help."

She reached for some, but I was already walking across the library. "I said I got them."

I reached the librarian's desk and dropped the pile. Using my library card, the whole checkout process took a couple of minutes.

Outside, thunderclouds loomed on the horizon. It was only five o'clock, but already the sky had darkened. Clover and I walked together to my new Jeep. The insurance check had come through the week before, and I'd picked up the replacement two days later. I loved not having to bum rides anymore or borrow the truck from the store. Looking up at the sky, I thanked whatever instinct made me pull up the soft top that morning. Otherwise, we'd have a wet ride home.

I started to put the books inside, but Clover stopped me. She silently searched through the titles before pulling one from the stack. I rolled my eyes. "Can't you wait until you get home to read it?"

"I need to do something."

"What? We're about to get dumped on."

"I know. I'll be quick." She slid the book under her jean jacket and took off.

"Clover!"

But she was already running up the street. I dropped the books in the Jeep and followed, cursing under my breath. When I got to the end of the street, I found her just around the corner. My jaw dropped. She leaned over Jaywalking Pete and offered him the library book I'd just checked out with my library card.

"You said you liked mysteries," I overheard her say. "So I picked this one. It's about a soldier, like you, who comes back after the war and becomes a detective. He helps solve crimes, and there's a mystery lady. I think he falls in love with her."

Pete's eyes welled with tears. He took the book with reverence, like she was giving him a priceless gift. "Thanks, Clover. I'll take real good care of it."

Thunder rumbled in the distance, and she jerked. "It's

going to rain soon, Peter. You need to go somewhere you can stay dry. Here." She pulled a few bills from her pocket. "Buy some supper and stay inside until the rain stops."

"Thanks, and thank you for the muffins yesterday."

She patted him on the shoulder, and shame filled me. Clover, who'd been in our town for only a month, who barely had a cent to her name, had taken the time to get to know Pete, to see him as a person. The rest of us were content to walk past without really looking. That night I vowed to talk to Dad about Pete. Maybe there was something he could do at the store. I'd be leaving for college at the end of the summer. Maybe they'd need extra help.

Clover and Pete said their good-byes, and she walked back to me. I grimaced. Whatever Clover's secrets were, I'd no right to pry them from her. She deserved more. Over her head, Pete caught my eye, a whole lot of meaning in his expression. His message was clear. Pete knew Clover was a special person, and he wouldn't sit by and watch anyone hurt her.

I tucked her under my arm, and we walked back to the Jeep. More thunder boomed, closer now, and she shivered.

"Is it the thunderstorm?" I whispered in her ear.

She nodded. Her fingers gripped my T-shirt.

"We're almost to the Jeep."

I walked her to the passenger door and pried her hand from my shirt. She'd put Pete's well being in front of her own fear, a fact that shamed me even more. I closed her door and sprinted to the other side. Lightning streaked across the sky, and the first drops of rain plopped on the soft top.

"Let's get you home."

She didn't answer. Her eyes were closed tight, and her fingers clenched the seat belt.

"It'll be fine. The storm can't hurt you."

I put the Jeep in gear and waited for a car to pass before pulling out. The slap of the windshield wipers filled the silence. I glanced over at Clover, regretting my decision to go with a standard. I wanted to hold her hand, to reassure her, but the constant gear changing on the town streets made it impossible. Damn, I hated feeling this powerless.

The rain intensified, and I flicked the wipers up to high speed. We drove toward the worst of the thunderstorm. A clap of thunder boomed close by. When I glanced over this time, she'd opened her eyes, but her skin looked almost gray.

"Mom used to tell us that thunderstorms happened when God was moving furniture in heaven. Growing up in Florida, I started thinking that God must be really into interior decorating."

My attempt to lighten the mood fell short. Clover's head fell back against the seat. Her lips trembled, and I heard her teeth chatter. The drive to Gran's house seemed to take forever, but it was probably only five minutes. I pulled in the driveway and turned off the Jeep. The rain lessened but still beat down on us.

"Do you want to make a run for it?"

She shook her head, and her eyes squeezed shut. She didn't look so hot. This was more than a little fear.

I reached over, pried her fingers from the seat belt, and unclipped it. Sliding my seat back as far as it would go, I pulled her into my lap and wrapped my arms around her. She buried her face in my neck.

"Shhh…it's okay. You're safe. Nothing's going to happen."

I spoke the type of meaningless reassurances Mom used to say to me when I was little and scared or sick. I held her tight until her shaking stopped, along with the thunder. Outside, the sky brightened, but I knew it was likely a break in what could be a long line of thunderstorms. I hated to think of her going through this over and over.

"Is it like this every time?"

"Yes," she whispered.

"What do you do when you're alone?"

She didn't say anything, but I already knew the answer. She panicked every time, except there was no one around to comfort her. I held her tighter.

A few minutes later, the porch light came on. "Gran obviously knows we're back."

Clover blushed. "I'd better go in. She warned me about doing inappropriate things with her grandson."

I chuckled. My thumb traced the smattering of freckles on her cheek. "If she only knew the truth."

Clover shuddered and pressed her lips against my throat. Then she lifted her head and kissed me properly. Her soft, sweet kiss lasted only a few seconds, but it still made me shift in my seat. She climbed back to her side, and I sucked in a steadying breath before we both hopped out. I reached in back for her books and followed her up to the veranda.

She stopped at the door and reached for her stack. "Thanks…for the books and for everything else."

I hugged her, hard. "You could talk to me about it, you know—the reason you're so afraid."

She tensed in my arms, tilting her head back to look at me. "Just being with you helped." She kissed my cheek and slipped inside the house.

For a long moment, I stood on Gran's porch, thinking about thunderstorms and feeling helpless. Storms hit Florida all the time. What would she do when I was miles away in Georgia?

Maybe I'd talk to Gran, but as much as I loved my grandmother, she wasn't exactly the comforting type. She was a poster child for the tough-love approach.

I sprinted down the steps and climbed in the Jeep, slamming the door behind me.

What I really wanted was to comfort her myself, but as I already knew, wanting something and getting something were two different things.

# Chapter Eighteen

"Thanks for your help."

Sam grinned. "No sweat. Had nothing better to do on a Saturday morning than wade through slime up to my knees and have my blood drained by bat-size mosquitoes."

"Yeah, that part *sucked*," I said, laughing at my own corny joke, "but at least we were successful." I referred to the mud-encrusted typewriter I now lugged through town.

As a surprise for Clover, Sam and I found her car and dug through her mucky belongings. Her books, papers, and pictures were beyond salvage, but I hoped that Dave at the repair shop might be able to fix the typewriter.

"I'm dying of thirst, man," Sam said as we passed a convenience store. "Want a Coke?"

"Sure."

I dropped the behemoth typewriter on a bench and sat next to it, while Sam disappeared inside. Slumping back against the seat, I stretched out my mud-spattered legs and tilted my head toward the late-afternoon sun.

A shadow crossed my face, and I sat up straight. "Hey…

Mr. Alexander." The older man paused, a blank look on his features. "I'm Daniel Hudson, Ginny King's grandson."

Recognition flickered in his eyes, but his expression never changed. The frown on his lips and furrows in his forehead appeared to be permanent.

"Daniel…I remember you. I met your sister a few weeks ago. She and her friend left abruptly."

Clover? They hadn't mentioned it to me. "How did you make out during the hurricane, sir?"

"Fine. Lost a few trees on the property, but I've weathered worst. I read about your escapade in the paper." I didn't take his bait. I wasn't sure what he'd read, but he made it sound like I'd gotten stuck in the park just for the fun of it. "Next time a hurricane heads our way, maybe you should act smarter."

I'd forgotten how unpleasant he was. I wanted to tell him where to stick his self-righteousness, but I'd been taught to respect my elders, so I gritted my teeth. "I'll try to remember that, sir."

"Hmmph." He shifted his leather briefcase from one hand to the other. Was he still working on cases? My grandfather retired a couple of years before he passed away. I hoped Mr. Alexander would continue walking and leave me to enjoy my sun, but his gaze fixed on the bench. His eyes widened.

"Where'd you get that typewriter?" He reached down to wipe away some mud and reveal the brand name.

"It belongs to a friend of mine."

His eyes leaped up and pinned me to the bench. "A friend…" He swallowed, and his Adam's apple bobbed up and down.

I nodded. "Yeah."

His greedy gaze returned to the typewriter, and I laid my arm across it, staking my claim. Why was he so weirdly fascinated with Clover's typewriter?

He pointed to the muddy keys. "Why does it look like

that?"

"Hurricane Delores."

His eyes misted, and he cleared his throat. "These typewriters are quite rare." He spoke in a gruff voice. "I owned one for many years. It originally belonged to my father."

"Where is it now?" I hadn't planned to ask the question, but it hung in the air between us before I had a chance to snatch it back.

"I gave it to my daughter on her eighteenth birthday." He looked at a spot over my head, but I could tell he was seeing something else completely. "She wanted to be a writer. When she was little, she'd visit me in my office. She'd sit at my desk and pound away at the keys. So I decided to give it to her."

"That was nice of you."

He grimaced, looking old and tired. "She didn't think so. She wanted a new car, not an old typewriter."

"Oh." What was I supposed to say? That I'd probably have felt the same way? "So what happened to the typewriter?"

"I don't know." He gave Clover's typewriter another fierce look. "My daughter left town with it a year later, and I never heard from her again."

A sinking feeling spread through my belly. I looked down at my sneakers, avoiding his gaze.

"Who did you say your friend was?" he asked.

"I didn't," I hedged. "There must be lots of these things around, though."

"Not lots. Mine had a deep scratch on the back where my father dropped it."

My fingers spread wide along the back of the typewriter, feeling its surface. "Must be a different one. This one has no scratches."

Mr. Alexander's shoulders hunched, disappointment etched on his face. "You're sure?"

"Yeah."

The older man started to say something more, but Sam showed up.

"Sorry I took so long. There was a line." He tossed me a can of soda.

"Thanks. Hey, do you know Mr. Alexander? This is Sam Garrett."

Mr. Alexander frowned. "Garrett...any relation to Andrew Garrett?"

"He's my dad." Sam offered his hand, but the older man ignored it.

"Didn't realize he had kids as old as you."

Sam dropped his hand and busied himself with popping open his soda. "Well, it's just me."

Mr. Alexander grunted. He pulled a handkerchief from his pocket and wiped it across his face. "I'll be going now. I have an appointment."

"Nice talking to you," I lied.

He gave a half wave before turning and heading down the street.

Sam looked at me. "What was that about? Did I say something wrong?"

I shrugged. "He was my grandfather's law partner, and he's always been like that. I wouldn't worry about it."

"So, onwards to the repair shop?"

I stood and picked up the typewriter. "Change of plans, actually. I have to get home. I'll take it in tomorrow."

If Sam was surprised by my decision, he didn't say anything. He only shrugged and followed me back to the Jeep. He climbed in the passenger's seat, while I laid the typewriter in the back. Using the end of my T-shirt, I wiped at the mud until the gouge in the back of the typewriter showed up.

I wasn't exactly sure why I lied, probably my instinct to protect Clover. I just knew that I needed answers before I told Henry Alexander anything. I needed to know who his daughter was and why Clover ended up with her typewriter. I had my suspicions, but if I was right, what possible reason did she have for hiding her true identity?

Clover insisted on keeping her secrets, but I couldn't ignore them anymore. Not this time.

I dropped the typewriter at home, showered and headed straight for Gran's, but Clover wasn't home when I arrived. She and Amelia were out shopping. So I planted myself in Gran's kitchen, in the same seat I'd been using for as long as I could remember. The room never changed, the familiar scent of fresh bread and beeswax making me feel like a kid. Gran set a glass of milk in front of me, along with a platter of Clover's cookies. I snagged one off the plate and popped it in my mouth.

Gran took the seat across from me. "I'm glad we have this moment alone."

One look at her serious face made me choke on my cookie. What was I in trouble for now? I gulped down some milk, which only made it worse. I'd barely started breathing again when she hit me with her question.

"Does Clover know about your plans?"

"My plans?"

"Daniel Hudson, you know what I mean. Is Clover aware that you're leaving the state in a couple of weeks?"

I slouched in my chair. "It's not exactly a secret, and we're just dating."

Gran folded her hands. "That girl has clearly not had much experience with boys or a lot of other things we take for granted. I'm not sure what you leaving will do to her."

My hand gripped the glass. "You think I want to see Clover hurt?"

Gran sighed. "Not intentionally, but she relies on you. The closer you get, the harder it's going to be. If you're going to let her down, you need to do it soon."

Hadn't Clover said almost the same thing that day on the beach? I released the glass and drummed my fingers against the tabletop. "What if I don't want to let her down at all?"

Gran looked over at me, a fierce light in her eyes. "You're still young, Daniel. You worked hard for this scholarship, and we all expect you to take advantage of it."

My head bowed under the weight of life and the decisions in front of me. Gran was right—I'd been living in the moment, but it couldn't last. In a few short weeks, I was leaving Florida, and I had no idea what that meant for Clover and me.

Gran patted my arm and gave me a sympathetic smile. "You're a good boy. I know you'll do what's right."

She sounded so certain, but I wasn't even sure what the right thing looked like. I rubbed at my neck, but it didn't help with the tension I felt or the difficult conversation still looming in front of me. My finger swiped at the condensation on my glass. "I ran into Henry Alexander today."

Gran raised an eyebrow. "Hmmm. Amelia and Clover ran into him a few weeks ago."

"He mentioned that. He also talked about his daughter, and I wanted to know more about her."

Gran's spine stiffened, and her hands splayed on the table. "I don't know what's going on here, but I don't want any part of it."

Confusion bubbled up inside me. "What are you talking about?"

"Don't pretend you don't know. Clover also asked me about Henry's daughter. What are you two up to?"

I frowned. "I didn't know Clover asked, and I don't know why she did." But of course, I was lying. Clover told me that she'd come to town looking for someone. She told me the typewriter belonged to her mother. Henry Alexander gave the same typewriter to his daughter. The logical conclusion was that Clover was Mr. Alexander's granddaughter, but I needed proof.

Gran stood. She picked up my empty glass with a shaky hand and brought it to the sink. "I know Clover's hiding something, something that upsets her. Sometimes at night, she wakes up screaming, and she won't tell me why."

I stiffened. Clover never mentioned this.

"I like Clover," she continued, leaning back against the counter. "I want to believe she'll tell us the truth when she's ready, but I can't welcome her in my house if she's planning to do something to Henry."

I straightened and rubbed my palms against my thighs. "I don't think it's like that."

The sounds of laughter reached the kitchen. Amelia and Clover had returned.

"Please don't say anything to Clover, Gran. Leave it with me for a couple of days. I promise I'll figure it out and tell you everything."

She didn't move, but her mouth tightened into a straight line.

"Please. Give me…one day."

The girls appeared in the kitchen doorway, still giggling about something.

"Hey, Gran," Amelia called out.

I looked at my grandmother, silently pleading with her. Then her stance loosened, and I knew I'd won. She stepped away from the counter. "Good shopping trip?"

"Excellent," Amelia answered, dropping a kiss on her cheek.

Clover hovered in the doorway, her fair skin bronzed from the weeks she'd spent in Florida, her hair even whiter from the sun. Gran's cooking had helped her fill out. She looked less frail and healthier. She also looked happy. Gran was right. I would hurt her when I left, but maybe a reunion with her family would lessen the blow.

She smiled at me. "I didn't know you were coming over."

"I just came by to talk to Gran." I gathered my nerve. "I was thinking we could head to the beach this afternoon."

Clover looked at me and then at Gran. "Sure. Just let me get changed."

"You can wear your new bathing suit," Amelia suggested. "Maybe Sam and I will come, too."

"Another time," I jumped in. "I think it's better if it's just me and Clover."

Amelia rolled her eyes. "Okay, little brother, don't have a conniption. It was just a suggestion." She winked at Clover. "I guess he wants you all to himself."

Clover didn't smile. Instead, she gave me a long, silent look before turning to head for her room.

Amelia, Gran, and I made our way to the living room. Amelia and Gran sat, but I paced, rehearsing various scenarios in my head. I tried and rejected at least three opening lines by the time Clover reappeared, her beach bag slung over her shoulder. From the way she dragged her feet, you'd think she faced a firing squad rather than an afternoon with me.

She climbed in the passenger seat of the Jeep and tossed her bag in the back.

"Did you have fun with Amelia?"

She nodded. The radio blasted when I turned the key in the ignition, and she reached over to turn it down. We'd barely made it out of the driveway when she confronted me.

"What's wrong?"

"Nothing."

She frowned. "The muscle is twitching next to your right eye. It does that when you're upset about something."

It did? I rubbed at the spot with one hand.

"Please…just tell me. Whatever it is."

I sighed and pulled off to the side. So much for my beach plans. "I saw Henry Alexander today."

"Oh." She stiffened, and her gaze darted to the window.

"I wanted to surprise you, so Sam and I spent the day looking for your typewriter."

This caught her attention. Her expression brightened. "You found it?"

I nodded. "I was on my way to get it repaired when I met Mr. Alexander. When he saw it, he recognized it. He said he'd given it to his daughter."

She paled, and her face turned back to the window. Her hands curled into fists in her lap.

"Are you his granddaughter?" I blurted out, tired of being tactful. "Is that why you came to Canna Point?"

She didn't respond.

I banged one hand on the steering wheel, and she jumped. "You can't just ignore this. I want an answer."

More seconds ticked by, and I began to wonder if she really planned to avoid this conversation, even after I'd finally uncovered the truth.

"Does he know about this?" she asked finally.

"If you're talking about Mr. Alexander, then no. I covered for you."

"Thanks," she mumbled.

I huffed. "I covered for you, but it doesn't mean I'm going to let it go. You've avoided every question I've asked about your family, but I deserve answers."

She turned on me, her blue eyes flashing. "You 'deserve' answers? Why?"

She really expected me to justify myself. Unbelievable! "Because I've stood up for you and been there every time you needed help. Christ, you're living with my grandmother."

She snorted and rolled her eyes. "So because you took

pity on me and helped out the poor charity case, I have to tell you my whole life story? I never asked for your help."

I gritted my teeth. Her angry sarcasm made my blood boil. I wasn't used to this Clover. "You may not have asked for it, but you never turned it down."

She squeezed her eyes shut. "Maybe I should have." When her eyes opened again, the anger had dissipated, replaced by sadness. "Take me back."

"No. I want to talk about this. We're not done."

She shook her head. "I think we are."

The finality in her words made my stomach clench. Maybe she was right. I stared out the window, the afternoon sun low in the sky. "So, you're not going to tell me the truth?"

I asked the question, already knowing the answer.

When she shook her head, my eyes burned. My voice was gruff with the disappointment clogging my throat. "I can't do this anymore, Clover. I told you about Grace because I trusted you, but I can't be in a relationship with someone who won't trust me back."

The silence lengthened between us. Part of me regretted my words, but part of me felt relief. What did that say about us?

She sat stiffly, her spine ramrod straight. "We haven't discussed it, but you're obviously leaving for college in a couple of weeks. Maybe it's best if we end it now."

I wanted to argue with her, to tell her she was wrong, but I couldn't find the strength or resolve to counter her position. Keeping her secrets was obviously more important than our relationship, and I was tired of fighting this battle.

I put the Jeep in gear and pulled a U-turn, heading back toward Gran's house. Clover hopped out the moment I stopped in the driveway. I slid out and slammed the Jeep door, slowly following her to the house. My mouth filled with a bitter taste. I finally knew where I really stood with Clover.

# Chapter Nineteen

Amelia waited for me on Gran's front porch. "What did you do? She ran in here crying."

Anger stiffened my spine. I hadn't planned to hurt Clover. I'd just asked the questions we'd all been wondering, so why was I the bad guy? "I don't want to talk about it."

Amelia glared for a full minute and blocked my path, but she eventually sighed. "I can't help if you won't tell me what happened."

I jerked a hand through my hair and tried to slow my racing heart. "I asked her some questions about her past. She refused to answer. I got mad. She got mad. Then we agreed that since I'm leaving in a couple of weeks, its best to call it quits now."

I stepped around my sister and headed to the living room where Gran still sat. Judging by her expression, she'd overheard everything.

I jammed my hands in my pockets. "I don't know what else to do, Gran. She won't trust me. She won't tell me anything."

"It's okay, Daniel. You couldn't avoid that conversation

forever."

Maybe, but why did it feel like the steel band around my lungs was back?

Amelia dropped down next to Gran and propped her chin on her hands. "I feel terrible. There must be a way to work this out."

I shook my head, not knowing what to do next. Part of me wanted to leave, but I couldn't bring myself to walk out.

Someone knocked at the front door, giving me an excuse to do something other than stew. I rounded the corner.

Sam's dad stood on the veranda, dressed in his uniform. "Hey, Mr. Garrett." I pushed open the screen door.

He pulled off his hat, not returning my smile. "Daniel, I need to speak to Clover. Is she here?"

"Why? What's up?"

"This is official business. I need you to step aside and let me in."

Mr. Garrett sounded stern and formal, different from the man who'd taken Sam and I camping more times than I could count. For once, I understood Clover's fear of him. I let him in, but only because I had no choice.

Amelia jumped up. "Mr. Garrett, what's wrong? Did something happen to Sam? Is he okay?"

"No. Sam's fine. I believe he's working this afternoon."

"Oh…good." Amelia sank back on the couch, looking embarrassed by her outburst.

"Good afternoon, Ms. Ginny." Mr. Garrett nodded at my grandmother. "I'm actually here to talk to Clover. I need to ask her some questions."

Gran and I exchanged a look, but none of us made any move to get her.

Mr. Garrett shifted his weight. "I know you've all become friends with Clover, but I am here in an official capacity."

He looked me directly in the eye, and something there

made me sick to my stomach—something heated and personal. The steel band squeezed tighter. The nagging fear I'd had since the beginning, that maybe Clover had been running from the law, reared its head, making my vision narrow.

"Did Clover ever mention her parents to you?" he asked. "Did she ever mention what happened to them?"

"No." Did I sound defensive? I worked at moderating my tone. "I mean she's talked about them in passing, but nothing specific. It's not a crime to be a private person."

"You're right, it's not. But skipping town when you're wanted for questioning by the authorities is a definite no-no."

My knees turned to rubber, and I braced the wall.

"Is that what you're saying Clover did?" Amelia spoke up, her face pale.

Mr. Garrett still focused on me. He'd always worn a gun when he was in uniform, but this time, I couldn't take my eyes off it. "When you boys were out at the park this morning, Sam mentioned to me that her car had Virginia license plates. I had the park staff go out and find the plate number."

I straightened, and my jaw tightened. "Why?"

"Because we know nothing about her. She just appeared in our town, without any family or belongings, and now…" He looked around the room. "You're all spending a lot of time with her."

"So you…investigated her?" I choked out.

"You may not understand or appreciate this, Daniel, but it's my job to be suspicious. It's my job to protect my family, my friends, and the public."

"From Clover?"

His nostrils flared. "She hasn't been honest about who she is. She hasn't been honest about why she picked this town."

He sounded so harsh and sure of himself. Did he already know about her connection to Henry Alexander? But that didn't explain why she'd avoided the authorities in Virginia.

What else was she hiding?

"I ran the plates and found the owner of the car was a Jason Scott. Jason was married to Lily Scott." He looked at my grandmother. "Before Lily married, she was Lily Alexander."

Gran frowned. "Henry's daughter?"

"Yes. She's Clover's mother."

So I'd been right, but it didn't explain why Mr. Garrett grimaced at the mention of Lily Alexander, like he was in physical pain.

"Why wouldn't she tell us?" Gran asked. "Why keep that a secret?"

"Because that's not all she kept secret." Mr. Garrett rubbed his thumb and finger back and forth on the brim of his hat. "Both Jason and Lily have been reported missing. The sheriff's office in Virginia suspects foul play. When Clover skipped town, she became a possible suspect in their disappearance."

Someone whimpered behind me.

I spun around, already knowing what I'd find—Clover on the stairs, her face pasty white, her eyes too bright. Her fingers wrapped around the railing. I jerked toward the stairs, reeling like the night before my eighteenth birthday when I'd had way too many beers.

My eyes never left her. She shook her head. Her mouth opened and closed, but no sound came out. She turned to run back up the stairs, but I was already there. My shaking fingers circled her wrist. My brain tried to wade through the shock and form words to reassure her, but nothing emerged. I held both her hands, leaning forward until my forehead rested against hers, hoping she'd hear my thoughts. *We'll figure this out. You couldn't have done anything really bad.*

"Clover…" It was Sam's dad. "You'll need to come with me."

Her whole body shook, and I held her tighter. "It's okay,"

I whispered. "I'll come with you." Our earlier conversation no longer mattered. I wouldn't leave her alone.

"No! I can't." She shrank away from me. Her lips tightened in a stubborn line, and I recognized the near-hysteria in her eyes. I'd seen it on the beach before the paramedics arrived. I'd witnessed it during the thunderstorm. Just like the other times, I knew what I needed to do.

I backed down the stairs, tugging at her resisting body, all the while pleading with my eyes for her to calm down. Freaking out wouldn't help. She needed to answer their questions and straighten this whole mess out.

At the bottom of the steps, I turned, keeping one arm wrapped around her. Sam's dad waited for us.

"I'm going with her."

Amelia and Gran stood in the living room, looking dazed.

Mr. Garrett shook his head. "I don't think it's a good idea."

"I wasn't asking." I tightened my grip on Clover.

He shoved his hat back on his head. "Fine. You can follow us down, but Clover rides with me."

Before we left the house, he read her Miranda rights. Clover barely seemed to notice.

I gritted my teeth. "Do you really have to do this? She's not a criminal."

Mr. Garrett gave me a grim look. "There are procedures in place for a reason."

We reached his car, and he used one hand to protect her head as she sank into the back of his cruiser. The door slammed shut.

I tapped on the window. "I'll be right behind you. Look at me." But she stared straight ahead like I wasn't even there.

At the sheriff's office, I followed Mr. Garrett and Clover inside. She seemed unaware of her surroundings, lost in her own world. Mr. Garrett led her into a room, and the door slammed shut.

I paced in the waiting area, my mind racing. I poured some lukewarm, stale-tasting coffee, and stared at the most-wanted flyers on the wall. Faces blurred in front of me. The room smelled like disinfectant, and I kept imagining what might be happening behind that closed door.

Twenty minutes later, Mr. Garrett strode out. "She's refusing to say anything. She also refused a lawyer."

I looked past him into the interrogation room, expecting concrete and steel. Instead, it looked like my dentist's waiting room, only smaller and not quite so nice. Clover sat at a table. Both hands covered her face.

"This is not helping her. When she refuses to answer, it looks like she has something to hide." His fingers dug into my arm, demanding my attention. "Do you understand? She needs to start telling the truth."

My eyes tracked back to Clover. Her hands were now clenched into fists. Her shoulders slumped, and her eyes were red-rimmed.

He glanced around. "I shouldn't be doing this—Christ, I could probably lose my badge for this—but I need to know what happened to Lily." How did Mr. Garrett know Lily Alexander? "You have ten minutes to convince her to start talking."

Maybe I should have questioned his motives, but I was already striding into the room, barely aware when he closed the door, locking me in. I pulled up a chair, sitting so close, our knees touched.

"You have to explain to Sam's dad. Tell him it's just a big mix-up, so he can let you go."

She stared down at the table.

"Is this about Henry Alexander? You came here to find him, didn't you?"

She nodded.

"It's okay. You can't get in trouble for looking for your family. Just tell them what you know about your parents."

She looked up at me finally. Her haunted expression made me shiver, like someone was dancing on my grave. "It's my fault," she whispered, her voice shaky and hollow.

The air thinned around us, making it hard to suck in a full breath. "What's your fault?"

"Mama." She breathed. "And Daddy."

My eyes darted around the room, landing on the camera in the corner. Who was behind the monitor, watching and listening?

"Clover, stop. I know you didn't do anything wrong."

"I'm sorry," she choked out. Her eyes filled with tears. "You don't understand about good and evil."

"So explain it to me."

"It lives inside of you. No matter how hard you try to escape."

"I don't buy it. You don't have an evil bone in your body."

"You always do the right thing, but I wasn't strong enough."

I gripped her shoulders and forced her to look at me. "Clover, where are your parents?" She didn't answer, so I shook her a little. "You need to tell me."

Her lips moved, but I couldn't hear, so I leaned closer, close enough to make out her faint, horrifying answer.

*"They're in the woods."*

A chill crawled down my spine.

"Daniel! Where are you going? What did she tell you?" Mr.

Garrett yelled at me after he let me out of the room.

"Nothing," I lied. "I have to go." Sam's dad called out to me, but I didn't stop. I ran out the door and into the parking lot. I reached the Jeep, jumped in, and jammed the key in the ignition. The engine sprang to life. I avoided looking back until I reached the street, afraid to find him following me, but when I finally glanced in the rearview mirror, the street behind me was empty.

I drove without thinking, my mind too busy reliving my last few minutes with Clover. After she'd whispered in my ear, I hadn't moved. I didn't say anything, frozen by her words, but then my need to protect her kicked in.

"Don't say anything to anyone until I get back. Do you understand?" She'd looked up at me, her gaze unfocused. I gripped her shoulders so tight, I probably left bruises. "Promise me!"

She'd nodded, but I could only hope she'd follow through. Somehow it didn't matter what she'd done to her parents. Later, once it had a chance to sink in, when the full story came out, it would matter. Now, I only needed to help her.

My cell phone rang, and my sister's picture appeared on the display. I should have ignored it, but I hit the speakerphone before I had a chance to think clearly. "Yeah."

"Where are you?"

"Driving."

"Where's Clover?"

"She's still at the sheriff's office."

"You left her there?"

"I needed to. I'm going to get her help."

"From who?"

I slammed my hand against the steering wheel. "She's in real trouble, Amelia. She needs a lawyer."

"Henry Alexander?" she guessed.

"Yeah." I gritted my teeth. I dreaded the conversation I

was about to have with the cranky old man, but what choice did I have? Clover's grandfather had the greatest motivation to help uncover the truth.

"I'll meet you there."

"No! I'll do it myself."

Heavy silence filled the Jeep. Maybe I'd hurt her feelings, but I couldn't worry about that now. "I called Sam," she said finally, determination in her voice. "He can bring me to the station."

I sighed. "Amelia, I know you're trying to help, but it's a bad idea."

"Why?"

"Because you can't put Sam in the middle. He's a good guy. He'll try to do the right thing, but this is more complicated than we thought."

"Why are you being so cryptic? What aren't you telling me?"

I hit the brakes and stewed at a red light. "I can't explain it all right now. You just need to trust me."

"So you want me to sit at home while you run around helping Clover?" Her voice thickened. "She's my friend, too."

The light turned green, and I stomped on the gas. "I know she is."

A sniff came through the speaker, and I blew out a breath. I worked to steady my hands on the steering wheel.

"Look, I'll call if there's any news. I promise."

She didn't say anything, but I'd reached the house. "I've got to go." I hung up without waiting for a response.

I pulled past the lions guarding the driveway, and stones crunched under my tires. It took a few minutes of pounding on the door before Mr. Alexander opened it. He stared at me, his trademark frown already plastered on his face.

"Daniel. What do you want?"

"Nice to see you, too, Mr. Alexander."

The older man grunted, unimpressed with my sarcasm. "If you're looking for a donation, I gave one at the office."

"I'm not looking for money." My hands curled into matching fists. "It's about the typewriter."

He stiffened. "What about the typewriter?"

"I lied this morning." I shifted my weight and prepared for battle. "It did have a scratch across the back, about four inches long."

He paled. "Why would you lie?"

"Because I wanted to figure out the truth about my friend before I told you." Losing a little of my nerve, I stalled. "Can I come in?"

He released his grip on the door and let it swing wide. I followed him down a wallpapered hallway and into a living room that would have overlooked the front garden if not for the heavy drapes blocking the view. The silent house smelled like a mausoleum—old and stale. I glanced around at the formal-looking furniture and finally chose a high-backed chair covered with pink flowers.

"I'm not known as a patient man," Mr. Alexander said. He sat on the sofa opposite me.

*Or a friendly one.* I shifted my butt on the chair, trying to find a more comfortable position. Mr. Alexander glared, so I started. "The friend who owns the typewriter is a girl... Clover."

His nostrils flared, and he straightened. "The girl I met a couple of weeks ago."

"Yeah. That's her. She arrived in town at the beginning of the summer. She was living out of her car in the county park when I first met her. She's the reason I was in the park during the hurricane. I went to make sure she was okay." I leaned forward, my heel bouncing with nervous energy. "When she lost everything she owned in the hurricane, she started living with Gran and working on the town chronicles. Because it meant a lot to her, Sam and I went to the park today to see if we could find her typewriter, but I had no idea what would happen next."

"You mean meeting me."

"Yes…and other things," I muttered. If I hadn't decided to find her car, she wouldn't be sitting in custody right now.

"So how did she get the typewriter?"

I gripped the arms of the chair and braced for the moment of truth. Would he help me or kick me out? "It belonged to her mother…Lily."

"Lily," he repeated in a whisper. His shoulders sagged. "So this Clover girl is my granddaughter?"

"Yeah."

He shook his head and slumped forward until his elbows rested on his knees. "But why didn't she tell me? I met her and she ran away." His gaze fixed on mine, looking for answers I didn't have.

"I don't know." But I had my suspicions. If she admitted her identity, she'd face questions about her parents, questions she clearly wanted to avoid.

"Why are you telling me this now? Does she know you're here?"

I shook my head.

"So she doesn't want me to know. Did Lily tell her to stay away? Does she think I'm still mad? It was so many years ago, and I said angry things, things I didn't mean, things that drove her away. I've spent years looking for her. You don't know how sorry I am, how much I wish I could take it all back."

His eyes glistened, and unexpected tears slid down his cheeks. I looked away, stunned by the emotions buried under his cranky exterior. God, how did I tell this man his daughter was missing, probably dead, and his granddaughter was somehow involved?

"As far as I know, Lily didn't send Clover." My voice

sounded too loud in the quiet house. I shifted again and stared down at the floor. "She came on her own."

"What aren't you telling me?"

I glanced up to meet his stern expression. So much for exposing his softer side. I cleared my throat. "Mr. Garrett came to the house today."

"Garrett…what did he want? What does he know about Clover? I want him to stay away from my granddaughter." Anger bolstered his voice, and his cheeks flushed red.

"He came because he'd looked up the license plate of Clover's car. Apparently, the car was registered to Jason and Lily Scott."

"Jason Scott!" Mr. Alexander jumped to his feet. "Are you telling me my daughter ran away with Scott? That she married him?"

"I guess so…who is he? I mean, besides Clover's father."

Mr. Alexander shot me a strange look. He wiped one hand across his face. "Jason Scott came into town the summer Lily disappeared. He worked as an insurance salesman, good-looking and smooth talking, but there was something off about him. He was interested in Lily, always sniffing around, but I never thought she returned his feelings. I was obviously wrong."

"There's more to the story. Parts you're going to like even less."

"Get on with it then," he barked. How had my grandfather managed to work with him for so many years?

"Mr. Garrett said that Jason and Lily went missing." I swallowed, my throat as dry as the bunker next to the seventh hole at the local golf course. "The authorities in Virginia questioned Clover about it, and when she left town to come here, she became a suspect. She's in custody right now…"

"Finish it, Daniel. Just tell me the rest, whatever it is."

"Fine." I nodded and let the awful words flow out. "She

needs a lawyer. I think she may be in serious trouble."

Mr. Alexander didn't say anything, but he swayed on his feet. Was he going to collapse on me, maybe have a heart attack? He was pretty old, but then he seemed to steel himself. He walked out of the living room without saying a word, leaving me to stand and wonder. Was he refusing to help his granddaughter?

I'd just about given up and decided to leave, when he reappeared. He stopped in the hall and put a yellowed envelope in his briefcase.

"I'm ready to see her. There have been too many secrets for far too long. It's time the truth finally comes out."

*Clover*

# Chapter Twenty

*"I'm not leaving."*

*Mama brushed the tear from my cheek. "I don't want you to go, but you can't stay. There's nothing for you here."*

*"You're here." I wrapped my arms around her, afraid to let go.*

*She kissed my forehead like I was still a little girl, but I wasn't. I was old enough to decide, and I wasn't leaving without her. "I can't leave with you. He'd find both of us. If I stay, I can convince him to let you go."*

*I frowned. "This is all Daddy's fault. I hate him," I whispered.*

*"Don't. Don't hate him. He wasn't always like this. He's just gotten sicker over the years. In his own way, he's trying to protect us."*

*I shook my head and clung to my anger and fear. "How can you say that? How can you defend him?"*

*Mama seemed to shrink, like she always did when we talked about Daddy. She became smaller, her spirit fading a little. I hated him most for this—what he did to Mama.*

*"I'm doing the best I can and, right now, that means getting you out of here."*

*"Where would I go?"*

*I needed to find the holes in her plan, but there weren't any.*

*"To Florida. To your grandparents—Henry and Rose Alexander. I've arranged everything with Mrs. Bell. Her nephew is a trucker. He'll bring you there."*

*"Florida? I can't go all the way to Florida on my own. These people might not even like me."*

*"Sweetheart, they're family. They'll love you."*

*"But what about you?"*

*She gripped my shoulders, her expression fierce. "Once you leave, don't look back. Stay away. Live an incredible, happy life, but don't come back here."*

*"No! There has to be another way."*

*"There's not. Promise me, Clover." Her fingers dug into my shoulders, hurting. "If you really love me, promise me. Now."*

*I nodded, afraid of the desperation I saw in her face, afraid to disappoint her, and inside, my heart broke into tiny, little pieces.*

"Clover!" A hand slammed on the table in front of me, and Mama disappeared. Mr. Garrett leaned closer. "Ignoring me will not make this go away. If there's an explanation, you need to tell me."

My stomach twisted. My mouth felt numb. I couldn't form the words even if I wanted to.

"What did you tell Daniel?"

I shuddered and wrapped my arms around my heaving belly. What did I say to Daniel? I tried to remember, but reality and my memories blurred. How long had it been since Daniel left? It felt like days since we talked in his Jeep, since he confronted me about my grandfather, since we agreed to stop seeing each other.

Pain burned through my lungs and scorched my skin. I'd lost Daniel. Did it matter now if they found out everything? Did it matter if they learned what I did? I pictured Ms. Ginny and Amelia. I imagined my world without any of them—lifeless and colorless.

Someone knocked, and Mr. Garrett yanked open the door. "What?"

My eyes widened. Henry Alexander walked into the room, shoulders back. He dropped his briefcase on the table. Daniel followed on his heels. Is that where Daniel had gone? To get my grandfather?

"Clover's my client," my grandfather said. He looked fierce and determined and nothing like Mama. "I'm advising her to not answer any of your questions at this time."

Mr. Garrett threw his hands up in the air. "Fine. She hasn't said anything anyway. But you should advise your granddaughter that she'd better start talking soon."

My grandfather grunted. "We'd like a few minutes in private."

Mr. Garrett strode toward the door. He stopped only to talk to Daniel. "You shouldn't be involved in this, son. You don't need this trouble in your life."

Daniel stiffened but said nothing. I wanted him to defend me, to say that I wasn't just trouble, but I couldn't expect more than a person was able to give. Maybe it meant something that he didn't leave. He stayed.

My grandfather sat in the chair across from me, and suddenly the moment I'd dreaded for so long was here. Problem was I still wasn't ready.

"You should have told me who you were."

I searched his face, but I wasn't sure what I was looking for. "I didn't know how."

"Because of Lily?"

Tears clogged my throat. I nodded.

He rested his hands on the table. They were wrinkled and gnarled with age. "We've all suffered enough, Clover. It's time now for the truth."

But the truth would only lead to more suffering, suffering he'd never be ready for, no matter what he said.

*"I know what you're planning. You think you can leave me?" Daddy yelled at Mama.*

*There was a picture of Mama and Daddy in their room, so I knew he used to look different—handsome, like a prince in a fairy tale. Now his face, half covered by his bushy beard, contorted with rage, his scraggly hair brushing his shoulders.*

*Mama shrank against the wall. "No. I promised I wouldn't leave."*

*"You're lying."*

*"No," she whispered. "It was just Clover. It was never me. I wanted her to see things outside this house."*

*I cowered in the corner, but his angry stare still found me. I hated him for making me feel like this—small and helpless. I wanted to scream at him, to tell him all the thoughts swirling inside my head, but I froze, unable to move.*

*"Clover is where she belongs." His eyes—crazed, obsessed—met mine. "There's nothing out there for her, nothing but evil and poison and tyranny." He turned back to Mama. "Don't you see that I'm just trying to protect you? Both of you? They can't find us here. No one can. We're safe here." He stroked one finger down Mama's face. His hand came to rest at the base of her throat. His fingers encircled the fragile flesh there, and her eyes widened. "You and Clover belong here with me. I'll never let you go."*

*Mama blinked back tears. Mine clogged my throat, making it hard to breathe. Her shoulders slumped, and she nodded.*

*Daddy leaned over to kiss her neck, to place his lips on the same spot where his fingers had gently squeezed. His hands moved to remove the pins holding up Mama's long red hair. It fell around her shoulders.*

*Mama's eyes met mine, wide with fear and pleading. "Clover," she whispered. "Go. Pick some berries."*

*I didn't want to leave, but I didn't want to stay.*

*"GO. NOW." She mouthed the words at me.*

*What I really wanted was to pick up the shotgun behind the front door and shoot Daddy right through the heart. The thought made my mouth taste like metal. Forcing my feet to move, I ran from the house, panting, not stopping until I reached the river. I threw up in the bushes, just missing my sneakers.*

"Clover." Daniel knelt beside me. His hands covered mine, pulling my fingers from the edge of the table. "You have to tell your grandfather what you told me...about your parents."

I shook my head, angry at myself. I'd been stupid to think I could change my story. I'd come to Florida wanting to find Mama's family, hoping to finally fit in, but my grandfather would never accept me unless I trusted him with my truth. And if I confessed my sins, he'd hate me.

I stared at my grandfather. "Why did she leave here? Didn't you love her anymore?"

The color left his face, and he looked almost gray under the fluorescent lights. "I made a mistake. My pride made me say things—mean, hurtful things that I later regretted. I loved her, but I chose to judge her rather than support her. Regret has eaten at me for years. It gets to the point that it taints everything you do. It consumes everything good in your life."

I understood about regret. I understood about reliving moments over and over again, hoping against all hope that the outcome would somehow change, but it never did.

"More than anything, I just want to see her again, to apologize and tell her how sorry I am. I want to tell her that I still love her." He swallowed and looked at me with such hope I felt it crushing me. "Please…just tell me. Will I ever see her again?"

I tried to remember how to become invisible. Why couldn't I fade into the tiled floor under my feet? My grandfather's wasted hopes taunted me. I gasped for air. My fingers dug into Daniel's hands.

Daniel leaned close. "Tell him. He needs to hear the truth, no matter how hard it is."

So I did it. I looked into my grandfather's eyes and shook my head, breaking his heart. He sagged in his chair, and his mouth went slack. His pain was too hard to watch, so I stood. I pulled away from Daniel and walked to the mirrored wall. The face in the reflection looked lost and scared.

"What about him? What about Jason Scott?"

I turned at my grandfather's question. He sat upright again, some unseen strength holding up his body.

"Daddy?"

A funny look crossed his face, and he nodded.

"He's with Mama." These words were sharper, colder, easier to say out loud, but I still turned away, not wanting to see the horror on Daniel's face.

*"Wake up, Clover."*

*I opened my eyes and peered into the dark. Mama stood above me. She shook my shoulder again.*

*"What's wrong?"*

*"Shhh…you have to be quiet."*

*Rain peppered the small window in my room, the night too dark to cast shadows, too dark for me to see the expression on Mama's face, but I heard her desperation. Her hand found mine, and she yanked me upward. Something covered my face. I reached up to help her with the sweater she'd jerked over my head.*

*Something landed on my lap. "Put on these pants. They'll keep you warm. Here, take your boots."*

*I yanked on my pants and sat back down to push my feet into my boots. "I don't understand. Where are we going?"*

*Her hand brushed my forehead, then felt its way down the side of my face. "Not we. Just you. You're going to Florida, like we planned."*

*"No! Daddy said no."*

*She sat next to me, and the bed sagged under her weight. "I know you're scared. I am, too, but this is for the best. You can't stay here." She handed me a backpack. Outside, thunder rumbled. "I saved up a little money. There's some food and a change of clothes. I'd give you more, but you need to travel light."*

*I shook my head. The darkness hid my tears. "If I go, Daddy will take it out on you."*

*When she hugged me tight, her body shivered against mine. "I'll take care of him. You just take care of yourself. I love you more than life, you know. I can't let my mistakes determine your story anymore. You're destined for better things."*

*My arms clung to her, but she untangled herself and dragged me to my feet. We left the bedroom, and I held my breath. Together, we tiptoed down the short hall. In front of Mama and Daddy's room, we slowed, careful to avoid the one squeaky floorboard.*

*I exhaled when we reached the tiny living room, although I shook so bad, I thought I'd drop the bag I held to my chest.*

*Mama unlatched the door, the sound swallowed by the rain pounding on the roof. I started toward the open door, but I screamed and stumbled backward. Mama turned, her finger to her mouth, but being quiet wouldn't help us. She hadn't seen what I'd seen, lit up by the flash of lightning—Daddy, sitting in the corner, waiting for us.*

"I'm sorry," I whispered.

"For what? What did you do?" Daniel stood in front of me. He pleaded with his eyes. He wanted me to say I was innocent, but I couldn't.

"She's dead because of me. They both are."

"No." His expression turned grim. "It must have been an accident. You couldn't have done it deliberately."

I shook my head. There was nothing accidental about that night. I still dreamed about it. I woke up soaked with sweat and screaming Mama's name. I looked past Daniel's shoulder at my grandfather. Besides his ashen color, he looked calm, like he'd already come to terms with the news about Mama, with the fact that she was never coming back to him.

The door opened, and Mr. Garrett stepped inside. "I've given you time. Is Clover ready to make a statement?"

I pulled back my shoulders. "Yes."

Daniel and my grandfather jerked. They stared at me like I'd gone crazy, but I knew it was time. I'd already confessed to the two people who mattered most. It didn't matter now if Mr. Garrett also knew the truth.

"Good." Mr. Garrett moved further into the room and pulled out the chair I'd vacated. He produced a pen, notepad, and even a machine to record my confession.

"Wait!" my grandfather interrupted.

Mr. Garrett huffed. "No more stalling."

"I'm not stalling, Garrett, but before Clover says anything, there's something you need to know." My grandfather pulled an envelope out of his briefcase. He gripped it so hard, it crumpled around the edges. "I should have told you years ago, but I always found some excuse. Now that my granddaughter is here, those excuses don't seem to matter."

"Out with it, Alexander."

Tension between Mr. Garrett and my grandfather filled the room.

"I'm trying to tell you, if you'd stop interrupting. It's about you and Lily."

Sam's dad froze, his face a tight mask. "What did you do, Alexander?"

"What I thought was best at the time." He slid the envelope across the table and waited in silence while Mr. Garrett picked it up.

"This has my name on it."

"Yes."

Mr. Garrett pulled out a single piece of paper and unfolded it. He turned rigid, unmoving except for the tremor in his hand. He read it out loud.

*"Dear Andrew,*

*I know what you think. You're angry right now, but there was only ever you. I really hope you believe me, because I'm in trouble. I've tried calling, but you won't talk to me. I know you're leaving for the training academy soon, but I'm pregnant, and I don't know what to do. If my dad finds out, he'll be furious. I know we never planned on this, but if there's a chance we could be a family, please call. I have too much of the Alexander pride to beg, but if you could find it in your heart to believe me, I think that we just might find a way to make this work.*

*Love, Lily."*

His voice broke at the end.

*What? Mama and Mr. Garrett?*

He glared at my grandfather. "Did you know what this said?" he ground out.

My grandfather nodded again. "I read it years ago when I intercepted it."

Mr. Garrett bent over like someone punched him in the gut. "Oh god, what did I do? I saw her with Scott and accused her of cheating. She called me over and over, but I wouldn't talk to her. I was so angry, and then I left for the academy. When I heard that she'd left town and Scott had also left, I thought it meant my suspicions were true. But she was pregnant…with my baby."

"I confronted her about the pregnancy," my grandfather confessed. "We argued. I said mean, terrible things…" His voice faded, but then he cleared his throat. "I never told her how I found out. She never knew I had the letter, that it never made it to you. It's probably why she turned to Scott. I took away her choices, leaving her with nothing else."

"Bastard. You had no right. I'd have married her if I'd known the truth." My grandfather flinched but didn't look away from Mr. Garrett's fury.

"Don't you think I know that? There's nothing you could do or say that would be worse than the regret I've lived with for nineteen years. The last words I spoke to my daughter were hateful, and they'll haunt me to my grave. Now I'll never have the chance to make it right."

"What do you mean?" Mr. Garrett pinned me with his furious stare. "What did you say? What do you know about Lily?"

"She's gone," my grandfather answered for me. "I think I already knew it. I felt it."

"How?" Mr. Garrett turned back to me. "How? I want answers. What did you do?"

I planned to confess, but the bitterness and hurt in his words swallowed me whole, like the ocean did the day I fell off the pier. Mr. Garrett leaped to his feet. He pushed Daniel aside. He hunted me like Daddy used to. Anger poured from him. I shrank against the wall, helpless just like that night.

*Do something. Pick up the rifle and shoot him. Pick up the lamp and hit him. Stop crying. He's killing Mama. Can't you see him choking the life from her? Can't you see her hitting him, scratching at his face, at his hands? She needs you. Save her. Stop being a coward. Stand up. Move your feet.*

"Stop, Andrew." My grandfather yanked on Mr. Garrett's arm. "Don't you see what this means? Just look at her. She's your daughter."

"What?"

"It's in the letter. You and Lily made her, and it's time everyone knows the truth."

*No!* I stared at the blond, blue-eyed stranger in front of me and shook my head. Jason Scott was my daddy. Why else would Mama stay with him? Daddy's evil lived in me. It's why so many awful things happened in my life. It's why I lived in fear. I atoned for that evil every day.

I sank to the floor, despite the hands grabbing at me. I didn't even care who they belonged to. I buried my head in my knees and sobbed.

*"I'm sorry, Lily." Daddy knelt over Mama's body, her arms and legs not moving. He picked up her head and brushed the hair from her face. Her mouth and lips were purple. "I just couldn't let you leave me. I couldn't live without you. I love you." He kissed her forehead, her cheek, her lips. He kissed the*

*dark bruises on her neck.*

*I stared at Mama and Daddy, and I stared at the open door. A moment earlier, my legs wouldn't move. I couldn't find the courage to stand up for Mama, to save her, but now, to my shame, I found the courage to run.*

*He screamed my name before I even made it off the porch. He chased me, but I ran faster than I'd ever run in my whole life. My feet slipped on the wet leaves and the mud, but I never fell. I ran until the air wheezed through my lungs and his voice no longer taunted me. Skidding to a stop, I leaned over, holding my hand against the stitch throbbing in my side.*

*Thunder clapped through the night, and I wrapped my arms around myself. Icy rain soaked my hair and ran down my neck. I curled up under a tree, making sure I was hidden by the branches, and I stayed there, not moving, not crying, not thinking, and definitely not feeling.*

"Shhh…Clover. It's over. You're safe." Daniel's voice reached me in the dark place where I hid after confessing the awful truth about Mama and Daddy. His arm wrapped around me, keeping me warm. I clung to him, fighting my way back from the nightmare of that night. His lips brushed my cheek, his reassurances whispered in my ear. I tried to stay in the stuffy, airless room with Daniel, but instead I went back to the woods, back to Mama and Daddy.

*I snuck toward the house, the hunger pains in my belly forcing me back after so many days alone in the forest. My legs shook. I tried to be quiet, but I kept tripping and stumbling. My heart pounded, afraid of Daddy, afraid of what I'd find.*

*I crossed the porch, my footsteps too loud, and pressed*

*both hands against the window, peering inside. I tried to swallow the scream, but my throat was dry, and a little sound emerged. Mama still lay on the floor, like she had the night I left. Daddy lay slumped over the round wooden table, the rifle on the floor next to him. Blood soaked his hair and shirt and the ground below him. I wanted to run away, to be anywhere else, but instead I pulled the collar of my shirt up over my nose and pushed open the door.*

*It took me two days, but I buried Mama in an open spot by the river. I wrapped her in my favorite quilt and planted wildflowers in the dirt. I didn't want Daddy near her, so I buried him as deep in the woods as I could manage on my own. At first, I didn't leave anything to mark the spot, but later I went back and added a wooden cross—just two sticks nailed together. I never went back again.*

# Chapter Twenty-One

"Why didn't you go to the police?" Daniel asked.

I looked into his red-rimmed eyes. Had my story made him cry? "Daddy warned me so many times not to trust the law or the government. He said that they were bad, corrupt. He said they'd use their power to make our lives miserable. That's why he wanted us to be invisible."

Only he was never my real daddy. His blood and his evil never flowed through my veins. I looked at Mr. Garrett. I couldn't think of him as my father yet. It was too soon. He sat on the edge of the table, a shocked, sad look on his face, just like my grandfather's. If I'd hoped that finally sharing my secret would make it somehow better, I was wrong. It still lived inside me. It made a part of my heart feel dead, like when you sleep on your arm and you wake to find it heavy and numb and useless.

Daniel's hand brushed against mine, and I flinched. I made no move to get off the floor. My body felt drained. I wanted to lay my head down and sleep for a very long time.

"The authorities in Virginia will have to investigate and

corroborate," Mr. Garrett said finally.

I nodded again. The movement took all my strength.

He rubbed his hands over his face, looking grim. "I can't just let you go, Clover."

"Why not?" My grandfather straightened in his chair. "She wasn't responsible for their deaths."

"But I was. They wouldn't have argued if it wasn't for me. Daddy wouldn't have been so mad if Mama didn't try to help me leave, and if I'd been braver…" I closed my eyes. I saw the rifle in the corner and the knives in the kitchen.

"Then what?" Daniel asked.

"I'd have saved her."

"Or maybe you'd have just gotten yourself killed, as well."

I pinned him with a desperate look. "Did you think about that before you jumped into the ocean to save me? Or before you came for me in the hurricane? You proved your courage when it really counted." I closed my eyes and shuddered. "But I was…I am just a coward. I thought it was because of him, because he was my father, because his evil ran through my blood, but now…" I looked at Mr. Garrett. "I don't even have that excuse."

I hated their looks of pity. I wanted to disappear.

"You've misplaced the blame," my grandfather said. "If it wasn't for me, your mother would have stayed here in Florida. She probably would have married Garrett, you would have had a happy childhood, and your mother would still be here. If we need to cast stones, throw them at me."

But his words didn't change the guilt scratching at my insides like a hungry dog at the door.

Mr. Garrett closed his notebook, pain clouding his eyes. "I think there's more than enough blame to go around. Unfortunately, none of this changes the fact that Clover's confessed to concealing a murder and a suicide. She knowingly tampered with the scene of a crime rather than informing the authorities."

My grandfather frowned and wiped at his forehead with a handkerchief. "She's only a kid. She was traumatized."

"Unless my math is off, Clover's eighteen."

"For Christ's sake, Garrett." My grandfather slammed his palm on the table, making me jump. "She's your daughter. Look at what she's been through. She needs our help, not our condemnation."

"I know that she's my daughter...now." Mr. Garrett glanced down at the letter, and my grandfather had the decency to flush. "Trust me when I tell you that I'd like to let her go, but the rules can't be different for her."

"She can't stay here," Daniel argued. He gripped my hand, but my shoulders still slumped.

"It's okay." I looked at Daniel. "You've done so much for me already." It didn't matter that I had to stay. "Maybe this is where I deserve to be."

"Bull," Daniel said. "No one in this room believes that."

Maybe they didn't, but I also didn't see anyone opening the door to set me free.

"You're going to have to show us where they are," Mr. Garrett said.

I jumped to my feet. "No! I'm not going back."

"Garrett, you can't put her through that," my grandfather argued. "There must be another way."

"I never said she had to go there." He looked at me. "I can get aerial photos of the property from the sheriff in Virginia. From those, can you show me the spots where you...buried them?"

My heart slowed a little. "I know where Mama is, and I think I can find Daddy. It's been a long time."

Daniel raised an eyebrow. "What does that mean? How long has it been?"

I shrugged. "Maybe two years."

My grandfather's mouth fell open. "We assumed it just happened."

Daniel looked shocked, maybe even more upset than when I first told him about Mama and Daddy. "I don't understand. Where were you all that time?"

"There—in our cabin."

"For two years?" Mr. Garrett asked. "How could nobody notice? Didn't the authorities get involved?"

I shook my head. They didn't understand. I didn't want people to know, and in the mountains of Virginia, people kept to themselves. It's why Daddy had picked the remote area to begin with. I'd always been home-schooled, so there was no one to miss me.

"People were used to our family keeping to themselves. They didn't question anything."

Mrs. Bell had been the closest thing to a friend to me. She lived five miles away, and she'd known what Daddy was like. She kept chickens and cows and always had eggs and milk she was willing to trade for. She was the only one I ever trusted with the truth.

*I spent the whole bike ride to her ramshackle house coming up with a story to explain Mama's absence. Then I crossed the yard, and Mrs. Bell opened her screen door.*

*"Clover, I haven't seen you for a few weeks. Is everything okay? Where's Lily?"*

*I saw the worry on her face, and all my plans fell to pieces. Tears streamed down my cheeks. Mrs. Bell pulled me into her arms, her gray hair and plump body smelling like the fried chicken she'd been cooking on the stove.*

*"Hush, child." She rocked me back and forth until my sobs turned to sniffles. "You're going to make yourself sick."*

*Once I was calmer, she sat me down at her kitchen table and poured me a glass of iced tea. One of her five cats curled around my legs.*

*I took a long swig and then blurted it out. "Mama and Daddy…they're gone."*

*Mrs. Bell fell into the chair across from me. Our eyes met, and I saw the unspoken questions there. "You mean that they're…"*

*I nodded. I couldn't say the words out loud. "It was awful. I hate him so much. I hate him for what he did." I left out the part about hating myself for being a coward.*

*"Honey…I'm so sorry. I always told Lily that one day Jason Scott would be the death of her."*

*Had I always known that, too? Had I understood what Daddy was really capable of? For a few moments, Mrs. Bell and I sat in silence, both lost in our grief.*

*"What will you do now?"*

*I shrugged. I'd wandered around our cabin, staring at everything that reminded me of Mama. Days passed in a blur until hunger drove me to Mrs. Bell's.*

*"My nephew passes through again in a month. He can still get you to Florida."*

*I shook my head. I couldn't leave her. I couldn't leave the only home I'd ever known. I couldn't leave her smell and her belongings.*

*"So you'll stay?"*

*"Yes."*

*"I'll do what I can to help. You can stay here if you want."*

*I looked around Mrs. Bell's cluttered farmhouse. "No. I'm good there."*

*"You want me to call anyone for you?"*

*I knew what she was asking—police, my grandparents, anyone?*

*I shook my head, and she just nodded. Folks around these parts were used to dealing with things on their own. Mrs. Bell wouldn't tell anyone what happened if I didn't want her to, and I didn't want anyone to know.*

I leaned back against the wall and closed my eyes, shutting out their disbelieving looks.

Daniel's question still reached me. "But how did you survive for two years on your own?"

My mouth snapped shut. I'd confessed what I'd needed to, but I didn't want to tell him the rest—tending the garden Mama and I had planted alone, trading preserves when I was desperate, going to bed with an empty belly or frozen toes, writing stories during those long, lonely months, knowing that if I ran out of paper, I'd probably go insane.

Daniel gave me a questioning stare, but I stayed silent. Fortunately, my grandfather broke our standoff.

"What changed your mind? Why did you leave Virginia?"

I didn't mind answering this question.

"For some reason, the local police showed up looking for Mama and Daddy. Mama had told me where she came from and where to find you. So I packed up and drove Daddy's car here."

*I knocked on Mrs. Bell's door, still panting from my furious bike ride through the mountain roads.*

*"Clover, what's happened?"*

*She pushed open the door, and I stepped inside. "The sheriff…he came to my house…asking questions. He's looking for Mama and Daddy. What do I do?"*

*Mrs. Bell frowned.*

*"What?" I didn't like her look one bit.*

*"Come over here and sit down."*

*I followed her to the kitchen table, my insides numb.*

*"Lily was my friend, and I've let her down."*

*"What do you mean? You didn't do anything."*

*She shook her head hard enough that the extra flesh under her chin jiggled. "I know. When you came here two years ago, I didn't do anything. I let you live up in that cabin by yourself and never said a word, but it's not right. You deserve more. Lily was trying to get you out because she thought you deserved more."*

*I said nothing, stunned by her speech. "Did you...call the sheriff?" I almost choked on the words.*

*Mrs. Bell's eyes widened. "Of course not, but maybe this is a sign that you need to move on. Go to Florida and find your grandparents."*

*"By myself? How would I even get there?"*

*She frowned. "My nephew won't be back through for another few weeks, which will be too late. What about the car?"*

*Daddy's car wasn't in great shape, but I kept gas in it for emergencies, and I'd taught myself to drive it on the dirt road around our cabin. Still, I couldn't imagine taking it on the highway and putting Virginia in the rearview mirror.*

*"I don't even know how to get to Florida." But the numb feeling inside had begun to turn to something else—a prickle of excitement. Could I really do it? Could I pack up everything I owned in Daddy's car and drive to Florida? Mama had told me stories about the sun and the ocean. I didn't even know how to swim. The river out back wasn't deep enough to learn in.*

*Mrs. Bell shuffled to a cupboard and dug through a stack of papers. She returned with a Virginia road map. "Head south. You can buy a better map at a gas station on the highway."*

*Gas! Gas required money, and I only had about a hundred dollars saved up. My stomach turned back to lead. I'd never make it far, not even far enough to hide from the sheriff when he came back.*

*"What's wrong?"*

*My fingers crinkled the map. "I don't have enough money."*

*Mrs. Bell gave me a long look before disappearing into her bedroom. She came back with a tin can clutched to her full chest. She pressed it into my free hand. "It's everything I have saved up. It's not much, but it should get you to Florida."*

*"I can't," I whispered. I pushed the tin back toward her, but she refused to take it.*

*She caught my face between her hands. "You're a good girl, Clover. You need to go and find your family. Go live your life."*

*I shook my head. Tears clogged my throat. "It's too much."*

*"No...it's just enough. And Clover, once you get there, don't ever look back."*

*I nodded, trying not to cry or think about the night Mama had said the same words to me.*

I'd never gotten the chance to repay Mrs. Bell for everything she did, so instead I paid it forward, giving what I could to anyone who needed it. I wished I could have taken Mrs. Bell's advice—the part about never looking back. I'd tried, but today had proved that you can't run forever.

Daniel rubbed his hand across his neck. "I still can't believe that you were alone for two years. When we first met, you said you'd learned to make yourself invisible. It was bad enough when I thought you were crazy, but this is worse."

I remembered telling him that the day before the hurricane hit. "But I can't do it anymore. I can't make myself invisible."

Daniel sighed and pulled me into his lap. We still sat on the floor, and I pressed my face into his neck and breathed in his scent. I didn't care who saw us together. In Daniel's arms, I felt like there was the smallest chance that somehow everything would be okay.

"That's because you were never meant to be invisible." His words whispered past my ear, making me shiver. "Since the first day I met you, I've never been able to look away."

My fingers tightened around his neck, afraid to let go. "But I lied to you for so long."

He brushed the hair back from my forehead. "And now I know the truth. You can trust me, Clover. You always could."

Hope sprung inside me. Maybe the truth hadn't set me completely free, but it also hadn't made Daniel run for the hills. Earlier, in his Jeep, he'd blamed my secrets for keeping us apart, but now he knew almost everything. Maybe it wasn't too late to work things out between us. I rested my forehead against his, closed my eyes, and listened to his steady breathing.

A warm feeling spread through my chest, but it didn't last.

Someone cleared his throat, and when I looked over at my grandfather and Mr. Garrett, they were both staring at us and frowning.


My grandfather left to start on some paperwork for my case, and Daniel stayed while Mr. Garrett went to request the photos. "This room is under surveillance," he warned, right before he left us alone.

"Yes, sir," Daniel said.

We sat next to each other at the table and held hands, his thumb stroking back and forth against my palm.

"How does it feel—to not have to worry about keeping everything secret anymore?"

I closed my eyes and focused on the feeling of his thumb moving across my skin. "I don't know. Maybe I'm supposed to feel relieved, like it's finally all over, but I don't. Not really."

I was still holding so much inside—awful memories of my

life in Virginia—that I'd no intentions of ever sharing with anyone. Even worse, the guilt still writhed and flourished deep inside me. My grandfather and Daniel seemed to think that I'd done nothing wrong, but they didn't understand how I just watched, frozen with fear. I was too scared to stand up to Daddy, even to protect the person I loved most in the world.

I shook my head. He wasn't "Daddy" anymore. He was Jason Scott.

I opened my eyes to see Daniel's grim expression. "When Grace died, people kept telling me that things would get better with time. So I gave myself milestones to look forward to. I told myself that after the funeral, I'd feel better, but nothing changed. So then I told myself that once summer ended and I got back to school, I'd feel normal again."

"How long did it really take?" Fear of the answer made my words shake, or maybe it was just exhaustion.

He pinched the bridge of his nose with his free hand and chuckled, a bitter sound with no real humor. "I don't know. Ask me ten years from now, and I might be able to tell you."

For a long moment, neither one of us talked. Then he leaned closer, stopping when his glittering green eyes were so close I could see the gold and brown flecks in them. "I don't know if this is true or not, but lots of people told me after Grace died that it helped to talk about it, to open up to someone. I didn't. I kept it inside and let it fester."

My muscles stiffened, and my mouth pulled into a straight line.

But Daniel kept talking. "I can't imagine what your life was like, but I'd listen, if you ever wanted to tell me. I wouldn't judge. I'd just listen."

Tears burned my eyes, and I lowered my head.

He squeezed my hand. "You don't have to say anything now. Just think about it."

We sat in silence. I don't know what Daniel was thinking,

but I kept thinking about the fact that as much as I didn't deserve him, the thought of him leaving hurt like a knife right through my heart.

Mr. Garrett eventually came back with a stack of photos. I still couldn't think of him as my father.

"Daniel, you'll have to leave now."

He folded his arms across his chest. "I want to stay." I swallowed back a smile. His insistence made me feel ten feet tall.

Mr. Garrett didn't look nearly as impressed. "I've been lenient so far, but this is official business. You're leaving."

Daniel's eyes flashed. "What about after?"

"Henry's talking to the judge, but it looks like she'll have to spend one night here until we get this all figured out. You'll be able to see her in the morning."

A knot formed in my belly. "I have to stay here?"

"Don't worry." Mr. Garrett looked at me, and his tone softened a little. "I'll personally make sure nothing happens. You'll be in a cell of your own. You'll be safe."

I turned away from Mr. Garrett's concern. I didn't want to think about how things could have been different if he and Mama had married and he'd raised me all along. If I let myself think about the life I'd never had, if I let that image into my heart, the unfairness of it all would choke me. I lived with enough regrets already.

Daniel grunted. "I guess I have no choice." He stood, and I squeezed his hand once before letting it go.

"I'll be fine." I tried to keep my voice strong.

He nodded, jammed his hands in his pockets, and then left me alone with my…father.

Mr. Garrett took Daniel's seat and spread a pile of photos out in front of me. My finger traced the route I'd taken from the porch, through the trees, to the riverbank. I used a black marker to draw an *X* on the spot where Mama lay covered in wildflowers that bloomed yellow and purple in the spring. I was proud that my hand shook only a little.

Daddy was harder to find. I had to study the photos, but eventually I found him, too.

Mr. Garrett hesitated when I handed them back. "I'm sorry, Clover. I want you to know that if I'd known, things would have been different."

My heart curled into a fetal position. It was the last thing I wanted to think about…the bright, shiny life I could have had.

He stared at the photos, and his eyes glistened, like maybe he was going to cry. "Was she ever happy with him?"

I rubbed my palms against my shorts and swallowed. The bad memories blotted out the good ones, and I had to dig deep to find one. "There were times when he was better. When I was younger, his good spells lasted longer." I still remembered when he used to take me and Mama to town. We'd shop at a real grocery store and eat at a real restaurant. Those trips became scarcer and scarcer until they stopped completely.

"And you…did you have friends, did you have fun as a kid? You went to school, right?"

I shrugged. "Mama taught me at home." Was I supposed to lie to make him feel better? To tell him the best times were the days when I didn't go to bed with an empty belly, the times when Daddy was too busy brooding to watch everything me and Mama did? "Sometimes it's best when you don't know anything different."

But I should have known the truth about Jason Scott and Andrew Garrett. Mama could have told me that much. I looked over at my real father. Did we look alike? Besides DNA, what else did we share in common? "She should have told me about you. I deserved to know."

His hands twisted together. "I've been thinking about it. Maybe Lily was afraid that if you knew, you might throw it in his face one day. God knows what he might have done. But she also knew you'd find out the truth when you came to Florida. Maybe that's why she risked so much to get you here."

Was he right? Had Mama been worried that Daddy would hurt me? In the end, he'd done that anyway. He'd stolen Mama from me. He'd robbed every bit of joy and happiness he could from me and replaced it with fear.

"I don't know what we're supposed to do now," Mr. Garrett said.

He wasn't talking about Mama and Daddy anymore. He was talking about him and me.

I pictured Sam and Mrs. Garrett. "We don't need to tell anyone else, if you don't want."

He frowned. "Is that what you want?"

I squeezed my hands together under the table. "I don't know. When you believe one thing your whole life and it gets turned on its head, it's hard to know what you're supposed to feel or want or think."

He nodded and laid the photos down. "I want you to know that Sam is a good kid, and I never cheated on my wife with your mother. I was hurt when Lily left, and Cheryl started out as a way to fix my heart and my ego, but then she got pregnant with Sam."

He stopped and looked away. Was he embarrassed to admit that he'd gotten two girls pregnant only months apart? He cleared his throat and looked back at me. "Anyway, we got married, and somewhere along the way, we fell in love. I'm not worried about telling either of them about you. You're my daughter."

I stared down at the table. "But I don't feel like I am."

"Maybe we just need to give it some time. Sam deserves to know he has a sister. You look like him, you know."

I nodded. In a short space of time, I'd picked up a grandfather, a father, and a brother, but would they ever feel like family? Would they ever feel like anything but strangers?

# Chapter Twenty-Two

The next morning my grandfather talked the judge into releasing me into his custody. Once the endless paperwork was taken care of, we drove straight to his big, brick house. We spent most of the trip in awkward silence. I stared at his profile and tried to find something of Mama in his face. Maybe they shared the same nose and lips, but Mama smiled a lot more than my grandfather did, so it was hard to tell. The first time I called him "Mr. Alexander," he asked me if I'd consider calling him "Grandfather." I'd agreed, but still stumbled over the word.

When we arrived, he gave me a tour of the first floor. Our entire cabin back in Virginia would fit in the living and dining rooms. I tried to picture Mama growing up in this big house, but it felt too stuffy and formal for her. I stopped in front of the family portrait hung on the wall—a larger version of the one Mama kept hidden in the picture frame.

"It's the last picture we had taken together." My grandfather stood next to me, also staring at the moment captured in time. "My wife—your grandmother—died ten years ago from cancer."

I'd long ago committed the image to memory—the way Mama leaned toward her mama and the way my grandfather held himself apart from his family. "Do you believe they're together now?"

He frowned. "I've never been a regular churchgoer. I never believed I had much to thank God for, but I'd like to think that they're together now, waiting for me on the other side."

The thought brought a smile to my lips. For a moment, the awkwardness disappeared. I'd found a connection to the man standing next to me—we both loved Mama.

"Did she ever talk about us, about her life here?" he asked.

I shook my head. "But just because she didn't talk about you doesn't mean she didn't think about you. I think it probably hurt too much to say it out loud."

He nodded, the wrinkles on his face more pronounced when he frowned. "I'm not sure how to be a good grandfather. I don't think I was a particularly good husband, and I know I messed up as a father. I feel like I've been given a second chance, but I don't know how to make it work."

He seemed so sad and lonely.

"Does it help that I don't know what a grandfather is supposed to do?"

He chuckled. His eyes lit up, confirming my earlier suspicion. Mama and he did share the same nose and mouth. It somehow made me feel better.

"Well, in this circumstance, it would probably help if I feed you and show you where you can sleep tonight. We also need to arrange to bring your things from Ginny's house."

"And my dog."

My grandfather grimaced, his features pinching together. "No one mentioned a dog."

"Caesar's pretty independent. He just needs a place to sleep and some food in a bowl."

He sighed. "There's never been a dog in this house. Your grandmother was allergic."

"That's too bad, but you're going to love him. Everyone does."

He grunted and headed up the stairs. I followed, my fingers trailing along the shiny wooden banister. At the top, he turned left and opened a door at the end of the hall. Decorated in yellow-flowered wallpaper, the bedroom smelled stale, like it hadn't been used or disturbed in a long time. Dust swirled in the air, lit by the sunshine streaming through the large picture window. The white lace curtains matched the lace bedspread on the wrought-iron bed. A few teddy bears sat propped against the pillows. On the mahogany dresser, covered in a lace runner, some mementos remained—pictures in colorful frames, a jewelry box, a miniature china tea set, ribbons and awards. In the far corner, a set of tall shelves overflowed with books.

"This was your mother's room. Your grandmother never had the heart to pack her things away."

I wandered over to the door in the corner and peered into the small closet. Mama's clothes still hung inside. Scarves and sunhats perched on knobs on the back of the door. I pulled the end of a scarf up to my nose and breathed in, disappointed by the slight musty odor that smelled nothing like Mama.

"Would you like to sleep here, in her room?"

I nodded. No matter how much it hurt to be surrounded by her memories, I couldn't bring myself to shut the door on her past. I couldn't walk away from the chance to learn who she was before me, before Jason Scott crushed her.

I picked up a picture from the dresser—Mama at the beach with a group of girls. She looked young and happy. "By the way, did Daniel call for me?"

My grandfather frowned. "Not that I know of. You and Daniel seemed close at the station yesterday."

I put down the picture and moved to the bed, testing the mattress. "Yes. Before yesterday, I'd driven Daniel away with my secrets, but now I'm hoping it will be different."

"What does that mean?"

I sat on the lace bedcover and stared up at him, unsure of how honest to be. We'd just met, but after living with so many lies, maybe it was past time to be open about things for a while. "It's hard to put it in words, but Daniel makes me feel like everything will be okay. He's amazing in every way, and I think I love him. I'm hoping he loves me, too."

My grandfather rubbed his hand over his chin. "But you just met a few weeks ago. You're so young, and it's awfully early to be talking about love. Isn't he leaving for college in the fall?"

Yes, his leaving would be a problem, but there had to be a solution. I knew people had long-distance relationships and made them work.

"And how do you know it's really love?"

I picked up a teddy bear and held it in my lap. "I don't know for sure, but I know that I think about him all the time when we're apart, and when we're together, he makes me feel safe and not so alone."

And now, there was nothing standing in the way of us being together.

I'd lain in the cell by myself in the dark, thinking about many things, but mostly I'd thought about Daniel. Sometime during the night, I'd made a decision. I was going to tell him how I really felt, that I was falling in love. Maybe I was young and maybe we hadn't known each other long, but I was certain about my feelings. I'd wait as long as it took for Daniel to return from college and for us to figure out a way to be together.

I imagined Daniel's face when I told him. Would he be surprised? Would his eyes turn bright green with happiness? He'd never said that he loved me, but when we kissed, he was always reluctant to let me go and, at times, he stared at me with such intensity. He'd been angry that I hadn't trusted him, but in the end, he said he understood. He'd held me in his lap after I'd confessed, and he hadn't left until my father forced him to. I didn't know much about relationships, but I took these as good signs.

"Hmmph." My grandfather snorted. "You don't need a boy to make you feel safe or good about yourself. You have family now."

I appreciated what he was trying to say, but it wasn't the same. Not even close. I hugged the teddy bear to my chest, and my lips lifted into a smile. I couldn't wait to see Daniel again.

Later, I met Mary. She came to Grandfather's house every afternoon to help with the cleaning and cooking. My grandfather left the house to take care of some things, so I was alone when she arrived. Her short gray hair clung to her head in a modern style, and she wore jeans and a button-up shirt. She looked to be in her sixties, but when she smiled, she seemed a whole lot younger.

She found me in the kitchen making tea. "You must be Clover." She laid her hand on top of mine. "I was so sorry to hear about your mother. I can't imagine what you've been through, poor thing."

I looked down at our hands, not knowing what to say. Her skin was soft, her nails painted light pink.

"So, are you planning to stay here with your grandfather for a little while?"

Outside the kitchen window, a hummingbird hovered near a feeder. Its wings beat so fast they blurred. "I think so."

Mary laid one arm across my shoulder and gave me a quick squeeze. "I hope you stay as long as you can. I know Henry will want that. Now which room are you staying in?"

When I hesitated, she gave me a knowing look. "Your mother's, of course. It will need some freshening. I'll change the bedding this afternoon."

The phone on the counter rang, and Mary moved to pick it up. She cradled the receiver against her ear. "Good afternoon, Alexander residence."

She listened for a second, and her eyes widened. "One moment, please." She turned and offered me the phone. "It's for you."

I held it to my ear, hoping it was Daniel. "Hello?"

"Oh my god, Clover, I'm so glad I found you." Amelia's anxious voice shot through my ear, and I winced, holding the phone a little farther away.

"Amelia, what's wrong? Is Daniel okay?"

"He's fine, but I'm so sorry. I didn't mean for it to happen. It just did."

I squeezed the phone. "What just happened? What did you do?"

She continued like I'd never interrupted. "Don't blame Daniel, but I pestered him until he told me the whole story, even the part about, you know…"

"No, I don't know."

She huffed. "You know, about Sam's dad and the fact that you and Sam are related."

"Oh." That part.

"Yes, well, Sam came over this morning. We were talking, and I might have let it slip."

That didn't sound so good. I chewed on my lip. I was pretty sure Sam's dad wanted to tell Sam himself. "What did he say?"

"He was pretty quiet, which isn't like him. Then he left."

"Where did he go?"

"That's the thing." She hesitated. "I'm pretty sure he's on his way to see you."

"I'll get it," I told Mary when the doorbell rang. There was no time like the present to face my new brother. Still, my hand shook when I turned the knob and yanked open the door.

Sam stood on the step. He looked awkward, like part of him wanted to stay and part of him wanted to run. I understood exactly how he felt. Even I could see the features we shared, now that I knew who he was—the straw-colored hair and blue eyes.

"Hey, Clover." He met my gaze, and I felt sorry for him. He'd done nothing to deserve this sudden fuss in his life.

"Do you want to come in?"

"I…well…I just wanted to…" His voice trailed off, and he combed trembling fingers through his hair.

I tried to help him out. "Amelia called. She told me that you know about us."

He blew out a breath. "Yeah." He opened his mouth, but no words came out. Eventually, he snapped it shut, turning to stare out across the yard.

I stepped out into the midday heat and shut the door behind me. "It must have been a surprise for you."

He glanced down at me. "And for you."

My chest ached, and I pressed against the spot. "I believed Jason Scott was my father. I don't understand why Mama never told me the truth." Mama could have spared me so much pain. She could have told me that Daddy's sickness and evil didn't live on in me.

"Amelia says your grandfather plotted to keep your mom and my dad apart. She said that my dad never knew about you."

I nodded. I looked out at the perfect blue sky dotted with billowing clouds. The forecast called for rain showers in the afternoon, which would help with the humidity, but God, I hoped it didn't thunder. I moved to sit on an iron bench wedged between two potted plants, the metal hot against my skin.

"She also told me what happened to your mom. I can't imagine how hard that must have been."

I stared down at my palms and remembered the blisters I'd gotten from scrubbing at the bloodstains on the table and floor. They'd taken weeks to heal. "You do what you have to do."

"For some people, it would have been more than they could handle."

"That's the trouble. I never really handled it. I see that now. I hid it and, in the end, I ran from it."

My brother sat next to me on the bench. He smelled like sun and coconuts and chlorine. Up close, his eyes were translucent. "Maybe you're looking at it wrong. Maybe instead of running away, you ran *to* something. To all of us…here."

It was a nice thought. "Maybe."

"So are you okay with all of this unexpected family?"

"Are you?"

"I wish I'd heard it from my dad first."

I plucked at my top, pulling the material away from my sweaty skin. "That's my fault. I asked for more time."

He snorted. "I guess Amelia didn't get that memo."

"Are you surprised?" I asked, rolling my eyes.

He chuckled. "Not really, but her heart is in the right place."

"You really like her."

He blushed and cleared his throat. "I've actually liked her for a long time, but I couldn't work up the nerve to act on it."

I leaned forward, sitting on my hands. "Why?"

He shrugged and pulled his feet closer. "I guess I was never that great with girls. Maybe that would have been different if I'd grown up with a sister."

I looked away. He painted a picture of a family that could never have existed. "You know we could never have grown up together."

Sam frowned. "Why not?"

"If your dad had known about me, I think he might have married my mom. Then he would never have met your mom, and you wouldn't be here. So maybe things happened this way for a reason."

"You think so?"

I nodded, although I didn't truly believe it. How could this moment make up for everything else I'd been through? But the exercise of weighing Mama's death against Sam's existence was a useless one. The past could never be changed. Time kept right on marching forward.

"So, do you know what you're going to do?"

"For now, I'll stay here with my grandfather. It feels right."

Sam smiled. "That's good. It'll give us a chance to get to know each other."

"I thought we kind of did."

"Maybe…but it feels different now. I mean, we're both the same people we were before, but we're also different. Does that make any sense?"

He had such an eager and earnest look on his face that I had to nod. Our newfound connection obviously meant more to him than it meant to me, and I smiled to hide my guilt. Maybe one day I'd be excited to have a brother. Right now, it was still too much to take in.

Our tentative sibling moment was interrupted by a car

pulling into the driveway. Amelia jumped out and ran up to the steps. When she reached us, she stopped to catch her breath, her cheeks pink.

"Oh my god…" She panted. "I'm so sorry. I didn't mean to spill everything the way I did."

Sam and I stood, and she launched herself at both of us, forcing us into a group hug.

"Isn't it better, now that everyone knows?" she asked, when we finally broke free. She glanced at me, but her gaze lingered on Sam. When he nodded, a wide grin broke out on her face. "I can't believe it. My boyfriend and best friend are secretly brother and sister. Someone should write a book about this. No, probably not," she said, shaking her head. "No one would ever believe it."

*Daniel*

# Chapter Twenty-Three

"I think you'll be really pleased with this driver, sir. It should add yards to your stroke."

I completed the sale I'd been working on for the last twenty minutes and turned around to find Henry Alexander.

I looked around the store for other customers, any excuse to avoid him, but there was no one. So I rolled my shoulders back and prepared to take whatever he was there to dish out. He dropped his straw hat and briefcase on my display counter, and his face sported his trademark frown. If he had a softer side, he was saving it for his granddaughter. For the rest of the world, his crankiness ran deep.

"Daniel."

"Mr. Alexander."

"I suppose you're wondering why I'm here."

"You suppose right." I didn't know why he was here, but I already knew I wasn't going to like it.

"I'll get right to the point." He leaned against the opposite side of the counter. "Do you have feelings for my granddaughter?"

I rocked back on my heels. Geez. Talk about putting someone on the spot. "I'm not sure that's any of your business."

"My granddaughter is my business." His eyes narrowed. "You're leaving in a few weeks, right?"

Impatience straightened my spine. "Yeah. I'm leaving for college."

"And what will happen to Clover then?"

I frowned. "People have long-distance relationships all the time."

"You're right—people who are in a committed relationship. So maybe my question should be more to the point." He paused and looked me right in the eye. "Do you love her?"

My lungs deflated. I'd been all set to defend our relationship, but his question snatched the wind from my sails.

I loved being with her—hanging out, talking, making out. When we were apart, I thought about her. If something funny happened, I filed it away so I could remember to tell her. I loved the way she made me look at everything differently. She made me appreciate things I'd taken for granted. Not just the physical things, but my family, my friends. She made me think about my place in the world. Yeah, I played in the charity golf tournament, and I shared the occasional sandwich with Pete, but did I spend more time taking than giving? Had Grace's death made me afraid of living? I loved that Clover made me think all these things, but did I love her? I wasn't sure.

Mr. Alexander's expression softened. "You obviously care for my granddaughter, so shouldn't her well-being come first right now? God knows she's suffered enough hurt for one lifetime."

"And you think I'm going to hurt her more?"

"Can you promise me you won't?"

I couldn't, of course, but he already knew that. No

guarantees existed. "Clover's strong. Look at what she's survived already," I argued.

Mr. Alexander took a hankie from his back pocket and wiped it over his face. "I'm not saying she's not, but are you willing to take that chance, especially considering your previous relationships?"

Wow. Low blow. "Hey—"

He held up one hand. "I know, I know. That was unfair of me, but I just got my granddaughter back. She needs a chance to get to know her family, to figure out what she wants to do with her life, to discover who she wants to be. Think about the way she's attached herself to you and your family. You were the first person to befriend her. Don't misunderstand me. I'm grateful that you did, but it's not the right basis for a relationship."

I cringed at his words, because he gave voice to my own doubts. Still I wasn't ready to give in. "Don't you think you did enough damage when you interfered with your daughter's life? How do you think Clover would feel about this?"

He didn't even flinch. "There's nothing I can do or say to change my actions all those years ago, but this is different."

"Why?"

"For starters, I assume that my granddaughter is not pregnant." He shot me a questioning look, and heat flared in my face. I shook my head. "That's what I thought. Secondly, I'm not telling you that you can't see my granddaughter. I'm asking you to think about her best interests."

"You think it won't hurt her if I break it off now?"

"I'm sure it will, but she'll have lots of people to support her, and it's better if it happens before she gets even more attached."

I said nothing.

"Think about it. I get the feeling that in the end you'll do the right thing." He picked up his briefcase and slipped his hat back on his head. "Thanks for your time, Daniel."

He left without waiting for my response. Standing there, I suddenly realized why my grandfather kept him as a law partner for all those years. The old man made one hell of an argument.

For the next couple of days, I avoided Clover. I ignored her calls and didn't listen to the messages she left. She was probably confused and hurt, but I needed time to think about Henry Alexander's visit. All summer long, I'd been jumping into things, which wasn't like me. This time, I needed to make the right choice.

Problem was, I already knew the "right" path. I just didn't want to take it. It didn't help that I already missed Clover. It would only get worse when I left for Georgia.

From Amelia, I knew that Clover and Caesar had settled into their new digs. She'd taken a little time off her work for Gran to get adjusted to her new life. I'd also heard that Clover would not face any charges from the authorities in Virginia. According to Mr. Garrett, they'd acted like they were doing her a favor, when they were really just covering their own failures. They'd neglected to investigate anything that had happened in that house for so many years.

That night I headed to the beach for a bonfire. I'd debated staying home, not sure if Clover would be there, but in the end, I went. I had so few days left with my friends. I'd spent most of the summer with Clover, Amelia, and Sam. Luke and Jacob had to be pissed. We'd all head in different directions in a few weeks, and as much as I wanted to get out of Canna Point, I understood what was happening—it was the end of an era. Sure, we'd see each other again, but it would never be the same. We'd text and video chat and see each other on holidays, but we'd never hang out at our lockers or sit together in the cafeteria or make fun of Mr. Baker's stupid jokes in Biology. That was the problem with life. It constantly changed.

I drove to the beach with the top down, a perfect blazing display of stars overhead. When I got there, I trod barefoot through the sand, the fire and music leading me to my friends. Sparks popped and flew into the night air. Jacob and his girlfriend, Rachel, swayed together off to the side. She'd returned from vacation with her family, and Jacob looked like he couldn't keep his hands off her. *Great.* Morgan and a few of her friends sat in a small circle on the far side, talking and laughing. *Outstanding.* No sign yet of Clover or Sam or my sister. *Fantastic.* I dropped down on the sand next to Luke.

"Hey, man."

"Daniel!" He punched my shoulder. "Where have you been? Feels like I haven't seen you in ages."

"Yeah, I know. Sorry about that."

He shrugged. Luke wasn't one to hold a grudge. "No problem. Mom's had me working on the house all summer anyway. I swear she had me paint every surface at least twice. I need to go to boot camp to catch a break."

I winced at the mention of the army. I hated thinking about Luke in danger, fighting for our country. "She just knows that once you leave, she won't have anyone to help her."

Luke's face turned serious. "I'm not sure how often I'll get home." He threw a piece of driftwood into the fire, and it sent a shower of sparks upward. "I know you're leaving, too, but maybe you can check on her when you're back? Just to make sure she's okay."

I nudged him with my knee. "Don't worry. We'll all keep an eye on her, although I'm not promising to paint your house."

He nudged me back, but harder. "Slacker! Hey, I've been

hearing rumors about Clover. Do you know what's going on?"

"Yeah, but do you mind if we talk about something else?"

He frowned but nodded. I stared into the fire, mesmerized by the glowing coals. A breeze came off the ocean, kicking up sand along its way.

Farther down the beach, steady waves rolled in on the shore. I remembered the day Clover had fallen in and Sam had frantically worked on her. I remembered praying she wouldn't die. Did I know even then how much she'd mean to me?

"Wanna swim?" Luke asked.

I shook off the memories and grinned. In one movement, I jumped to my feet and peeled off my T-shirt. "Race?" I called over my shoulder, running toward the water.

"No fair. That's cheating." Behind me, Luke was already on his feet, running and stripping off his shirt.

The cold water hit my bare skin, but I didn't slow. I dove into an oncoming wave and cut through the water. I surfaced a distance from shore and grabbed a quick breath. Something splashed close by, and Luke's face appeared next to me, lit by the full moon.

"I think we started a trend."

Back toward shore, a trail of bodies backlit by the fire ran into the ocean. Squeals and laughter carried across the water. Morgan reached us first. She splashed water in my face and dove under before I could retaliate. She popped up behind me, treading water.

"So, where's Clover tonight?"

"Not sure. I think she's coming later."

She slicked her hair back from her face, her expression unreadable. "Trouble in paradise?"

"Nope. Last time I checked, Canna Point is definitely not paradise."

She snorted and fired another handful of water in my

direction. "That's not what I meant."

I wiped my eyes against the sting of salt water. "I know, but I'm not planning on talking about it. So let's move on."

"Geesh. No need to be grouchy."

She was right. I worked at getting the scowl off my face. Where had Luke disappeared to? A clump of heads bobbed closer to shore, but Morgan and I were alone this far out.

She swam closer and touched my cheek with one hand. "That's better." Her leg brushed against mine. Her hands moved to my shoulders.

"Morgan…" I warned, but she shot me a smile, her perfect white teeth illuminated.

"Hey, I'm just trying to help you out of your obvious funk."

"I'm fine." I reached for her waist to hold her away from me, but her hands slid around my neck. Her familiar touch felt wrong.

"You don't look fine. You look tense. I can help you relax, you know."

"Yeah. How?" Stupid question, but curiosity got the best of me.

She grinned and dipped her head backward into the water. Swells rolled past us, and we swayed together.

"Oh, honey, I know exactly what to do." Her whisper drifted past my ear, and I shivered.

I cleared my throat. "Yeah?" When did my voice become so hoarse?

"Yeah." She looked into my eyes. "This…"

Her legs wrapped around my waist. Her hands circled to the top of my head, and she pushed down. Her feet pushed me farther under, and she kicked off me, propelling herself toward shore.

I came up, coughing and sputtering. Shaking the water out of my ears, I chased her laughter back to the beach, my need for revenge outweighing my common sense. I caught up. My tackle sent us both flying into the shallow waves. We rolled around a few times, and when we stopped, my head lay on the sand, the rest of my body in the water. She was on top, her wet body pressed against mine. She sat up and straddled me.

A wave hit her from behind, and she fell forward. Her hair trailed across my chest. Then her lips pressed against mine. I should have told her to stop, but for one second, I was curious about what life would be like without Clover. Could I ever move on to someone else? But I already knew. This felt so wrong.

Morgan's tongue darted out to lick at my lips, but my mouth stayed closed, shutting her out. Her hands moved across my chest, and I reached up to hold them in place. I shifted a little, aware of the sand scratching my bare back and the numbness of my toes from the ocean.

Morgan lifted her face a couple of inches. "Daniel?"

"Yeah."

"Am I boring you?" Her sarcasm didn't quite hide the hurt in her voice.

"Sorry."

She rolled off me, and I sat up next to her. Her chin quivered, and I felt like the jerk I was.

"Sorry," I repeated. "I shouldn't have let things get that far."

She turned and shot me a half smile. "It's still her, isn't it? Clover?"

I shrugged.

"No offense, but I don't get what you see in her."

I knew Morgan would never get it. "You'll find the right guy. It's just not me."

"Honey, the last thing I need from you right now is a pep talk. I know I'll be fine, but you need some serious help.

You're too much of a nice guy, and that girl is going to suck you down and stomp all over you."

She pushed to her feet and turned to face me. Something on the beach caught her eye and made her smile. She stuck her hands on her hips and did her best model pose. "It's been fun, Daniel." She flicked her wet hair over her shoulder. "Call me if you ever get the taste for something more exciting."

I swung around, a sinking feeling in my stomach. Behind me, I heard Morgan dive into the water and swim out to her friends, but my eyes never left Clover.

She stood about thirty feet away, frozen, one hand on Caesar's leash, the other pressed to her mouth. Sam and Amelia stood on either side of her. I jumped up, and she jolted into action, stumbling away and pulling Caesar with her.

I started to follow, but Sam blocked my path. "Don't even think about it."

# Chapter Twenty-Four

"Get out of my way." Impatience attacked my control. "I need to talk to her."

Sam didn't move. "You've done enough for one day." I tried to sidestep him, but he blocked me again. "You need to leave her alone."

"This is none of your business."

He stuck out his chin. "I disagree."

"Why?" I poked my finger into his shoulder, and he knocked it away. "Because you're suddenly her brother?"

"Don't go there, man."

"Why not?" I straightened to my full height. "What are you planning to do about it?"

"This." He charged.

His shoulder hit my stomach, and the air whooshed from me. We both landed on the sand, but momentum rolled me on top. I cocked my arm, ready to swing, but someone pulled me back.

I fought the hold, until Luke's steady voice reached my ear. "You don't want to do this."

Sam jumped to his feet, and Clover stepped between us, shouting at us to stop. In the moonlight, her disappointment was clear. My heart sank into my gut, and my brain started working again. What the hell was I doing?

I shrugged out of Luke's hold. "I'm fine. I just need to talk to Clover."

Sam started to protest, but Clover shut him down. "It's my choice, and I want to hear what Daniel has to say."

I would have felt smug at her decision, except I knew what was coming. I'd decided her damned grandfather was right. Breaking it off now was the right thing, no matter how much I dreaded it.

Sam stepped to her side. "Are you sure?"

She looked up at me, trust there that I didn't deserve, and nodded.

Slowly, the small crowd around us dissipated, leaving only Clover and I. Caesar nudged his nose against my leg, but I couldn't look away from her face.

"What you saw with Morgan was nothing. It was her kissing me. I stopped it." She didn't respond, but I could see her disappointment, and I felt like shit. "I know it was wrong. I'm sorry."

Her blue eyes flashed up at me. "Fine. You're sorry. Is that all?"

"Don't do that." Sand clung to my skin, and I brushed at it, frustrated.

"Do what?"

"Pretend you don't care, when I know you do."

She made a strangled noise. "What do you want me to say? That seeing you with Morgan hurt so bad I could barely breathe? That after being at the sheriff's office with you I thought we had a chance together? That I've waited for days for you to call me back, and when you didn't, I had to wonder?"

Leave it to Clover's directness to cut me off at the knees. "Wonder what?"

"If maybe you thought I was a terrible person?" she whispered.

I stared up at the stars, kicking myself for being fifty types of jerk. "How can you possibly think that?"

"Because I don't know why else you'd avoid me." She tightened her grip on Caesar's leash. "But maybe it's because of Morgan. Do you still have feelings for her?"

I jammed my fingers through my hair. "Not in the way you mean. It really was her kissing me. There's nothing going on between us. You have to believe me."

She stared at me for a long moment, looking as lost as I felt. "I do," she said, finally, "but I don't understand anything else. I don't know what you want."

"Clover—"

She sucked in a deep breath and cut me off. "So I'll tell you what I want. What I said in your Jeep, about us breaking up, I said it because I was scared to tell you the truth. Now you know my secrets, and I don't need to hide anymore." Her hand brushed against my fingers. "I've thought about it a lot, and I want us to stay together. I know you're going away to college, but Amelia says people have long-distance relationships all the time."

I dug my toes into the sand and pulled my hands to my side, out of her reach. "They do, but we've only known each other a few weeks, and now you have a new family and new opportunities. You deserve space to figure it all out." I stared at my feet. Clover had called me brave, but meeting her gaze required a courage I didn't possess.

"So, you're giving me space?"

I finally looked up at her pinched features and nodded, encouraged that she understood but disappointed that she'd accepted my decision so easily.

"And you're making this decision for my own good? Without asking me what I think?"

Crap. "Yeah, I guess, but you make it sound like a bad thing."

Her hands squeezed into fists. "Daniel. Maybe I wasn't clear. I—" Tears glistened in her eyes. "I love you," she whispered. "Nothing will be better if you leave me. I need you. I can't do all this without you."

I gritted my teeth. Her raw confession pulled at something deep inside me. My fingers ached with the need to touch her, but I couldn't. I had to be strong enough for both of us. "You can't be with me because you *need* me. It's not the right reason. You have to figure out what I already know: you *can* do this by yourself. You can do anything you want."

"Except be with you." A tear escaped, tracing a lonely path down her cheek. She swiped it away, and my stomach clenched. "Do you love me?"

I jammed my hands in my pocket, trying to ignore the growing ache in my chest. I remembered Henry's words and, for some reason, I remembered exactly where I'd been the moment I'd heard about Grace—in my room, packing my bag for school, completely unaware that she'd been dead for hours. I'd told Clover that happily-ever-after only happened in books and movies, and I'd meant it. My own experiences had proven it. "I care about you, but I'd be lying if I said it's love. I'm not even sure what that means. Maybe we all say it too easily." I'd told Grace that I'd loved her, but maybe I'd said it because it was expected of me.

Her lip jutted out, but I saw the pain behind her defiance, pain I'd caused. "You may not be sure, but I know what I feel."

"How?"

She stood ramrod straight and looked at me. The light from the fire didn't quite make it to our stretch of the beach, but the moonlight was enough for me to see the raw feeling on her face. "Because if it's not love, why does it hurt so much?"

Something clogged my throat, making it difficult to swallow. I stared at the ocean. Most of my friends had made their way back to the bonfire. Sam and Amelia hovered just out of earshot, waiting to swoop in if needed. I didn't blame Sam for wanting to protect Clover. I just hated that he felt she needed protection from me.

"I'm sorry it turned out this way, but it will get better. You deserve everything good."

Her shoulders sagged, and Caesar whined. Did he understand that I'd just broken his owner's heart?

There was nothing I could say to make it better, but somehow I couldn't bring myself to walk away. "Clover, please say something. Tell me you'll be okay." *Please, I can't walk away if you don't.*

Her eyes squeezed shut, the night wind tugging at her hair. When she opened them, she looked small and alone. "I told you that day on the beach—I lived without you before and I'll figure out a way to do it again."

She'd given me what I needed—permission to leave. But the grim determination in her voice made me feel even worse. Still, I forced my feet to move, to carry me away from her.

"Daniel."

I stopped. "Yeah?"

Her mouth opened and closed a few times. "I never thanked you for bringing my grandfather to me. You helped me, when you should have been thinking the worst."

"I knew you couldn't have killed anyone, at least not intentionally."

She stared out at the dark water. "I never expected to find you or Amelia or my family."

*I never expected you, either.*

I rubbed at the tightened cords in my neck. "You asked me once if I regretted the day you walked into my store, and

I can tell you now, I don't. No matter what else happens, I'll never regret meeting you."

Sadness crept over her face, pulling down the corners of her mouth and darkening her eyes. I wanted to hold her and take back everything I'd said. I wanted to explain that it was all Henry Alexander's fault, but some part of me knew that this was for the best — for both of us.

I sucked in a breath and tilted my head to stare at the stars. I couldn't look at her anymore. If this was the right decision, why was the steel band squeezing my chest? I turned and stumbled through the sand. Then I was running like the devil himself was chasing me.

At home, I stopped in the kitchen to dump my keys on the counter and snag a bag of chips and a can of soda. The family room was thankfully empty when I dropped my stash on the coffee table and fell on the sofa, exhausted in every possible way. I dug under the cushion for the remote and flicked on the TV. A cop drama appeared, and I changed the channel, stopping at a mindless sitcom — anything to distract me from the look on Clover's face when I left.

"You're home early." Mom stepped in front of the TV, blocking my view. "I thought you were going to the bonfire. Your dad's still at the store."

I motioned for her to move out of the way, but she only worked her way around the coffee table and pushed at my legs. With a heavy sigh, I swung them to the ground and made room.

"So who was there?"

"Pretty much everyone." I popped the top on my soda and took a long drink.

"Was Clover there?"

"Not at first, but she came later."

My eyes drifted back to the television and, for a moment, we both watched in silence. She reached for the chip bag, and I handed it over. The characters on screen said something funny, followed by the predictable laugh track.

"How's she doing? She's been through so much."

"Yeah, and I just made it worse. I broke things off with her."

Mom rubbed my shoulder. "Oh, honey, I'm sorry. How did she take it?"

"Not great. She probably thinks I'm a jerk."

Mom shook her head and frowned. "Impossible. You're a great kid, and she must know it. Look at all you've done for her."

I slumped back in the sofa and spun the remote on the cushion. "When she came tonight, she saw me kind of kissing Morgan."

"Oh…" She twisted toward me and pulled her knees up to her chest. Her chin rested on top—classic "listening pose" for my mom. "What does 'kind of kissing' mean?"

"It means that Morgan was kissing me, and then I stopped it."

"And that's why you broke things off with Clover? Because of Morgan?"

"Not really." I sent the remote into another spin and replayed my conversation with Henry Alexander. "Clover says she loves me, but I'm not sure I feel the same way."

Mom sighed. "You're young, and you haven't known her that long. Was she angry at you for not feeling that way?"

I shook my head. "Disappointed and hurt, but not angry."

"And that's why you broke up with her?"

"Not really. Well…kind of." She raised an eyebrow, and I grunted in frustration. "All I know is that I'm leaving town and she needs space to get to know her family and figure out the rest of her life. I think it's better for her if we make a clean break."

"But she doesn't agree?"

"No. Not now, but I think when she has some time to think about it, she'll see it the same way."

"I'm sorry, Daniel, you're a great kid, but none of this sounds like you. It sounds like — "

"Henry Alexander?" I blurted out.

Mom's mouth hung open for a second and then snapped shut. "Exactly. Let me guess. He talked you into this decision."

"Kind of, but what does it say about my feelings for Clover if it didn't take much to convince me? It's not like he threatened me."

Mom bristled. "I should hope not."

"He didn't. He just made me think about my own doubts."

"Which are?"

I didn't answer right away, because I'd never said it out loud. Mom waited patiently, though, until I finally gave in. "Fine. I'm worried that Clover doesn't really love me. I'm worried that she needs me, because I was there when she had no one else. I don't want her to see me as some kind of knight in shining armor, because I don't know if I can always be there for her. When I go away, I'll be busy with school and golf. What if I don't have time to talk to her? What if I'm too busy to come home to see her?"

Mom rubbed my arm. "Honey, she's not Grace."

I fisted the remote. "I know that."

"Do you?"

My eyes found the high school picture on the top of the entertainment unit. Grace's face looked back at me, her eyes sparkling and mischievous, a half smile on her lips. What had she been thinking? I'd thought I knew her, but she'd kept secrets. She'd hidden her dark and depressing thoughts, and I'd been oblivious, completely missing the signs. I dropped my head back on the sofa.

"Honey, Clover's been through a lot. She grew up in an environment we can never begin to understand. She witnessed her mother being murdered. She survived on her own for two years and then made it here all by herself."

I picked up my head and looked over at my mother. "I know all this."

"So if she's strong enough to survive all that, don't you think she's strong enough to handle whatever happens between the two of you?"

My stomach dropped. "So I was wrong to break it off?"

She shook her head. "I can't tell you that. I can only tell you that you shouldn't make your decision out of fear. No matter how long you agonize over it, you'll never know what Grace was thinking. It's long past time you forgave yourself and her. You need to let it go."

My jaw tightened, and the characters on screen made another witty comment that got the fake audience laughing again. It had been a long time since Mom and I had talked about Grace—more evidence of how deeply and profoundly Clover had changed my life.

"Did you know her—Lily Alexander?"

Mom nodded. "Our dads worked together, so there were family picnics and parties. She was five years younger, though, so we weren't really close."

"What was she like?"

She shrugged, a wistful smile on her lips. "Beautiful, and I mean *really* beautiful—long red hair, blue eyes. She was smart and popular. I think she could have charmed anyone...except her father."

"They didn't get along?"

Mom smoothed her hair back with her hands, working it into a ponytail with the band she always kept around her wrist. "It's been a long time, but I remember them always butting heads. Everyone else was intimidated by Henry Alexander, including myself. He looked so stern, but Lily didn't seem to have any trouble standing up to him."

"Do you remember when she left?"

"I remember Rose being really upset, and Henry becoming even more distant than he'd been before, but I was a newlywed, with you on the way. I had other things on my mind."

"It's strange to think that if she'd stayed, Clover and I would have grown up together, gone to school together."

"And Sam probably wouldn't be here."

"Yeah."

I gave the remote another spin, thinking about how Clover's life could have been if her mother had made a different choice, a life surrounded by family and friends. I still hadn't allowed myself to picture Clover hiding in the corner of a house in the woods, watching the man she thought was her dad choking the life out of her mom. I knew the facts, but it was different than picturing it. It took a lot of self-control, but I kept the image away. I'd done it with Grace, too, never picturing the last moments of her life. I didn't want to know if she'd been in pain or if she'd regretted her decision in the end, if she'd tried to get help but realized it was too late. I didn't want to know if she'd been scared or crying when she took her last breath.

"Do you think there's some master plan out there somewhere, that things work out the way they're meant to?"

Mom shook her head. "Some people say that everything happens according to God's plan, but I find it hard to believe that what happened to Lily or to Clover was meant to happen. But I also think that regrets and second-guessing is a waste of time. We can't change the past. All we can do is move forward."

I knew my mother was right, but not believing in regrets and not feeling them were two different things.

*Clover*

# Chapter Twenty-Five

Rain trickled down my cheek and dripped off my chin. My grandfather held a large, black umbrella over both of us, but it wasn't quite wide enough. Water pooled on the strip of outdoor carpet we stood on. It was meant to save us from standing in the sodden grass and mud on either side of the fresh grave, but my toes were still soaked inside my new pink ballet flats.

I would have preferred to be anywhere else, but this ceremony was for my grandfather. He'd wanted to bring Mama home and bury her next to my grandmother. He'd asked my opinion, and I couldn't say no. After all, I'd had her to myself for so long and it was time I shared her with the other people who loved her. I'd begun to think of her as two different people—the girl who used to live in Florida, who had dreams and friends and ambitions, and the one I knew, the woman who'd given up on happily-ever-afters. This ceremony was for the girl her family lost.

My green and blue striped dress stood out like a beacon in a depressing sea of black and gray. Raised eyebrows and frowns met my dress choice, but I didn't understand the need to wear somber mourning clothes. Wasn't this day about Mama? She hated dreary colors. I looked up at the overcast sky. She also hated rain and dull days. Around me solemn faces bowed in prayer—my father and Sam and his family, Ms. Ginny and Daniel and his family, Mary. I recognized a few others, like the men I played chess with in the park, and Peter, but many were strangers.

My wandering gaze stopped on Daniel for the tenth time since he'd arrived. His hair was plastered to his head, his cheeks red. I hadn't seen him since he walked away from me at the beach, and my greedy gaze couldn't get enough. I'd started working with Ms. Ginny on the book again, but somehow Daniel managed to never be there at the same time. He'd even had Amelia drop off my repaired typewriter. It now sat on the desk under the window in Mama's old room— finally home again.

He felt my stare and looked up. The minister's voice continued, but I wasn't listening. "You okay?" Daniel mouthed at me, his hazel eyes filled with concern.

I shrugged. Was I? I looked down to find my hands clenched in fists. I felt boxed in, trapped by a black wall of strangers.

"Henry, would you like to say a few words?" the minister asked.

My grandfather tightened his grip on the umbrella and nodded.

"I wanted to thank everyone for coming. I've waited a long time for Lily to come home." His voice broke, and he stopped. Should I try to comfort him? But my limbs wouldn't move. Wet hair fell in my eyes. He cleared his throat and started again.

"Lily was a special person, loved by many, including her mother and myself. For those of us lucky enough to have known her, we will always remember her—her smile, her laughter, her stubbornness, her beauty. This is not the way I'd prayed to have my daughter come home, but I have to be thankful for the blessings I've been given. While Rose is no longer standing here with us, I know she is thankful to have her daughter back, lying next to her. And I'm thankful to have found Clover, my granddaughter. In the midst of tragedy, she has returned to me."

His arm came around me and squeezed my shoulder. "Clover, would you like to say anything?"

I brushed the hair off my forehead and looked at the expectant faces huddled together under umbrellas and hoods. Amelia stood with Sam, holding hands, tears in her eyes. She gave me an encouraging smile. My father frowned, his eyes red-rimmed.

Directly in front of me, a bouquet of white roses spilled over the sides of the shiny black coffin. My mother's bones lay inside, but her soul had left a long time ago. My heart raced. I found Daniel's eyes over the top of the wet casket. He took a small step toward me, but I squeezed my eyes shut and shook my head. Somehow, his kindness only made everything worse. I didn't need him, and I didn't want to speak.

I opened my eyes and shook my head, more firmly this time. Fortunately, the minister started talking and the stares drifted away from me, allowing me to breathe again.

"Clover?"

My grandfather's voice forced my attention back to the service. He offered me a lily and kept one for himself. He stepped forward and brought the flower to his lips before laying it on top of the casket. He placed both palms on the wet surface and whispered something to his daughter, something I couldn't hear.

He turned to me, and I realized I was expected to do the same, only I couldn't. I felt the uneasiness I'd been fighting swell inside me. It forced the air from my lungs. I needed to be free of the stares and sadness and the rain and the shiny coffin. I turned and forced a path through the black and gray bodies. I blocked out the shocked and sympathetic looks on their faces. I needed space. I needed... I didn't know what I needed, not really.

I ran until I reached the shelter of the pavilion at the far end of the cemetery. I sank down on the farthest bench and shivered in my wet dress, clutching the flower to my chest, not sure how many minutes passed before footsteps approached.

"Clover..."

I looked up to find Ms. Ginny. In the distance, a huddle of people still stood around Mama's grave. Had Ms. Ginny been nominated to check on me?

"Are you okay?"

I sniffed and wiped at my tears with the back of one hand. She pulled a package of tissues from her handbag. "Here."

I took one and blew my nose. Outside, the rain eased. It no longer drummed against the roof of the pavilion, and the afternoon sky brightened.

"Better?" She leaned against the railing.

I nodded and balled the tissue into a wad.

"This must be a tough day for you."

I stared out at the rows of headstones. Fresh flowers brightened some of the graves, while others were barren, aged, and crumbling. I made a silent promise that Mama's grave would never look like that.

Ms. Ginny sank down on the bench next to me. "Clover..." she prompted. "Whatever's bothering you—it will help to talk about it."

Maybe. Had talking about Mama's death helped? I'd lost Daniel, but gained a family. Was that how life worked? A constant trade-off. Nobody had warned me that the downside of love was the heartbreak you felt when it ended.

Ms. Ginny waited with an expectant look, and I didn't want to disappoint her. So I blew out a breath.

"I used to think I was evil."

"Oh, honey…how can you say that?"

"Because I believed he was really my daddy. I believed I shared his blood, and the evil lived inside me, too. I worried that anything might set it off. Every time I felt angry or afraid, I thought it was starting."

Ms. Ginny shook her head. The sympathy in her eyes made me feel small, the same way I used to feel around him. "I never knew Jason Scott," she said, "but I'd be surprised if he was ever evil. I suspect he suffered from a mental illness."

"I know. The police contacted his family. They said he had paranoid schizophrenia. His family tried to get him treatment, but then he left town and they lost track of him." The afternoon sun crept inside the pavilion. It warmed the back of my shoulders, but it didn't melt the ice in my veins when I thought about him.

"It doesn't excuse the things he did, but maybe it'll help you understand him better."

I nodded. "I looked it up online." I read about the symptoms and thought about Mama. She'd told me he was sick, but I wondered if she'd known the truth, or if she'd ever tried to get him help. I inhaled a lungful of fragrant air, rich with the scent of fresh rain and flowers.

"Ms. Ginny…" I stared down at my wet shoes.

"Yes?"

"Why did she stay?" The question seemed so simple, just a few short words, but the answer haunted me. It teased and tortured me, always just out of my grasp. It ate at my insides and kept me awake at night.

"Oh, Clover." Ms. Ginny blinked a few times and leaned closer. She pressed her hand on my knee. "I wish I had an answer, but I can't say what your mother was thinking. I can only tell you that she's not alone. Many women in her situation…in abusive or controlling homes also stay. Maybe she was too afraid or too worn down. Maybe she believed she could help him or that he'd change. She probably loved him at one point, or maybe she felt like she had nowhere else to go."

"But everyone here talks about how smart and driven she was."

"That's because people don't like to speak ill of the dead, but no one is perfect. As time goes by, we tend to overlook the bad things and just remember the good." She leaned away and tightened the sash of her coat. "I knew your mama since she was a baby. She was a good girl, a beautiful child, but she was always one to leap first and look later. I know that being pregnant and unmarried wasn't easy, but she had choices. She happened to choose wrong. I suspect she didn't recognize what was happening until she was already in an impossible position."

I tried to imagine it—knowing I was going to have a baby, not sure if the father loved me, having my own father disapprove of me. I tried to sympathize, but I kept thinking about the small house in the woods and Daddy's "rules" and Mama's silent tears and all the things I'd missed—school, friends, family. Familiar anger welled inside me, followed by the ever-present guilt.

Ms. Ginny grasped my hand in hers. "You can tell me, whatever it is. I promise you I won't judge. I'll just listen."

I looked at the sincerity in Ms. Ginny's eyes, and I wanted so badly to believe her. Maybe I could finally confess my last secret—the one I still carried deep inside.

"Clover?"

In the distance, the crowd around Mama's grave broke up. People wandered back toward the parking lot. Had Daniel left already?

I looked up at the roof of the pavilion. In one corner,

a bird had built a nest, but it seemed deserted now. Empty. Gathering my courage, I allowed the forbidden words to form. "I'm mad at her."

I waited for Ms. Ginny to look shocked or horrified, but she didn't. She just looked patient, waiting for me to finish. So I cleared the lump from my throat and found the nerve to continue.

"I'm mad at Mama...for staying with him. She could have tried to leave, but she didn't. She just stayed there, until he killed her, and then she left me alone." Problem was that once I started, the words wouldn't stop. "She died trying to protect me, and I stood there and watched. I did nothing to save her. I let it happen. So how can I be mad at her? But I am. I feel the anger inside. What kind of person does that make me?"

"Oh, Clover..." Ms. Ginny wrapped her arms around me and pulled me close. "It's okay, sweetheart."

"But it's not. Don't you see? I don't deserve any of this." I choked on my tears. Ms. Ginny's fingers stroked the hair from my brow, and she rocked me back and forth like Mama used to. "I don't deserve Grandfather or a new father or Sam or Daniel or Amelia. They won't love me if they find out the truth."

"Clover, look at me." She held my face between her two hands. "Take a deep breath. In and out. That's good."

My chest still heaved, but my crying slowed.

"You have to stop blaming yourself. Of course you were angry at your mother. She was supposed to protect you, look out for you. She didn't do those things. If you believe that her spirit lives on, then you have to know that she's mad at herself for putting you through all that. She loved you. I know that much, and if she can see us now, I know she'd be even more upset that you continue to suffer. You have to let it all go—the guilt and the anger. You have to accept the amazing second chance you've been given and make the most of it."

"I don't know how," I whispered.

"One day at a time. You learn as you go. You accept the advice, love, and support of your family and friends, and you don't give up."

I sniffed. "Are you just saying this to be nice?"

Ms. Ginny snorted. "Ask Daniel. He knows I save my sugarcoating for the kitchen. It's a prerogative that comes with age. You're a good person, Clover, a bright and beautiful girl. Don't let the mistakes your mama made or the terrible actions of Jason Scott take away your future. Don't you think you've all suffered enough?"

I was tempted by her words. I was tired of dragging these feelings around like a ball and chain, but I didn't know how to do it. How did I let it all go?

# Chapter Twenty-Six

I walked home from the cemetery, turning down several rides, including one from my father and Sam. My dress dried in the hour it took me to reach the small café next to Grandfather's house. I stopped and ordered iced tea and sat at one of the outdoor tables. After, I paid the waitress and walked home. Late afternoon gave way to dusk. Caesar met me halfway up the driveway.

"Hey, boy. What have you been up to?" He barked and trotted beside me all the way to the front door. It was locked, so I dug in my pocket for a key. Silence greeted me in the front hallway. Someone had pulled the drapes in the living room. "Grandfather! Mary!"

No one answered. I kicked off my shoes and wandered down the hall, my bare toes sinking into the carpet runner.

I heard a noise in the study. Knocking softly, I cracked open the door.

In the murk and shadows, my grandfather sat slumped in his armchair. Fear shot through me, and I ran to him. I touched his shoulder, and his head swiveled. The glass in his hand shook, and liquid sloshed over the side. The smell of alcohol burned the inside of my nose.

Grandfather blinked a couple of times and peered at me. "Clover, is that you?"

"Yes." I grabbed for his glass just as it slipped, almost knocking over the half-empty bottle of scotch on the end table. "Where's Mary?"

"I sent her home. Lily hated the rain," he mumbled.

I set the glass next to the bottle and knelt in front of him. "I know she did."

His mouth quivered, and his eyes were bloodshot. "I didn't know what to say."

"You did great." I could barely remember his words.

"I should have said the truth. I should have told everyone that I drove her away, that everything was my fault. How could I have been so stubborn and stupid? She was still a child, and I turned my back on her." He shuddered, and his head dropped into his hands.

"I was angry at her," I whispered, confessing for the second time in one day. "I look around her room and see everything she left behind. Why did she take me away from here? Why didn't she try harder to come home? She died trying to get me out, and I repay her by thinking badly of her. I thought you'd hate me if you knew the truth."

My grandfather shook his head. His shoulders slumped further. Tears trickled down his face, following the lines and troughs etched by age and sorrow. "How could I ever hate you when it was always my fault? My god, when I think of all you've been through. If you want to be angry at someone, it should be me. You should hate me for what I did to you and your mother."

Sadness and pain and regret mixed inside me like some toxic cocktail, more debilitating than anything my grandfather was drinking. The easy way was to let the poison take over.

The harder path was to fight back, to let go of the past, and to think about all the good things I'd found in Florida. I stood up and reached for the switch on the lamp. Light flooded the room, and my grandfather jerked.

"Come on." I reached for his hand and tugged. He didn't budge, so I pulled harder. "We're going to the kitchen. I'm fixing you supper and a cup of tea."

He stumbled to his feet. "I don't understand."

"Mama wanted you and I to find each other." I wrapped my arm around his waist. Looking over at him, I realized that I didn't care about his grumpiness or gruff exterior. I loved him already. I didn't expect it, but somehow it happened anyway.

"She never blamed you for anything. If she had, she wouldn't have sent me here." I pressed his gnarled hand to my cheek. "It's not easy to say good-bye to guilt and regrets, but maybe if we try together, we can do it. We can be thankful for our second chance and make the most of it."

He shuffled with me toward the kitchen, and I tightened my grip on him.

"Where is this coming from?" he asked.

"I got some great advice today from Ms. Ginny."

My grandfather snorted. "That woman always thinks she knows best."

I chuckled. "Maybe it's because she does."


A few days later, Mary laid a steaming lasagna in the middle of the dining room table. The rich aroma made my mouth water.

Mary reached for my plate and spooned out a big piece. "I overheard Amelia and Sam talking about the dance this weekend."

*The dance.* I'd tried not to think about it, but it was near impossible when Sam and Amelia kept chattering on about it. They weren't trying to be mean, but it still hurt every time they mentioned it. I was supposed to go with Daniel. It should have been perfect.

Mary handed back my plate. "Did you know your grandfather is a member of that club? He has been for years."

Grandfather mumbled something under his breath, and I held mine. What was Mary up to?

"It's open to all members. Isn't that right, Henry?"

"I suppose. I haven't been in more than a decade."

Mary huffed. "So maybe it would be nice if you took your granddaughter." She glared at him and dropped his plate in front of him, harder than usual.

He grunted. "She probably doesn't want to go."

Mary planted one hand on her hip. "Maybe you should ask her first."

"Fine." He huffed and looked over at me. "Do you want to go?"

"I don't have anything to wear." It was the easiest excuse I could come up with, but also true. I pictured Amelia and her beautiful dress. I owned nothing that fancy.

"That's not what I asked. I asked if you wanted to go."

Of course I wanted to go. I wanted to wear a pretty dress and listen to music and maybe even dance, but I wanted to do all that with Daniel. "No…I don't."

"Clover, why not?" Mary asked, hovering next to the table.

Because going without Daniel and possibly seeing him there, out of reach, would be like having him stomp on my heart all over again. "Because I was supposed to go with Daniel."

Mary gave me a sympathetic look. "Aw, honey, I'm sorry. Maybe I shouldn't have said anything."

I figured the discussion was over, but my grandfather

dropped his fork on the table.

"That's no reason. Don't let a boy stop you from anything you want to do."

"But it won't be the same without him."

Grandfather leaned forward on his elbows. "Of course it won't. It'll be different, but that doesn't mean it won't be worthwhile." His voice thickened. "And it would mean a lot to me."

Maybe he was right. I couldn't stop living just because Daniel had decided he didn't want me anymore. "I still have nothing to wear."

Mary squeezed my shoulder. "Oh, honey, that's why God gave us the good sense to invent stores and credit cards."

Three nights later, I sat in front of Mama's dresser mirror and stared at my reflection. Amelia and I had spent the afternoon in a salon, getting manicures and pedicures. A lady with bright red hair and a nose ring trimmed my hair, evening out my own attempts. She added bangs and layers and curled it with an iron. Amelia produced a small glittery clip and pinned back the curls on one side. I looked glamorous, like a movie star, with my soft blue eye shadow and pink lipstick.

Amelia called my dress "retro," but to me it was just beautiful. Royal blue chiffon draped around my shoulders, narrowing to a fitted waist and then flaring to just below the knee. It swirled when I spun on my toes. I wore a gold necklace I'd found in my mother's things, a fine chain with a sparkling pendant.

My grandfather's eyes glittered with tears when he met me in the living room, dressed in a dark gray suit. "You look beautiful—like an angel."

I blushed. "Thank you. You look good, too."

"No. I look old, but I am, so that's okay." His gaze rested on the necklace, and he reached out to pick up the pendant. "We gave this to your mother on her sixteenth birthday. She liked to wear it on special occasions." He frowned, and his face sagged with regret. "How could I have forgotten that she'd left it behind?"

"Well, it's found a perfect new home," Mary said, stepping into the room and breaking the sad moment. She held a camera in one hand. "We need pictures before you go."

Grandfather looked disgruntled, but allowed Mary to fuss around us, fixing our poses for a full five minutes, before he barked, "That's enough. We're leaving."

Mary winked at me. "No problem, Henry. I was finished anyway."

We drove to the dance in a shiny convertible with leather seats. It normally resided in the garage under a cover, so it was my first time seeing it in all its glory.

I climbed in, and my grandfather shut the door for me. I slid my hand over the polished interior while he slipped into the driver's seat. "What kind of car is it?"

"A '67 Mustang. Open the glove box."

Inside, I found a silk scarf.

"Your grandmother always kept one there for her hair. I hope it's not musty."

I brought it to my nose and inhaled the scent of roses. "No. It's perfect."

Grandfather drove with one arm resting on the open window and the other on the wheel. He looked younger and happier than he had since I met him. I took a mental picture, knowing the image was important, something I never wanted to forget. The rush of wind made conversation difficult. The air along the coastal highway smelled like salt and summer. Overhead, an eagle circled in front of a sinking sun. And far off on the horizon, towering clouds built over the ocean. We'd have rain before morning.

At dusk, we pulled up in front of the club. My grandfather handed the car over to the valet, and I climbed out, greeted by the distant strains of music. A warm breeze played with the skirt of my dress, and lights twinkled around the grounds like fairy dust. This was a magical place inhabited by beautiful, wealthy people.

Grandfather offered me his arm. "I remember bringing your mother here. When she was little, she loved it when I danced with her, but then she outgrew me."

I squeezed his arm. "I'll dance with you if you'd like to teach me."

Birds fluttered in my stomach when I walked through the glass doors, but unlike last time, I wasn't here as an outsider. This time, I belonged. So why did I feel like a little girl playing dress-up?

My grip on Grandfather's arm tightened. Waiters circled in the main reception area, offering champagne and hors d'oeuvres to the men in their suits and the women in their gowns and glittering jewelry. I froze like a deer in headlights, but he patted my hand and shot me a reassuring look.

"If you're feeling overwhelmed, just stick with me. I have a reputation for being grouchy, so most of these people avoid me."

I hid my grin behind my hand. There was a time when all I saw was his cranky exterior, but now I knew what hid beneath.

Amelia appeared at my side. She squealed in my ear and pulled me into one of her hugs. "Oh my god, you look amazing…seriously. We should have done this to you a long time ago."

She also looked fantastic. The corsage on her wrist perfectly matched the dress she'd picked out with me weeks earlier.

"Hey," my grandfather protested, overhearing her observation. "There was nothing wrong with the way my granddaughter looked before."

"Of course not," Amelia stuttered. "I'm sorry, Clover. I didn't mean anything by it."

Grandfather winked at me and whispered, "See, I've got to maintain my grouchy reputation." He straightened and released my arm. "I'm heading off to find a bar. I need a real drink and not this bubbly, girly stuff. Take care of my granddaughter," he barked at Amelia.

"Yes, sir."

As soon as he disappeared into the crowd, Amelia turned back to me. "That man is so intimidating. I know he's your grandfather, but how do you stand living with him?"

I shrugged, cherishing my secret knowledge of his soft side. "Beauty is in the eye of the beholder."

Her mouth fell open for a second. "I can't believe you find anything beautiful about that man." Then she shook her head. "Whatever. Let's find Sam." She tugged me across the plush rugs and into a large room decorated in silver and white. A low stage sat at one end, a polished wooden dance floor extending out from the raised surface. Music piped into the room through speakers.

"The live music starts soon," Amelia explained.

Sam and his family sat at a round table in the corner. Daniel's parents sat with them, but no Daniel.

"Clover!" My dad stood and came around the table, followed by Cheryl Garrett. He held me by the shoulders and kissed me on the cheek. "You look beautiful. Wow."

"He's right," Cheryl added, leaning in to kiss my other cheek. She acted kind and gracious, but I sensed the stiffness behind her smile. Not that I blamed her. I'd no doubt that my presence created a strain on her marriage. It wasn't easy when your husband's child by another woman suddenly appeared.

Still, I could see she was trying.

"Hey, Clover." Sam joined our family reunion. "I got this for you." Looking a little uncomfortable, he offered me a wrist corsage, a pale, delicate bloom in a clear case, tied with a royal blue ribbon. "Amelia told me what color to get."

"Thanks." I opened the case and slipped it on my wrist. I brought the flower to my nose and inhaled.

Daniel's mom waved to me from the table, and I smiled back. "Please join us," she offered.

"Umm…" I looked around the room for my grandfather, but he hadn't come back. "I'm not sure where my grandfather is sitting."

"Henry Alexander is a big boy," my father said. "He can take care of himself." He pulled out the closest chair for me, and I sat sandwiched between my dad and Daniel's mom.

Meredith Hudson asked me some questions about Ms. Ginny's book, and I explained the research I was doing. She seemed to know I felt out of place and worked hard to make me feel welcome.

"Good evening, everyone."

A female voice interrupted our conversation. My gaze landed only for a second on Morgan in a tight black dress that exposed miles of tanned skin, before moving on to Daniel, wearing a black suit and striped tie. He looked older and more sophisticated. He'd slicked back his normally messy hair, and his eyes glittered when they met mine.

I rubbed my hands together under the table. Why did the sight of him still make my palms ache?

"Daniel," his mom said, "we were starting to wonder when you planned on making an appearance."

He cleared his throat, using one finger to tug at his collar. "I was just…"

"Waiting for me," Morgan interrupted, linking her arm through Daniel's. "It's my fault. I can never get ready on time."

"Morgan called me at the last minute to ask for a ride. I didn't want to leave her stranded."

"Of course not," Meredith Hudson said, glancing over at me, "and you're here now. Why don't you join us? We can pull up some more chairs."

Morgan tightened her grip on Daniel's arm and shot an insincere smile in my direction. "Are you sure there's room?"

I stood up and met Morgan's stare. "Please, take mine." Protests sounded from around the table, along with offers to find other chairs, but I didn't flinch.

"It's fine. I have to go find my grandfather anyway."

Morgan might have won the upper hand with Daniel, but it didn't mean I was going to stick around and let her walk all over me. When I spun and crossed the room, I made sure to hold my head up high.

# Chapter Twenty-Seven

My grandfather found me on the veranda, leaning on the railing.

"Why aren't you inside dancing? What's wrong?"

"Nothing. I just needed some air."

He shook his head, his eyes clouded. "Don't do that. Don't lie to me. I thought we'd reached the point where we could be honest with each other."

He was right. I looked out at the edge of the golf course, where it disappeared into the darkness of the night. "It's Daniel," I whispered. "I keep expecting it to get better, but it doesn't. What's wrong with me?"

He snorted. "It's not you. Any boy would be lucky to have you."

I laughed, but it was a bitter sound. "No offense, Grandfather, but you're biased." I crossed my arms over my chest. "I love Daniel, but somehow I wasn't good enough for him."

My grandfather looked away. He loosened his necktie and leaned hard on the railing. When he looked back, he'd become more like the broken man I'd first met, a man weighed down with guilt. "Ah, Clover...I have a confession. I did what I thought was best. I did it for you, because I didn't want to see you get hurt."

My head jerked up, and my fingers dug into the railing. Frogs and crickets peeped, fighting with the sound of music from the band, but I only had ears for my grandfather. What had he done?

He heaved out a long breath. "I asked Daniel to give you some space, to break things off with you."

"No—"

He held up his hand. "I know it sounds bad, but you needed time to connect with your family, to figure out what you want to do."

My head shook, and my hand pressed against my chest. "It wasn't your decision to make." I thought I could trust him, but he'd betrayed me.

He straightened. "I'm your grandfather. It gives me the right to look out for your best interests."

"By going behind my back?" My voice carried across the veranda, hard and angry. "Didn't you learn anything from Mama?" I'd confided my feelings for Daniel, and he'd twisted them against me.

His shoulders sagged, and he deflated like a balloon. "You're right, but I had good reason. I just got you back. I didn't want to lose you again."

"That doesn't make sense."

"It does if you think your granddaughter will traipse after a boy who's heading off to a different state."

His honest admission thawed a tiny corner of my heart, but my anger was stronger. He had no right to interfere.

"I know it was wrong, and I'm sorry, but can you tell me one thing?" He stepped closer and reached for my stiff hand. "Daniel helped you when you needed it most. He made you feel like you weren't so alone in the world. Can you honestly tell me your feelings for him have nothing to do with the fact that he saved you?"

The question hung over me and left a bitter taste in my mouth. "No…" I mumbled. "I mean, I don't know. But even if that's part of it, why is that so bad?"

"It's not bad, but maybe it's not love you feel. Maybe it's gratitude."

I had no answer. Pulling my hand free, I stared out at the greens. His words spun and twisted in my mind for so long that when I finally turned, I was alone. Overhead, a patch of stars disappeared and reappeared. They played hide and seek with the scattered clouds skirting the night sky. I searched for the North Star, needing something familiar to anchor me, to make me feel less adrift.

"I've been looking for you."

I turned to find Daniel framed by the open terrace door. He'd shed his jacket and tie, undone his top button, and rolled up his sleeves.

I pressed my hands to my hot and swollen cheeks. "Well, you found me."

He stepped out on the veranda but hovered near the door. Was he afraid to be alone with me? Is that what my grandfather had done to us? Is this what we'd been reduced to?

"Are you okay?"

I leaned back against the railing and nodded, but I didn't feel okay.

"I didn't invite Morgan tonight. She called and needed a ride. That's all."

"You don't owe me any explanation. We're no longer a couple."

He frowned. "I know, but I still wanted to explain that she's not my date. Considering that I originally invited you,

I don't want you thinking I'm a total jerk." He paused and peered at me. "You changed your hair."

This was Daniel. So why did I suddenly feel so self-conscious? I reached up to smooth back a stray curl. "I got it cut."

"Wow. I kind of miss the whole 'attacked by scissors' look you had going, but this is also nice…and the dress. You look great."

More heat flooded my cheeks. Mama had been beautiful, but I'd never felt particularly pretty. Even now, I didn't care what other people thought about me, but with Daniel, it mattered. It mattered a lot. "I've never owned something like this." I lifted the side of my skirt with one hand and let it drop and swish around my knees. "I don't even feel like me. You look really nice, too."

He tugged at his collar and grimaced. "Yeah, well, these things are designed for torture."

Uncertainty paralyzed me. I wanted to tell him about my grandfather's confession, but nerves took over. What if it didn't change anything? What if he still didn't want me? Heavy air filled my lungs, weighed down by the static of the impending thunderstorm and my own doubts.

He turned to go, and I bolted forward. "Wait…"

I said it without thinking, without having a plan. I only knew that I needed him to stay. Ever since that night at the beach, my life felt incomplete and off-kilter, like the uneasy feeling you get after waking from a bad dream.

Daniel hesitated, one foot on the threshold, his hand on the knob.

My fingers reached back to find the railing. "I know what Grandfather told you. He confessed everything. He may have done it for the right reasons, but he was wrong to interfere."

Daniel sighed and turned to face me. "Clover—"

"All these things have gotten in the way of us being

together, but they don't need to, not anymore." I swallowed past the lump in my throat. I felt naked and exposed. He held the power to crush me or pull me back into the light, and I'd given him that power.

He stiffened, but then he crossed the veranda, stopping close enough for me to smell his aftershave. "I'm still leaving for college in the morning."

"I'll wait for you." The breeze picked up and lifted the bangs from my forehead. "I don't mind."

He wiped at the sweat on his forehead with the back of his arm and glanced around the empty veranda. "Why would you do that?"

"Because I love you." I stuck my chin out. "You and my grandfather don't believe me, but I know what I feel."

Daniel said nothing. He leaned against the railing, and my gaze wandered the width of his shoulders. He stared at the rose blooms below us, the pale flowers illuminated by the security lighting.

When he stayed silent, I needed to fill the void. "In the years after Mama died, I missed a lot of things. I missed her voice, her stories, and the smell of her baking, but mostly I missed her presence. Until I met you, I'd forgotten what it felt like to be held or touched or hugged. You gave that back to me." I slid my hand across the railing until my fingers brushed his arm. "You gave me my first kiss."

"Clover—" he choked out. He turned to me, one hand finding my hip. More than anything, I wanted him to kiss me again. In his arms, I felt safe and protected and loved. I felt pretty and worthy, but he winced like I'd hit him.

Not wanting to see any more, I laid my head against his chest. My arms looped around his waist, and I held tight. Under his thin shirt, his heart raced.

For a long moment, I didn't move, afraid he'd leave if I let go. Eventually, I raised my head, wrapped my arms around his neck, and pushed up on my tiptoes. I'd come halfway, but I needed him to meet me in the middle.

"Daniel…please."

His arms tightened around me. My feet came clean off the ground, and I gasped against his mouth. His lips claimed mine, and I kissed him with everything I had. He needed to know I loved him. Nothing else mattered. I closed my eyes, but it didn't block out the stars I saw. Tears burned my eyes, but my mind raced.

Was it possible to die from happiness and relief?

Did he finally understand that I loved him?

It ended as suddenly as it began. He set me back on the ground. His fingers brushed the hair from my face, and he kissed me once on the forehead. I wanted to cling to him. I wanted his warmth and scent and strength, but he took a step back, and I died a little inside.

"Clover…"

I'd never heard this tone before, this strangled voice filled with determination.

I knew what was coming. "Don't." Some protective instinct kicked in, warning me.

He stared at me, his hazel eyes darkened to brown. "Your grandfather may have warned me away, but in the end, it was my choice. I can't be your crutch. You need to figure out who you can be without me. You need to conquer your fears and start believing in yourself."

I stared up at the stars and ground my teeth in frustration. Everyone kept telling me to let things go, to believe in myself, to accept this second chance, but what did they want from me? I'd moved in with my grandfather; I'd made connections with my father and brother. What more was I supposed to do? "I'm trying, but why can't I have you, too? Please. I need you."

His features stiffened, and he took another step back. I knew then that I'd really messed up—in a way that couldn't be fixed, that couldn't be made right.

"We can't be together because you need me. I may have saved your life, but I can't fix you. You need to figure out that you're strong enough to stand on your own."

This wasn't happening. I shook my head, and my heart pounded. I lashed out. "You're afraid, too. You're afraid because of Grace. You're afraid of getting hurt again."

His mouth curved into a sad smile. "Maybe you're right. Maybe neither one of us is ready for this. You can't take two broken halves and expect them to fit together into something whole. I don't know much about love, but I'm pretty sure that's not how it happens." His hand lifted like he was about to reach for me, but it fell back to his side. "This is for the best. It may not seem that way right now, but it is."

And then he walked away.

I expected the tears to come, but they didn't. Tears happened when you felt pain and hurt and sorrow. Now, I just felt numb.


Grandfather tried to talk on the drive home, but I just sat and stared out at the darkness. Inside, I went straight to my room, stripped off my dress, and wiped off my makeup. I didn't belong in them.

I lay in bed, but my body thrummed with nervous anticipation, waiting for the storm to arrive. I felt it coming, like I always did, the unease building inside me like the static in the air.

Sometime past midnight, I slipped out of bed and stood at my window, watching the forks of electrical current light up the night sky.

Thunder boomed overhead, and my heart thudded. I tasted my fear—a sharp metallic flavor that wouldn't go away no matter how many times I swallowed. This uncontrollable terror had haunted me ever since that night.

Caesar whined at my side. He tugged at my nightgown with his teeth.

"Hush, Caesar. Not now."

A clap of thunder reverberated through my room, and I shivered. Daniel was right, at least about one thing. I still lived with the fear of that night. I'd never faced it or my guilt. I told Daniel I'd changed, that I was ready, but maybe it was time to prove it. Every fiber in my body wanted to hide from the storm until it ended, but for once, I needed to prove that I was stronger than my fear.

Fumbling in the dark, I pulled off my nightgown and tugged on my shorts and a T-shirt. My toe struck the corner of my dresser, and I swallowed back a holler. By the time I crept downstairs, the pain had dimmed to a dull throb, but fear still made my limbs shake.

Stopping at the back door to step into rubber boots and pull on my raincoat, I swallowed hard and slipped from the house, darting to the side of the garage where I kept my bike. I gave myself a running start and jumped on. My legs pedaled hard, carrying me down the driveway, while lightning illuminated the towering clouds overhead.

I sailed past the café, and the first drops of rain hit my face. More and more came, and I wiped at my eyes, trying to see. My bike skidded on the rain-slicked streets, but I kept going. Bile rose in my throat with every thunderclap. Still, I biked until my muscles burned and my fingers ached from gripping the handles so tight.

I only stopped when the cemetery loomed in front of me. Sliding off the bike, I sank to my knees, fear and exhaustion seizing my muscles. Huddled under my raincoat, Daddy's voice shouted at me, screaming that he was coming for me, that he'd find me no matter where I hid. Lightning illuminated the cemetery gate, and I struggled to my feet, ignoring his screams. The gate was locked, so I found a place to hop the fence.

I landed in a small puddle and wiped the water from my eyes. My legs trembled only a little as I hiked through the rain-soaked grass, searching for Mama's new home.

The irony wasn't lost on me—I was alone on a stormy night in a cemetery, but it wasn't the ghosts of the dead that scared me. It was the ghosts of my past. Thunder rumbled again, and this time it brought an image of Mama, her face gray and lifeless, except for the angry bruises smeared across the fragile skin of her neck.

I tried to swallow, but tears clogged my throat. This wasn't the way I wanted to remember her. I didn't want to see her like that every time it stormed.

I sucked in a deep breath, slowing my sprinting heart, and pictured her smile instead. I saw her baking cookies. She hummed to the tune of a song on the radio, and her red hair tumbled past her shoulders.

Lightning forked overhead, but this time I tilted my head back, daring the thunder to come while I held tight to the image of Mama.

It cracked overhead, and rain streamed down my face. All the while, my good memory of Mama remained. *I could do this. I could defeat this fear if I really tried.* But this trip wasn't just about thunderstorms. It was about confessions and forgiveness.

My flashlight swept the area, settling on the artificial grass covering Mama's fresh grave. I dropped to my knees in front of the Alexander family headstone.

"Hi, Mama." I swallowed, fighting past the lump in my throat. "It's me…Clover." My fingers traced the newly etched lily in the top right-hand corner of the family marker. Then they found her cold, wet name—*Lily Margaret, Born 1978,*

*Died 2013. Beloved Daughter and Mother. Forever loved. Forever missed.* My chest tightened. In Virginia, she'd had only wildflowers and a simple wooden cross. Did she like this better?

"You're home now," I whispered, "back with all the people who loved you. Grandfather picked out the lily and the words, and I'm sure you'd like them. Grandmother is here, too." I touched the grave at my right. "Now, neither one of you have to be alone."

I held my breath, half expecting to hear her voice, but there was only the plopping of rain on my hood. Cold water ran down my legs and trickled inside my boots, pooling around my feet.

"You were right to send me here." I spread my hand wide across her name. Could she feel me here in the dark, fighting my fears and looking for her? "It feels like home, and Grandfather needed me as much as I need him. He messed up and made me angry tonight, but I love him anyway."

I sucked in a shaky breath and pushed back my hood a little. "He's spent a long time blaming himself, and it's eaten him up inside. I told him you still loved him, right to the end. I hope it's okay, but I told him it wasn't his fault—"

Lightning streaked across the sky and singed the night, leaving behind the smell of sulfur. I clung to the image of Mama smiling. The clap of thunder came quickly. The storm was closer.

Turning, I sat on the wet ground and leaned my head back against Mama's headstone. Mud and water soaked through my shorts, and I worked to steady my heart and organize my jumbled thoughts.

"I also met my real father." I pulled my hands up inside my sleeves and peered through the rain at the rows of headstones, silent soldiers standing guard over me. "We don't know each other very well right now. I know he wants to, but he already has a family. What if he doesn't have room in his life for a daughter?"

Another fork of lightning lit up the sky. This time, I opened my mouth and let the rain land on my dry tongue. Thunder rumbled over the cemetery.

I turned and leaned close to the stone. "The thing is, lying to me about Jason Scott was wrong. I had a right to know the truth." I squeezed my eyes shut and listened to the sound of my own breathing. "Maybe you were trying to protect me, but it only hurt me worse."

Could Mama even hear me? I wanted to believe in heaven. I wanted to believe that when I died, I'd see her again, that I'd feel her arms around me, but what if there was nothing? My shoulders hunched, and my eyes burned. What if when she died, she simply ceased to exist? When Jason killed her, maybe he took every part of her from me...everything, forever.

Another clap of thunder shook the ground, and this time Daniel's face kept the bad memories at bay—his crooked smile and hazel eyes—but just thinking about him hurt. "I have something else to tell you, Mama. I fell in love. He's brave and strong, and I never expected him." I shivered and breathed in the pungent smell of wet earth and grass. "You and I never talked about boys, and now everything's messed up. I love him, but he's leaving tomorrow." I pressed my fist against my chest. "I never knew a broken heart could hurt like this."

I was stalling, waiting for the courage to say what I really needed to. I twisted and sat on my bum, remembering Daniel's words. He couldn't fix me. I needed to do this for myself.

A gust of wind sent leaves flying past, and I shivered. "I also have a confession. It's the reason I came tonight." I forced the words out past my fears and guilt.

"I've been mad at you...all this time." My breath hitched.

"I don't understand why you stayed. What about the times when Daddy went out, when he went to town for supplies, or he went out hunting? We could have left together. You could have been here with me." My hands dropped to the ground, and I pulled my knees closer.

"Did you love him, or were you too scared? I needed you to protect me, Mama, to stay with me. When I was little, you promised you wouldn't leave, but you did. You left me alone." Hot tears streamed down my face, lost in the rain. "There was so much blood, and you were both so heavy. I didn't know what to do."

I stared into the dark clouds, and my heart raced. I tried to remember Mama's smile, but this time, I was back in the cabin, frozen by fear. "It's wrong to feel this way. I know it is, especially when I wasn't strong enough to save you. When Daddy was choking you, I should have stopped him, but I couldn't move. I was so scared…"

Memories stole my words. I hugged my knees but couldn't fight the cold that numbed my limbs. I huddled under my hood, trying to block it all out, but for many long minutes, the thunderstorm won. The panic was back, sharp and acrid tasting.

Finally, the storm started to move off. The rain eased up, settling into a steady drizzle. My panic lessened, and I unlocked my stiff limbs.

I wiped at my tears and turned back on my knees. "The thing is," I whispered, "I need to know that you forgive me." My hand gripped the marker. Its stone edges bit into my palm. "It's the only way I can move on. I need to know that you understand and you still love me."

I leaned my forehead against the headstone, closed my eyes, and waited.

Rain ran down my coat sleeves, and my knees sunk into the wet ground. Minutes passed.

I opened my eyes and a chill coursed up my spine, but it wasn't from her presence. It was just because I was wet and cold.

In front of me, the headstone remained the same—just a solid hunk of stone with words engraved on it, words put there by someone paid extra by Grandfather to etch them in time for Mama's memorial.

The realization hit me slowly…Mama was gone.

She couldn't fix my problems any more than Daniel could.

There was only me, and I had to figure out a way to forgive myself. I'd told Daniel that he needed to forgive himself for Grace's death. He needed to let it go.

I had to find a way to take my own advice.

# Chapter Twenty-Eight

The ride home seemed longer and darker than the ride to the cemetery. I'd left my grandfather's filled with determination to conquer my fears and earn Mama's forgiveness. How naïve and childish that plan seemed now. Healing the broken parts inside me would take more than a reckless ride to the cemetery in the middle of the night. Maybe Daniel had been right. Maybe I wasn't ready for love.

Trouble was I'd never thought of myself as weak or needy. I'd survived on my own for two years, but now I saw the truth. I'd hid for two years, burying my head in the sand. Sure, I'd found a way to feed and clothe myself, but I'd done nothing to make myself a better, stronger person. I'd done nothing to escape the mental chains of Jason Scott's actions.

Shoot. My bike slipped, and I barely caught myself. I tightened my grip on the handles and coasted for a minute, trying to catch my breath. Biking out to Mama's grave in the middle of the night had been foolish.

My tires sloshed through the sprawling puddles. I pushed off my hood and wiped the wet strands of hair from my face.

Maybe I shouldn't have left my cell phone at home, but I wasn't used to having one.

I rounded a bend and swerved to avoid a branch in the road. Headlights popped out from behind the curve. They swept the road and settled on me.

I stared at the bright light, blinded.

My heart stopped.

Tires screeched, and my bike locked up.

The headlights jerked toward the side of the road, but the pickup truck kept coming, sliding sideways, coming straight for me.

And then I knew.

This was my fate. I'd been cheating death ever since the night Jason murdered Mama. The ocean tried to claim me, the hurricane did its worst, and now I'd die in the middle of the road.

But before I became nothing, I wanted to forgive myself. I didn't want to be broken when I faced the great unknown, but there was no time now. Only seconds.

My eyes squeezed shut. My bike hit something hard. Then I was weightless, airborne.

The crunch of metal sounded miles away. My arms flailed, but there was nothing to find.

My body hit the ground. The air knocked from my lungs. I couldn't breathe.

My head hit the pavement, and the night got darker.

This was it.

*No regrets. I love you, Daniel.*


My fingertips scraped against wet asphalt. I wasn't dead, or at least, I wasn't in heaven. I groaned and tried to move.

My mind spun, registering and assessing each throb and

ache shooting through my body.

I rolled on my side, and my stomach heaved. Blood ran from my skinned hands. It mixed with the rain and flowed down my arms, like the day I'd washed the blood from the cabin floor.

I shook my head.

A sharp smell filled the night…gasoline.

I sat up, and the world tilted. The tail end of a pickup stuck out of the ditch. Its front end was wrapped around a tree, and a flicker of red came from the engine. Fire!

I pushed to my feet, but my knees gave out. "Hey!" I screamed. "Get out of the truck!"

No one moved.

I staggered to my feet again. The ground still listed and rolled, but this time my knees held.

Fire from the engine licked a little higher. I made it to the side of the truck. Black smoke burned my eyes, and I lifted my arm to block the heat. I inched forward.

"Hey! Are you okay?"

Someone groaned. I reached the driver's window and looked in. A blond head slumped against the steering wheel and a deflated air bag.

Wait. I knew that head.

Time stopped.

It was my father.

"Hey!" I yanked at the door handle, but it wouldn't budge. I banged at the window. He moved a little. "Wake up."

The fire spit and crackled, taunting me. Panic tunneled my vision.

"Clover?" Blue eyes stared out the window, confused.

"Dad!" I reached for the door handle. "Unlock the door. I can't get to you."

Blood streamed down his forehead, and he shook his head. I knew the exact moment when he realized. His eyes widened, and he glanced out the front windshield. His face turned back to me, and I saw his fear.

"Unlock the door!"

His arm moved, and pain flickered across his features. I heard the lock disengage. My fingers grasped for the door handle and yanked. It gave a little, but wouldn't open.

He pushed with his shoulder, and I pulled with all my weight. It wouldn't budge. The impact must have twisted the frame. The windows were automatic and wouldn't move without the engine running.

Smoke burned my lungs and made me wheeze. I started coughing and couldn't stop.

"Clover!" He pounded on the inside of the window. "Go. The truck could explode." I shook my head, but he pressed his palm flat against the window. "Please…"

The wind gusted, sending a roar of flames toward us. I staggered backward. The air shimmered with heat. I saw him lurch to the other door, but it was also stuck. He was trapped.

Oh god, I was going to watch another parent die.

I couldn't get to him.

I pictured Jason with his arms around Mama's neck. I'd felt helpless then, too—watching her struggle against him, watching her body twitch, fighting for oxygen.

I couldn't lose my father, too. We were supposed to have more time. If we didn't, what was the point in having found him?

Determination warred with panic. I'd lost more than my share. Anger fought my hysteria. I'd suffered more than enough, and I wasn't losing anyone else, not without a fight.

I stumbled to the back of the truck and climbed in. The truck liner was slick with rain, and I fell against the tool chest he kept in the back. In the dark, I worked at the latches, cursing and fumbling until they finally sprang free. I grabbed the largest object I could find—a massive wrench.

"Cover your face!" I swung the wrench, but it came up solid. Pain shot through my arms, and I screamed into the night. But yelling wouldn't save my father.

I braced myself against the cab and remembered what Daniel taught me about golf. I swung the wrench at the rear window as hard as I could, using the full weight of my body.

The window shattered.

I swung it again, making the hole bigger, brushing the glass away. The wrench clattered to my feet, and I leaned in through the gap. "Dad!"

He was slumped by the passenger door. Smoke filled the cab, and heat scorched my skin.

"Wake up!" I grabbed his shoulder and shook him. "Come on. I can't get you out alone."

He moaned.

"That's it." I lifted his face toward the opening, toward fresh air. His eyelids flickered.

"Dad! Look at me."

His eyes focused.

"We're getting out of here. Now!"

Awareness flooded back to his features. He grimaced and reached for me. I wrapped my arms under his and pulled.

For a long, agonizing moment nothing happened, and then he pushed with his feet. I fell back out through the window, and he landed next to me.

I wanted to just lie there, sucking in the damp night air, but we weren't safe yet. I scrambled to the tailgate and dropped it down. Dad was already moving next to me. I jumped to the ground and reached back for him.

He leaned on me, and together we stumbled to the other side of the road. I helped him sit, and then I fell down beside him.

He gasped for air, and his body convulsed with coughing. He reached for me, and I wrapped my arm around him.

Together, we stared at the flames consuming the cab of his truck. He held me tighter, and I buried my face in his neck. Tears streamed down my cheeks.

"Hey," he rasped. "I'm alive…because of you."

"I thought you were going to die." I was sobbing, and I couldn't stop. "I thought I was going to watch you die, too."

He stroked the hair from my face, and my sobs gradually turned to shudders. "It's okay." His voice was raw and gritty. "I'm still here."

I lifted my head and looked at him, his blue eyes a mirror of my own. "Are you okay?" Soot and blood covered his face. "We need to stop the bleeding."

He shook his head, his eyes overly bright in the glow from the fire. "I'm fine." He wheezed. "What about you? I was sure I hit your bike."

I pressed my shaking hand against the gash in his head. "I thought I was going to die, but I think I'm just bruised."

He swayed, and I helped him lie down with his head in my lap. "You don't look so good. Where does it hurt?" Oh god. What if he had internal injuries? If Sam were here, he'd know exactly what to do.

He looked up at me, pain in his eyes. "We need help."

I looked around the deserted road. I couldn't remember how far it was to the closest house. If my bike was still in one piece, I could get there, but I didn't want to leave him alone. "I forgot my cell phone."

"It's okay." He fumbled in his pocket and pulled out a phone. He punched in some numbers. "This is Deputy Sherriff Garrett." He gave our location, but then started coughing so badly he couldn't finish.

I took the phone from him. "We've been in an accident. His truck is on fire, and he's hurt. Please come quickly."

The dispatcher asked me a few more questions, and then she assured me that help was on the way.

I dropped the phone on the ground next to us and adjusted my father's head, trying to make him more comfortable. He looked up at me. "They're coming, sweetheart. We just need to hang on."

Something squeezed my heart. This is what being with your father was supposed to feel like…like he had my back and I had his. He had to be all right. We deserved years to get to know each other. My raincoat was a little shredded, but I draped it over us, trying to protect him from the rain. "What were you doing out here?"

His eyes jerked up to meet mine. "Henry told me what he did. He thought you'd run away."

I broke his stare, suddenly realizing this was all my fault. He was out on the road looking for me. "I wasn't running." My cheeks burned. "I needed to visit Mama."

More coughing wracked his body, and he winced. "Maybe you could have picked a better time to do it."

Guilt washed over me. "There were things I needed to say, and I thought it couldn't wait." My shoulders hunched, and I shivered. I should have left a note, but I'd been so sure I'd be back before anyone even knew I'd gone. "My bad decision almost got you killed. I'm so sorry."

"Clover." I jumped at his harsh tone, but then his fingers found mine. "Don't. We've all been drowning in guilt, and I don't see what good it's doing. It's not honoring Lily's memory," he rasped. "I was out here tonight because I'm your father. Period. I'd have done the same for Sam."

He was right. Maybe it was the hindsight of almost dying, but I saw it now—my guilt and regret were quicksand. If I even put a toe in, it sucked me in completely. I'd believed I was a coward because I couldn't save Mama, but I needed to accept that in that moment, I'd done the best I could. It wasn't my fault that it wasn't enough—it was Jason Scott's fault. Tonight my bravery had been enough, and it was past time I focused on all the good things in my life.

He drew in a shallow breath. "You saved me tonight. You pulled me out of a burning truck." His eyes squeezed shut, and tears burned in mine. "I'm proud you're my daughter." He smiled up at me through his pain. "And it meant the world when you called me 'dad.'"

I'd said it without thinking, but it felt good. My teeth chattered, and I squeezed his hand. "I've never told you this before, but I'm happy it was you. I'm happy he wasn't my real father."

"I am, too, kiddo." He pressed his hand against his side, and I knew he was hurting. "Next time you need anything, just ask me."

I nodded, my whole body shaking now.

"I'm serious. If you ever have a problem or need a ride to the cemetery in the middle of the night, call me…"

His words trailed off to a whisper, and I prayed for the ambulance to come quickly.

"I will. Just hang on," I stuttered the words.

I heard sirens echo in the distance, growing steadily louder.

"They're almost here," I whispered to my dad.

His eyes flickered open. "That's good." He chuckled, but it turned into a cough. "Lying on the road in the rain sucks."

A few minutes later, voices called out to us, and then we were surrounded by responders. Activity hummed around us, and it felt so good to not be alone. Firemen sprayed foam on the bonfire that used to be a truck, and someone else put a collar around my dad's neck. A warm blanket dropped around my shoulders, and gentle hands helped me to my feet.

"My dad, is he going to be okay?" Firemen helped load him on a backboard and then on a stretcher. Doubts crowded into my head. What if he was hurt really badly?

"We're taking good care of him, Clover. Now, let's take

care of you." The paramedic examining me looked familiar, and then I remembered why. He'd been there that day on the beach. I'd been afraid of him because of my past and my secrets, but now I only felt fear for my father.

The paramedic helped me onto a stretcher and slipped a collar around my neck. Then he loaded me into the ambulance. He smiled, his brown eyes crinkling in the corners. "Let's get you warmed up."

I nodded, and he slipped an oxygen mask over my mouth and covered me with blankets.

Somewhere on the way to the hospital, my teeth stopped chattering and my limbs stopped shaking. My body still ached, my chest hurt, and more than anything, I just wanted to sleep.

# Chapter Twenty-Nine

"I need to see her. She's my granddaughter." My eyes opened, and I turned my head in time to see my grandfather yanking back the curtain around my cubicle.

Our eyes met. His glistened with unshed tears. I held out my bandaged hand, and he walked forward to grasp it.

"Thank God you're okay. Don't ever scare me like that again. I don't think my heart can take it."

I squeezed his fingers. "I'm sorry."

He sank down on a chair, his shoulders slumping. "No, I'm the one who should apologize. I was wrong to interfere with Daniel. I should have learned my lesson with Lily, but I almost drove you away, too."

"You didn't drive me away." The doctor figured I had a mild concussion, because I felt drowsy and the bed kept spinning. They'd already done a bunch of tests and pricked me with needles. "I just went to see Mama, but it was a stupid idea. I should have waited."

Grandfather leaned closer and sighed. "Are you hurt? I heard you were thrown off your bike."

"I was lucky." Were my words slurring? I couldn't tell. "Just cuts and scrapes and bruises. I hit my head, so maybe a concussion. They want me to stay for a while."

Grandfather closed his eyes. "Thank God for small miracles. You should have been wearing a helmet. As soon as you get out of here, we're buying you one. What about Garrett?"

When we'd first arrived, we'd been so close, I could hear the doctor working on him—giving loud, hurried commands to the people buzzing around our stretchers in a blur of scrubs and hands and equipment. I'd been terrified for him, but through it all, he'd assured me. "I'm fine," he kept saying, his words muffled through his oxygen mask. Then they'd whisked us off in different directions to be X-rayed and scanned.

The doctor had updated me on his status just before Grandfather arrived. "They admitted him for broken ribs and smoke inhalation, but he should be fine."

Grandfather patted my hand. "That's good to hear. It could have been so much worse, and it would have been all thanks to my meddling."

The emergency room bustled with noises, beeps, and commands, but inside the curtain, it was only he and I. "Grandfather?"

He looked at me. "Yes?"

"I went to the cemetery tonight to ask for Mama's forgiveness, but I know now that we can only forgive ourselves." He stared at me for a long minute, while I searched for the right words. "So from now on, no more guilt and regret. Please?"

His mouth sagged, his forehead creased, and he looked so sad. I didn't want that for him, not anymore. I wanted us both to let go of the past. We deserved to be happy.

His head slumped forward until his cheek pressed against my hand.

"Grandfather?"

He lifted his head, and this time he nodded. "Okay."

"Really?"

"Yes." He gave me a determined look. "For you and for Lily."

"Thank you."

A warm feeling spread through my chest and limbs. Maybe it was the aftereffects of the accident, but it felt a lot like hope. For the first time in a long time, I knew Mama was there with us.

Tapping on my shoulder woke me. I blinked up into Amelia's worried face. Behind her, my eyes found Daniel's. Amelia's arms came around my shoulders, and she hugged me so hard it hurt. A groan slipped out.

"Sorry!" She let me go. "We were so scared."

"Don't smother her, Amelia." Daniel's hair stood up on end, like he hadn't combed it, and his black T-shirt was inside out.

I tried to smooth my hair and felt nothing but knots and tangles. I could only imagine how bad I looked. "You didn't have to come."

"Are you kidding?" Amelia nudged me, making room for herself on the bed. "Sam called to tell us about the accident."

"He was here earlier to check on me."

"I'm not surprised." Amelia clucked. "He was worried about you. How is Mr. Garrett?"

My eyes kept tracking back to Daniel. He'd been right to break things off, but how long would it take before I could look at him without this dull ache in my chest? My fingers twitched with the need to touch him.

I released a shaky breath. "He's stable. A few broken ribs,

a concussion, and they're treating him for smoke inhalation. Grandfather went to get a status report."

Amelia brushed the hair from my eyes with gentle fingers. "And you? Are you okay?"

I knew she was asking about more than just my physical injuries. I stared down at my bandaged hands. "I'm fine. Everything is mending."

She leaned over and kissed my forehead. "That's good. I couldn't take it if anything else bad happened to you," she whispered.

Daniel cleared his throat, and Amelia swung around to look at him. He lifted one eyebrow, and then she huffed and looked back at me. "I'm going to go call Gran. She wants an update, but I won't be far."

"Tell her we're all fine, and she shouldn't worry."

She gently squeezed my hand. "I'll try, but you know Gran. You can't tell her what she should or shouldn't do."

I chuckled and then moaned, because it hurt to laugh.

"Amelia," Daniel ground out.

She winced. "I know, I know. That was bad of me. I'm leaving, but I'll be back."

She slipped outside the curtain, leaving me alone with Daniel.

He looked around at all the medical equipment and monitors and shook his head. His cheeks flushed. "You had us really worried."

I cleared my throat and picked at the blanket. "I'm fine." I didn't tell him about the throbbing pain centered around the lump on the back of my head or that the world still tilted when I'd tried to stand up earlier. I didn't want him worrying about me anymore.

He pinned me with his stare. "You were lucky."

"I know." I lifted my chin. "You should go home. You're supposed to be driving to Georgia in a bit."

His eyes closed, and when they opened, the intensity there stole my breath away. He pulled the chair up next to my bed and sat down. He leaned forward, so close I felt his breath on my cheek.

"That's the thing. I can't leave if I don't know you're okay." He swallowed, his voice thick with emotion. "You ran off in the middle of the night and almost got yourself killed. I know it was because of me. I hurt you at the dance."

He looked grim under the harsh fluorescent lights, and I imagined how bad he must have looked when he heard about Grace.

At the dance, he'd told me we were over, but he clearly still felt tied to me. He felt responsible, and it wasn't right. If I truly loved him, I needed to let him go, so he could start over in Georgia.

I stared at a spot over his head, because the right thing wasn't always the easy thing. If I looked at him, I'd lose my will and nerve in those familiar hazel eyes. "You were honest with me at the dance. Never feel bad for that, and…you were right."

He jerked upright. "I was?"

"Yeah." I covered my chest with my hands, afraid he'd see my heart thudding through my thin hospital gown. "I thought that surviving what happened to me in Virginia meant I was okay. But when I watched Jason kill Mama, something inside me broke. Maybe it's unfixable, but I never even tried. I built a wall around it and avoided it however I could. It's past time I faced it. I'm tired of being afraid of things. I'm tired of the doubts and regrets. Tonight, when I pulled my dad out of that truck, I felt brave and strong and good about myself. I liked that feeling."

Daniel caught my bandaged hand in his. "You didn't need to risk your life to prove your bravery. You've been proving yourself ever since you came here. You do brave things for others every day."

His thumb brushed back and forth against my wrist, sending tingles shooting though my body. I wanted him to gather me in his arms. I wanted to press my face into his chest and stay there. But I could see now that my love for Daniel was like an addiction. I needed him because of the way I felt about myself when I was with him. I had to learn to feel that way even when I was alone.

I lifted my chin. "I want you to go to Georgia and know I'm going to be fine."

He swallowed, and his eyes glistened. Was he crying? "I don't know if I can."

I sat up, ignoring my aches and pains, and wrapped my arms around him. "Sure you can," I whispered. "Just get in your Jeep and drive." He buried his face against my neck, and I stroked the back of this head. He clung to me and, for once, it felt like I was comforting him. "Maybe you couldn't save Grace, but you saved me."

He lifted his head and captured my lips. I tasted his goodness and his salty tears, and my heart felt full.

Then he pulled away. He wiped his eyes, straightened his shoulders, and smiled at me—the crooked grin I loved so much. "I'll never regret meeting you, Clover Scott."

He stood up and walked out without looking back. I wasn't offended by that fact. I understood it was the only way he could bring himself to leave—quick and decisive with no room for second thoughts.

After he'd gone, I lay down and pressed the nurse's call button. I needed something for the pain in my body, but no amount of painkillers would ease the gaping hole in my heart left by Daniel. I just needed faith that each day it would hurt a little less.

Amelia, Sam, Grandfather, Mary, and my dad stood in the backyard, all looking a little sleepy. Sam and Amelia were both attending college in Tampa, and they came back most weekends to visit.

Amelia wore a suspicious and slightly disgruntled look. "I love you, Clover, I really do. But you need to tell me why I had to show up here so early and wearing old clothes."

My dad had been out of the hospital for three weeks, but his ribs were still sore, so I'd appointed him supervisor.

I clapped my hands together. "We're making a garden."

Amelia groaned, but Sam grinned. "Cool. What are we planting?"

"Herbs and vegetables." I looked at my dad and my grandfather, and they nodded. "We talked, and we thought this would be a great way to honor my mother. She loved growing things. I don't want to go to a cemetery anymore to remember her. I want to come here."

The idea had started in one of my therapy sessions. My grandfather had found a really nice woman, and I met with her once a week. I was ready to open up about my life in Virginia, and my therapist suggested I do it in a way that made sense to me. So the idea of the garden took root.

Amelia leaned on my shoulder. "It's a beautiful idea, and I fully support you, but couldn't I support you at a more humane hour?"

Sam snorted. "Stop complaining, Hudson. It's time to get those hands dirty."

Amelia gritted her teeth but accepted the shovel I handed her.

"By the way, I also made cookies and muffins and lemon loaf for all my volunteers."

Amelia grinned. "Well, you should have mentioned the lemon loaf first. Where do you want me to dig?"

For the next few minutes, I explained my plan. My dad

made a few suggestions, and then we got to work.

I don't remember who told the first story about Mama. I think it was my grandfather, but soon the memories came flooding out—her favorite things, the times she'd gotten in trouble, the things that made her special. My dad explained how they first met and how they fell in love. I shared the good times we'd had together. The garden wasn't a place for the bad times. I'd already decided that I'd write those down.

My grandfather looked up at the clear sky. "Lily would have loved this day. She loved sun and summer."

I nodded, knowing that we were finally honoring her memory in the way it deserved.

Eventually, we took a break. We washed up with the hose before heading to the patio where Mary had set out iced tea and all the goodies I'd made.

Afterward, we reapplied sunscreen and bug spray and worked for another few hours, until Amelia begged us to stop.

"I'm going to have blisters." She pulled off her gloves and inspected her fingers. "Too late. I think I already do."

"Let me see." Sam brought her hand closer for inspection. He frowned and blew on the red areas with a tender look that made me blush. "You're definitely done for the day."

My dad rolled his shoulders. "I think your mother will be massaging my sore muscles tonight."

"What's wrong, Garrett?" my grandfather asked. "You can't handle a hard day's work?"

I tensed at the insult, but there was a glimmer in Grandfather's eyes.

My dad chuckled. "You shouldn't have bothered wearing work clothes, Alexander. You didn't do enough to get them dirty."

"Hmmph." My grandfather's eyes narrowed, but then he slapped my father on the back. "Thanks for your help."

"Yes." I stepped between the two men, just in case.

"Thanks for your help. I couldn't have done it without all of you."

I looked around at what we'd accomplished and grinned. We'd cleared off the sod and turned over the soil, removing the rocks. Tomorrow, I'd add some more soil, and then I'd be ready for planting.

My father laid one hand on my shoulder and looked me straight in the eyes. "My pleasure."

I hugged him, and a tightness gripped my throat, making it hard to swallow. It still hurt to think about what I'd missed out on—Andrew Garrett teaching me how to ride a bike or swim, my real dad protecting Mama and me from all the bad things. I straightened my shoulders. The time for regrets was passed. From now on, I'd only look forward.

His hand squeezed my shoulder. "Okay, kiddo, I gotta run."

Back in the house, I showered and changed.

When I was done, I found a box and packed away Mama's things—her trophies and trinkets. It was time to make the room feel like mine. I dug through her clothes, keeping those that fit me and relegating the rest to a donation pile on the foot of my bed. I kept her photos and books where they were. Maybe I'd talk to my grandfather about painting the room— blue, like the ocean.

Later that evening, I sat in the desk chair and stared out the window. I reached for a fresh piece of paper, lined it up, and rolled it into Mama's typewriter. I pounded on the keys, letting the bad memories flow onto the paper. I'd add it to the small stack of papers I'd already started. Right now, they were just a string of painful events as I remembered them, like a journal of my past. But, more importantly, they were part of my healing—every page I added to my pile, every word I typed made me feel a little more whole. I was slowly becoming the person I had always wanted to be.

# Epilogue

I biked into the driveway and leaves crunched under my tires. The late October breeze bit at my cheeks, but it was still warmer than the mountains in Virginia at this time of year. I'd even had to stop halfway home, pull off my hoodie, and tie it around my waist.

It was Halloween, and I'd talked my grandfather into decorating the front of the house with pumpkins and a scarecrow. Mary explained that in past years, Henry refused to give out candy to the neighborhood kids, but this year would be different. Mary and I made candied apples and ghost-shaped gingerbread cookies. We'd stocked up on miniature chocolate bars and bags of chips. Grandfather frowned when we hung the little pumpkin lights, but he didn't stop us. He did tell me that he planned to spend Halloween with a glass of scotch and a good book. If we wanted to give out treats, it was up to Mary and me.

I was fine with being in charge of the trick-or-treaters. I even planned to wear a costume. Mary supported my excitement about my first real Halloween, knowing I was making up for all the things I'd missed. It's why I'd come home at lunchtime—to help her with last-minute preparations.

Leaning the bike against the side of the house, I bounded up to the front door. Inside, the scent of fresh bread made my mouth water. I dropped my backpack in the foyer, kicked off my sneakers, and headed down the hall to the kitchen.

Mary stood at the counter, rubbing butter on the loaves she'd just taken from the oven. She looked up when I came in. "How was school?"

"Great." I'd been attending classes at the local community college, working toward my GED. I still helped Ms. Ginny with her book on the weekends. "I think I've figured out what I want to do."

"Really?" Her eyes lit up, and her hand stilled. "That's something worth celebrating."

I climbed on a stool at the breakfast bar. "But you haven't even heard what it is."

Mary spent a lot of time at the house lately, and if I wasn't mistaken, she had a thing for my grandfather. He remained clueless. I'd offered to help, but she'd blushed and shooed my questions aside. Maybe she preferred to work at her own pace, but I knew how time could pass. I wanted my grandfather to be as happy as he could be, as soon as possible. We'd all wasted too much time.

"I know you, so it must be something creative and worthwhile. Otherwise, you wouldn't waste your time at it."

I blushed at her high praise. "Thanks."

She nudged my hand. "So…what's the plan?"

I sniffed her bread and sighed. "Well, first, I'm going to have a big hunk of this, then I'm going to finish my GED, and then I'm going to apply for college. I want to be a social worker or a therapist. I want to help other kids."

She stared at me for a long minute, and her eyes welled with tears. "Honey, I think that's a very noble plan. Your mama would be really proud, but it's not an easy thing. Helping other people with their problems may be a painful reminder of your past. Are you ready for that?"

"I know it will be hard, but it's important work. Maybe my experiences will help someone else. It's nice to think that maybe something good can come from all that suffering."

She reached across the counter to grip my hand. "Honey, I'm so glad you found us. You belong here, you know that, right?"

I nodded, but her words made me think of the package I'd couriered to Daniel two days ago. I'd finally finished writing down all my memories, and I'd packaged them up and sent them to him. I'd paid for overnight delivery, so he'd received it yesterday morning.

Maybe it was stupid of me. We'd only communicated through Amelia and Sam since he left. Still, I needed him to know about my past. He'd asked me so many times over the summer, and I wanted him to understand that it wasn't him I hadn't trusted. I hadn't trusted myself not to fall apart if I allowed myself to remember.

I'd thought about sharing it with my grandfather and my dad, but they knew and loved Mama. No matter how many times they said they wanted to know everything, I knew they weren't ready.

Grandfather had been upset enough when the packages arrived—several boxes of personal items from Virginia. He'd arranged to put the property up for sale, including whatever furniture was left. He'd worried when the first package arrived, offering to go through it for me, but as we sifted through the measly contents, it proved harder for him. I knew what to expect, but for Grandfather, it offered proof of the sad life his daughter chose.

"I don't understand," he'd said, when we finished with the last box. "Where is everything else?"

"This is it."

I sorted the contents into two piles—one to donate and one to keep. I'd taken most of the important things when I left the first time, so almost everything ended up in the donation pile. The only exception was Mama's baking supplies—her recipe box and ceramic cooking bowls.

Grandfather's shoulders had slumped, and his face paled. "I'm so sorry, Clover. I had no idea."

I couldn't see that look on his face again, so I sent my package to Daniel instead. It was unfair of me to make him read it. He'd started a new life at college. As much as I missed him every day, he'd moved on. Plus, I'd written about some very sad and awful moments in my life. It was wrong to burden him with my past, but despite all the reasons why I shouldn't, I'd still sent it.

But I hadn't heard from him. Not a single word. Now, all I could think is maybe I'd made a horrible mistake.


The doorbell rang, and I took the stairs two at a time, Caesar at my heels. "I'll get it, Mary."

It was early for trick-or treaters, and I hadn't finished with my witch's makeup. My long black frothy skirt caught under one toe, and I pitched forward, just catching myself against the railing.

The doorbell rang again, and Caesar barked. I chuckled at his enthusiasm. Maybe he thought Halloween meant treats for him. Not that he needed any. He'd gotten fat from all of Mary's spoiling. I'd need to put him on a diet soon.

With a laugh still on my lips, I pulled the door open.

Caesar barked again and jumped up on the visitor. I should have pulled him off, but I couldn't, because I couldn't breathe. My knees turned to jelly, and I sagged against the doorframe.

"I was hoping for an enthusiastic greeting, but I didn't know it would be from the dog."

His words kick-started my breathing, and I gulped in air. *Daniel.* On my doorstep. Petting my dog and looking nothing like a neighborhood trick-or-treater.

Dark smudges underlined his eyes, like he hadn't slept much. Was he taller than I remembered? He still smelled just as good. My fingers squeezed the doorknob. "What are you doing here?"

His hair brushed the collar of his jacket. It had grown out since the summer, and he looked even more handsome. "I came because of this." He held up my courier envelope. I hadn't even noticed it in his hand.

He thrust it at me, like he could barely stand to touch it. I took it from him and clutched it against my chest. The intensity of his stare made me retreat a step. Oh god. I'd really screwed up. "How did you get here?"

He grunted. "I finished reading it late last night, and then I drove straight here. I pulled over at a rest stop for a few hours of sleep, but I feel like shit."

I winced. He was so angry that he'd driven through the night to confront me. "I'm sorry. I should never have sent it. I can see now that it wasn't fair."

Daniel's forehead crinkled. "What?"

My shoulders slumped. Part of me felt alive to just be near him again, but it was also depressing to feel the familiar pain. It had been two months, and I was still no closer to getting over my heartbreak. "I'm sorry. You have every right to be angry." I laid the envelope on the foyer table and turned back to Daniel.

His eyes widened. "Wait. You think I'm mad at you?"

"Aren't you?"

Daniel jammed his hand through his hair. "God, no!"

His face turned red, and his jaw clenched. "I'm angry at that bastard, Jason Scott. He had no right to put you through all of that. When I think about it…when I think about him, I want to kill him with my bare hands."

Tears burned my eyes. "He's already dead."

His palm smacked the doorframe. "I know, but he got off too easy. He deserved to pay."

"Don't." I'd never seen Daniel this upset or angry, and my heart twisted. Something clogged my throat, making it hard to breathe. "I didn't share it with you to make you feel this way."

For a long moment, he just stared at me, his hands in fists at his side. I wanted to touch him, but he looked so hard and distant.

Finally, he blew out a breath and rocked back on his heels. Some of the tension left his body. Not much, but a little. "Why did you send it? Did you let anyone else read it?"

I shook my head, my witch's hat bobbing back and forth. For a moment, I'd forgotten where I was and how ridiculous I probably looked. I'd been so focused on Daniel. "No, just you. My therapist recommended that I write it all down, and when I was done, I wanted you to know the answers to all the questions you'd ever asked. Maybe it was selfish of me. Obviously, it was."

He stuffed his hands in his pockets and turned to stare at the yard. I tugged Caesar inside and followed Daniel out on the porch, shutting the door behind me.

"I heard from Amelia that you were doing really well," he said. "She told me you were happy."

I leaned against the porch railing, the breeze pulling at my skirt. "In some ways, I am. I'm proud of the person I'm becoming. I love my new family, and I want to make a difference with my life."

"So why was it so important that you share your past with me? Why not Amelia or Sam or your grandfather?"

He stood next to me at the railing. His arm brushed mine, and I squeezed my eyes shut. *Daniel.*

"I don't think I can say it out loud." I forced the words passed the lump in my throat. "It still hurts too much."

A heavy silence wrapped around us. I finally had the things I'd always wanted—a real home, family, people who loved me, dreams—but there was still this big piece missing. When Daniel went away, he'd left a hole in my life, a hole I couldn't seem to fill.

He released a long breath, like he'd been holding it for a while. "Then I'll say it. It's my turn anyway." He looked down at me, his mouth curving into a ghost of a smile. "Before I met you, people kept telling me that I needed to let go of my guilt over Grace, but I didn't know how. I thought that if I left Canna Point, I could finally escape it, but it didn't work that way."

"I'm sorry." My heart broke for him, and I wanted to take away his pain.

"Don't be sorry, because you'd already shown me the answer." He turned and sat back against the railing, his long legs stretched out in front of him. "Every day I spent with you this summer helped me let go of a tiny piece of my guilt—day after day, one day at a time, until I got to Georgia and I realized there was nothing left."

He looked over, and his hazel eyes met mine. "I knew then that I'd made a mistake."

The air stilled around us, and I was the one who forgot to breathe.

"I'd pushed you away because I was afraid of you needing me. But it was more than that. I swore after Grace that I'd never get that close to someone again, and you made me break that oath. Then Amelia and Sam kept saying how happy you were, and I figured that if I really loved you, it was best to stay away. Then you sent that package, and I got so angry reading it, and all I could think about was getting in my Jeep and driving here. Now you're dressed like a witch, and I feel so damn tired, and I'm scared shitless that I've messed things up for good."

He kept talking and talking, but my brain was stuck on one thing—the part where he said "if I really loved you." He'd never told me that before. I'd told him, but he'd never said it. I wanted to believe it, that maybe he loved me, too, but what if I'd heard him wrong?

"Daniel!" I grabbed his arm, and he jerked. "Stop talking and say that part again."

He frowned. "What part? I said so much, I can't remember it all."

I gritted my teeth and tried to be patient, but it felt like fireworks were going off in my heart. "The part about…you loving me."

His eyes widened, and he searched my face. I wondered what he saw there. "You've always known just how to put a guy on the spot." He tugged me over until I stood between his legs, chest-to-chest, face-to-face.

He plucked the witch's hat from my head and tossed it on the ground. "It's hard to declare your love for a girl who's wearing that."

My hands curled around his shoulders and touched the cool skin at the back of his neck. "Is that what you're doing? Declaring your love?"

He pressed his forehead against mine. I could feel his nervous, uneven breaths on my skin. "Yes, I am. I love you, Clover Scott, and I was a jerk to ever leave you in the first place."

I squeezed my eyes shut. My heart felt so full, I was sure it would split open. "Don't say that. You were right to leave. I needed to find out who I could be on my own. I know now that I love you because of who you are and not just because of how you make me feel or because you saved me."

"God, Clover, I never saved you. You saved yourself a long time before I ever met you."

I wrapped my arms around his neck, and he crushed me against him. Our lips met, and my life became complete. He kissed me softly, like I was something rare and precious, but I wasn't fragile anymore, and I wanted more. I wanted everything. His fingers traced the lines of my face, and I clung to the collar of his jacket, pulling him closer. He tasted like warmth and light and the promise of all the good things still to come.

"Ahem—"

Daniel pulled away, and I blinked.

I twisted my head to find my grandfather standing on the porch with a scowl on his face. Daniel straightened and tried to take a step back, but I wrapped my arm around his waist. I didn't care who saw us together. Not when we'd been through so much to get here.

Daniel stuck his hand out. "Good afternoon, sir."

Grandfather ignored it. "Is it really?"

Daniel's face tightened, but I hugged him and whispered in his ear, "His bark is much worse than his bite."

Daniel grimaced and tucked me under his arm. "Don't worry. It'll take more than Henry Alexander to keep me away from you this time. I have a plan for us. The long-distance thing will suck for a while, but this plan involves some weekend traveling, a lot of Skyping, and maybe even a few golf lessons."

"What are you two conspiring about over there?" Grandfather frowned, but I just laughed.

Daniel loved me, and it felt amazing. "We're not conspiring, and you need to make Daniel feel welcome. You're always telling me it's my home, too."

Daniel dropped a kiss on my forehead. "Speaking of home, I have to make a phone call. My mom will kill me if she finds out I'm in town and she doesn't know."

"Go." I leaned up to kiss his cheek. "I'll be right here waiting for you."

Daniel winked, and then he walked down to the front lawn, leaving me on the porch with Grandfather.

He pointed at Daniel's retreating back. "Are you sure this is what you want? What if he breaks your heart again?"

I crossed the porch to hug him. "Don't worry. I have more than enough room in my heart for both of you."

Grandfather grunted and hugged me back. "You'd better. Does this mean I have to get used to him being around?"

I stepped back, bouncing with happiness. "Yup."

Grandfather retreated into the house, and a few seconds later, Daniel bounded back up the stairs. I threw myself into his arms.

"Mom wants you to come for supper."

I pushed him back against the railing and linked my hands around his neck. "I have to give out candy first."

Daniel laughed. "Then I guess I'll have to help. Do I have to dress up?"

"No." The sky behind Daniel turned golden with late-afternoon sun, and I thanked Mama for all she'd done to get me here. "You're perfect just the way you are—"

His kiss stole the rest of my words, and I closed my eyes. I finally had everything I ever wanted, and I was done with looking back.

# Acknowledgments

So many people have supported me on this long and winding road, including my wonderful family, amazing friends, a great group of fellow writers, and lots of beta readers. You know who you are, and please know I am forever grateful. Thank you to my daughter, Elizabeth, for being my inspiration and secret plot weapon. I write YA because of you. Thank you to my sons, Jacob and Connor, for always supporting my dreams, and to my parents, for always being proud of me. Marilyn, thank you for caring enough to ask about my goals; you set me back on this path. Your actions remind me that we never know how and when we might make a positive difference in someone else's life. Lilian, Kerri, and Sharon, thanks for reading my early attempts. Sharon, don't worry. I won't forget my promise. To the Bean Team, I may be far away, but I love you all so much. To my CPs, Shelly Alexander and Rebekah Ganiere, I'm so glad I found you both. Thanks for all your sound advice and much needed encouragement. Thanks to my agent, Carrie Pestritto, for taking a chance on me, and thanks to my editor, Karen Grove. You saw the potential in this story, and with your help, Clover and Daniel's story has now come to life.

# About the Author

Originally from Newfoundland, Katherine Fleet gave up the cold winters of Eastern Canada for the year-round warmth of the Caribbean. The slower pace of island life has given her time to pursue a long-time goal—becoming an author. When she's not writing, she spends her time baking, chauffeuring her three amazing, talented kids around, and having sun-filled adventures with her husband and wonderful friends in Curaçao. She is also a very thankful breast cancer survivor. In 2007, she joined RWA and has enjoyed the support and camaraderie of the YARWA and OIRWA writing communities. She's participated in NaNoWriMo since 2012 and is an active supporter of the associated Young Writers Program. She is represented by super-agent Carrie Pestritto of Prospect Agency. *The Secret to Letting Go* is her debut novel. You can connect with her at www.KatherineFleet.com.

CPSIA information can be obtained at www.ICGtesting.com
Printed in the USA
LVOW12s0258220116

471815LV00001B/2/P

9 781682 810705